Praise for The Belvedere Club

"Snappy and full of sass, Briana Kaleigh fields the punches in *The Belvedere Club*, the evocative debut by Nicola Trwst. A girl with attitude who you want on your side when it comes to murder. I loved it."

—*Cara Black, author of the Aimée Leduc Investigations, set in Paris.*

Praise for Bolinas Bongo

"Nicola Trwst has created a quirky, fun character who thinks outside of the box when it comes to solving crimes: Murderers beware.
We look forward to seeing more of this offbeat character."

—*J. J. & Bette Golden Lamb authors of the Gina Mazzio RN -- medical thriller series.*

"Briana Kaleigh, the audacious journalist and accidental sleuth from *The Belvedere Club* is back with a vengeance in *Bolinas Bongo*. The story zips through Marin County to its secret beaches in a wave of snappy dialogue, outrageous humor, and murder. I can't wait to see what kind of mayhem she'll be up to next."

—*Cynthia Greenberg, author of Burmese Jade.*

Also by Nicola Trwst
Bayou Nights (2013)

Briana Kaleigh Mysteries
The Belvedere Club (2012)
Bolinas Bongo (2013)
San Rafael Sizzle (2016)

San Rafael Sizzle

By

Nicola Trwst

NgH Press
San Francisco, CA

San Rafael Sizzle
Copyright ©2016 by Nicola Trwst
All rights reserved

Discover more of Nicola Trwst's work at
www.nicolatrwst.com

Published June 2016 by NgH Press
978-0-9855208-6-1

Publisher's Note:
This is a work of fiction. Names, characters, businesses,
places, events and incidents are either the products of the
author's imagination or used in a fictitious manner. Any
resemblance to actual persons, living or dead, or actual
events is purely coincidental.

This book was a huge collaborative effort. I have many people to thank for their expertise and connections. Any errors in interpretation or use of information are totally mine.

For their connections:
Char Maassen & Melissa Lasky

For information on fires
Christopher Cooper-Fire Captain Station #5
Larry Luckham-Fire Commissioner/County Investigator
Werner Maassen

For information on stem cells:
Larry Lasky Ph.D.
Drs. Ove and Christine Peters

For sharing their critiques, ideas, and patience:
Margaret Lucke, Bette and J.J. Lamb, Shelley Singer,
Judith Yamamoto, Marie Roughan, Debbie Blasco

Many Thanks to you all.

CONTENTS

The Mess

I stepped over two balled-up men's socks and kicked a blue high-top out of my path. The shoe thudded against the baseboard. Neither socks nor shoe were mine. Neither socks nor shoe belonged to a lover or one-night stand because my sex life was dryer than burnt toast. That made me want to kick something else.

Instead, I yanked the cord of the dirty white blinds covering the front window of my apartment. As the vertical slats slapped together, they made a heck of a racket. Good thing I wasn't trying to be quiet.

At the table, I switched on my laptop, drumming my fingers as it booted.

The bell on Fifi's collar jingled as she trotted past me and into the kitchen. Fifi was a high-strung toy poodle with issues. She'd been willed to me by my best friend. Hard to believe a friend would do that to a friend.

Fifi stopped at her empty food bowl, twitched her nose, and turned to me with her paws on her hips. Well, not really, but if her paws could go on her hips, they'd be there.

I opened the music folder on the laptop and launched *Ha Ha You're Dead* by Green Day. I cranked up the volume, hoping to feel the floor beneath me rumble, but without real speakers that clearly wasn't going to happen.

Fifi backed away from her bowl and cowered near the fridge. My finger paused on the volume slider. Fifi's hearing was more sensitive and *she* wasn't my target. I slid down the volume a tad.

"What the hell, Briana?"

Ah. Conor, my soon-to-be ex-husband, stood half in the hallway and half in my living room. A stretched-out pair of briefs clung to his bony hips; otherwise he was naked.

"Oh, sorry," I said, "I forgot you were still here. By the way, when *are* you leaving?"

He scratched his scraggly hair, which made it stick up even higher. "I'm waiting on a call. You know that. Once I make the delivery, I'm out of here. Now, why don't you come to bed with me and let me relieve some of that stress?"

"Oh, baby, baby. I want you so badly… TO GO AWAY." I turned down the music a little more and stalked into the kitchen.

I picked up Fifi's bowl, forked a tablespoon of canned food into it, mashed the stinky mound into bite-sized chunks, and sprinkled in some dry nuggets. I set it on the floor next to her water bowl. Even turned down, the music drowned out the slurping sound she always made while scarfing up her food.

I switched on the coffeemaker and opened the cabinet for the bag of ground coffee. My formerly half-full bag now had barely enough for one cup. "Conor! I said you could crash here, not drink my coffee!"

Now wearing a pair of straight-legged jeans and a black tee shirt stenciled with the words *I Taste Like Chicken*, Conor shuffled through the kitchen doorway. "I had to drink it. There's nothing else. Not even a beer."

"I told you, I'm off the sauce. That's why I need my coffee!" I tossed the last of the grounds into a clean filter and threw the empty bag at him. I checked the water level, but was no longer in the mood. I switched off the machine.

Conor came up behind me. He ran a hand down the length of my ponytail and then stepped closer whispering, "Ginger." A nickname only he used, referencing my hair color.

He wrapped his arms around me. I smelled the scent of his skin. His embrace felt familiar and irritating at the same time. Once upon a time, I couldn't bear to be away from him. I needed to breathe the same air he breathed; I needed his touch to feel secure. He was my best friend, Haylee's, cousin. We'd started dating my last year of college and he'd proposed on graduation day.

Maybe if I'd grown up with a mom, instead of a father and six brothers, I would have known that our need to smother each other was unhealthy. I'd always envied Haylee and her "normal" family and with Conor's proposal I would become part of her family. What was there to think about?

I broke from his embrace. "Don't do that, Conor."

"What are you afraid of…you might like it? You used to love it. Come on now, come with me to bed, babe. Let me remind you of how good I can make you feel."

My body tingled at his words. Sex had never been the problem. "Fifi, let's go for a walk."

Fifi scampered past me to the apartment door.

"I'm here when you're ready," Conor said, and strutted off to his room.

"I'll be ready when you sign the divorce papers," I called, snatching up Fifi's leash. I hooked it on her collar and picked her up. After six weeks, she still hadn't conquered her fear of going down the outside stairs. Or maybe she'd trained me well.

At the bottom of the stairs, I put Fifi on the ground and she took off across the asphalt parking lot until the leash lead jerked her to a sudden stop. I chuckled. That never got old.

She swung her head around and gave me an annoyed look.

"All right." I walked faster. Fifi was one of those female dogs that prefers to lift her leg rather than squat, and today she lifted her leg and gave the tire of Conor's pickup truck a soaking. Nothing made him madder. My day was getting better and better.

We walked south to the patch of green between the apartments and the pier where the boats were docked. Two side hatches and the door of my friend Dusty's schooner were open, but he was nowhere in sight. About two months ago, when I'd left D.C. for Marin County, Dusty had found me this apartment in the small six-unit complex. So much had happened in the last two months that it felt as if I'd lived in California for half my life. I was actually getting used to the summer fog, although I'd forgotten my jacket again.

Fifi headed toward the pier.

One of the things that had happened was that Dusty and I almost lost our lives to a paid-for-hire killer. Another was that Dusty had kissed me, tickling parts I hadn't known I had. It didn't bother me much that he didn't remember the kiss; he'd been pretty drugged up. What did bother me was that since he'd left the hospital, he'd been treating me as if I were growing barnacles and fangs.

Fifi sniffed the concrete wall that ran along the sidewalk. Another few steps and her leash line would jerk again.

Dusty stepped out onto his deck. He was wearing a pair of chinos and a blue golf shirt the same robin's egg blue as the awning of his boat.

"Hey," I called.

He waved before turning to close the wooden door at the top of his boat. He snapped the padlock into place while I waited for him to come ashore.

"I have to run," he said, crossing to the dock.

"Something up?"

"Robbery at the drugstore near the station." He unconsciously touched the top of the gun holstered at his hip.

"But you're a detective." I said. There was no reason for him to take this call.

"I know, but it turns out there was an off-duty Fed in the store and he decided to claim the glory. Now, we have a hostage situation."

"Oh. Oh! Can I come?"

Dusty was a big guy, six-two and solid muscle. I had to look up at him and as I did the sun blinded me. I sidestepped so that his big, shaved head blocked the rays. He was a budding Buddhist monk and he shaved his head at the full moon.

He looked down at Fifi, who was baring her teeth at him. "What about your husband?"

"Ex-husband." I snatched up Fifi, ready to run her upstairs if he gave me the sign.

He started walking toward the harbor parking lot. "It's been a month and he's still there. Maybe you should rethink the *ex* part."

"I told you, I'm doing something for him so he'll do something for me."

What I hadn't told him was that I was giving Conor a place to crash until his job came through in exchange for Conor finally signing the divorce agreement. This was saving me a ton of money because I'd hired a detective to find Conor. Now, I didn't have to pay the detective since Conor had found me.

We reached the spot where I either had to cross over to the dock and walk with Dusty or head around the building to the apartment. "Let me run Fifi upstairs and I can ride with you. I might get a story out of this."

"I don't have time," he said, and kept walking.

The Holdup

I took the outside stairs two at a time. I'd had enough of Dusty's brush-me-off attitude. Without his help I wouldn't be able to get up close and personal to the crime scene, but at least, I'd be able to get as close as any other reporter.

I threw open the apartment door and found Conor stretched out on the psychedelic-colored cloth sofa. I dropped Fifi into his lap, but by his yelp, I realized I'd missed his lap and dropped her in a delicate spot. *Whoops.*

"Need you to watch the dog."

I ran to my room and grabbed my camera case. I glanced at my jacket hanging in the open closet. This part of California was known for its summer micro-climates. One minute it could be a sunny eighty-five degrees and the next, overcast and sixty-eight. This morning the fog was thick and looked like it might hang around. I yanked the jacket off the hanger and ran toward the door.

"What if I get my call?" Conor asked.

"We've been waiting for you to get your call for four weeks. You might never get it. For that matter, I'm not sure you're even waiting for a call."

"Why else would I be here?"

"That's what I've been trying to figure out. You *will* sign those papers, call or no call."

"I said I would, didn't I?"

I pushed my tongue to the roof of my mouth, allowing me to hold back what I really wanted to say. "Fifi has had breakfast and won't need to go out for another two hours. I may be back by then." I didn't wait for a reply, but slammed the door shut behind me.

My new car was in the third spot from the back. *New* was pushing it since it was a 1996 Honda Civic, but it was new to me. It had once been a shiny, cherry red; now it was a dull, rotten red like the color of dried meat. I turned the key and pumped the gas pedal and it groaned. A second time, I turned the key and pumped the pedal and waited for the engine to catch. It did. Two turns. Every time. Consistently annoying because each time I turned that second time I wondered, *what if it won't start this time?*

I pulled out of the lot onto San Pedro Road and saw a row of twenty or thirty blackbirds perched along the power line running from pole to pole in the center median. With the foggy backdrop, it looked like a scene out of Hitchcock's *The Birds*, which Dusty had told me was filmed a ways up the road in Bodega Bay. A shiver ran down my spine. I hoped it wasn't an omen.

* * *

The Marin County Sheriff's Department was housed in the Civic Center. Dusty had said the drugstore was close by. I knew the one he'd meant. It was across the highway and he'd once told me that it was always getting robbed. I steered clear of it after dark, but this was early morning. A weird time for a robbery.

The first thing I saw when I turned the corner near the store was two Highway Patrol cars pulling out of the strip mall lot. I parked across the street and jogged over on foot. Another sheriff's car was leaving when I reached the sidewalk. Officers, in different uniforms, loitered near the drugstore's entrance. A paddy wagon—that's what we called it in Boston, not sure what it was called in Marin—was also parked near the entrance with its rear doors open. It was empty.

Two sheriff's deputies were pulling down the barricade tape. The situation must have been contained. I looked around for Dusty. He was usually the odd man out.

He was alone, leaning against the rear of a San Rafael police car, talking on his cell phone. I headed over.

He shoved the cell phone in the pocket of his windbreaker. "What are you doing here?" he asked.

"I need some hairspray."

My red hair runs halfway down my back. The most I do to it is put it in a ponytail. Products dull the color. My lie was meant to be obvious and, hopefully, piss him off. I was building toward a showdown. This cold-shoulder attitude of his was growing old. I'd given him time to get over his injuries and to deal with the PTSD that comes with being taken prisoner, but no matter how sympathetic I was, no matter how patient, he acted as if I was a nosy neighbor he'd like to avoid, rather than the friend with whom he'd once shared a passionate kiss. Not only had he hurt my feelings repeatedly, he was now hurting my bank account.

Without a change of expression he looked away, glanced over his shoulder at the store. Two thick-muscled Mexican men were being led out, their hands cuffed behind them. Across the sidewalk, another man in khakis and a yellow striped shirt pointed at them. He was standing with two San Rafael officers.

"Is that the Fed who was taken hostage?"

"He wasn't taken hostage. The idiot caused the situation."

"Can I talk to him?"

"No!"

His tone, another slap to my ego. I gritted my teeth and told myself he didn't mean it, but I also started across the parking lot. He grabbed my arm and jerked me around to face him. "Briana, you're making me mad."

"Good, because you've been ticking me off for a couple of weeks. I've tried to be patient, but you've cut me out of all the cases you're working. You told me when I moved here that you'd help me find stories and now, suddenly, everything you do is a big secret."

He shook his head and puffed. "Pfff. Secret? That's choice coming from you. Perhaps you've forgotten that not so long ago your secrets almost got us killed."

"So that's it! You blame me. I also broke the case and got us rescued." *Barely.* I'd called for backup, but a little too late. To be honest, I also blamed myself, but we'd survived. Move on.

He leaned in. The smell of his aftershave caused my breath to catch. We hadn't been this close since our capture. For an instant, I thought of grabbing his lapels and planting a wet one on his lips—that might jumpstart his memory—but before I could, he jerked away as if sensing danger.

"If you'd told me about the phone calls," he said, "we wouldn't have needed rescuing."

"I was working a case, just like you." But he was right. I should have told him I was being threatened and that I had information he didn't, but growing up with six brothers I was never very good at sharing. And—I've been told—I may have control issues.

He took another step back and ran his hand over his bald scalp. "And then there's the husband. You told me you were divorced."

"We're in the process." *If he'd ever sign the blasted papers.*

"That's not what he says." Dusty looked past me and waved to someone.

I glanced over my shoulder and spotted a woman in a dark-colored pants suit coming out of the drugstore. From the distance, I couldn't see who she was, but something about her struck me as familiar. Probably someone from the Sheriff's Department. I turned back to Dusty.

"When did you talk to Conor?" I asked.

He held a hand up as if to stop my words, but it had the opposite effect. It was like greasing my jaws.

"I told you I'm helping him out," I said. "Haven't you ever helped out your ex-wife?"

"Not once."

He started to walk away, but he quickly twisted around, the hand still raised as if to push my words away. "It's your secrets, Briana. I never know what's true with you or what's just you running down a story. Bottom line: I can't trust you."

Ouch! Right hook to the solar plexus; a direct hit. I stood stunned, watching him walk toward the group of officers.

The Note

Conor was gone when I got home and he'd left Fifi behind. I picked her up and gave her a hug. I don't know why because we don't particularly like each other, but she was warm and her fur soaked up the tears of Dusty's lingering anger.

When I finished blubbering, I put her down, wiped my eyes with my sleeve, and went to the dining table to switch on my laptop. Fifi followed at my heels. I sat and she gave me her big brown-eyed stare. Had she mistaken my lapse as one more way to manipulate me?

"What?"

Her head flicked to the kitchen, then back at me.

"You've had breakfast. You don't eat lunch and we are *nowhere* near dinnertime."

She gave a short whine and trotted over to the sofa. She leapt up, gave me another glance, another whine, and curled into a ball facing the door.

Coffee. If I was going to work on my masterpiece, I'd need some strong brew. My masterpiece was a true crime book that an editor was actually paying me to write. It was about the case I'd recently solved; the same case that had driven a wedge the size of Nevada between me and Dusty. I'd already been paid a hefty advance and I had a two-month deadline for the first draft. After a week and a half, I'd written the opening paragraph.

I went to the kitchen and switched on the coffeemaker. I checked the filter to make sure the last few meager grounds were still in there. On the counter was a rectangular piece of torn paper towel. In bleeding black ink were the words: *got my call.*

"Yeah, right."

Something rubbed up against my leg. I glanced down and there stood Fifi, a big smile on her snout. "Forget it," I said, but she just stared. Maybe because she was a dog and couldn't understand English. Every dog owner I'd met contradicted this belief, especially the Mexican lady who lived up on the hill with three Chihuahuas. Her dogs—Juan, Marcos, and Fred—understood both English and Spanish.

Right.

I looked back at the note. Was it possible that I was finally going to be rid of Conor? I'd once loved him, cherished him, but that was another lifetime ago. Back then, we'd been one of those couples that others loved to hate. We didn't just finish each other's sentences, we prompted each other's stories. We'd laugh at private jokes from across a crowded room because we could read each other's smug thoughts with the glance of an eye.

And smug we'd been. Superior in our love, knowing that it was the real thing, the kind of love that comes from the souls of similar spirits. Our bond was unbreakable.

Then we broke.

Not like a jar falling off a shelf to smash into pieces, but like the nuts and bolts of a chair that slowly come loose, causing the other parts to realign to the change of force until the nuts and bolts pop off and the chair collapses.

We were two young parents adoring the new baby our union had produced. We were so happy it gave me nightmares, not because I believed that we didn't deserve that much happiness; of course, we did. We were young and in love. But that much love was scary.

Early one morning, Conor went to bring Siobhan, our beautiful girl, to our bed so that the three of us could greet the day in each other's arms. Siobhan meant little elf and she was ours, her smile spreading a magical glow over everyone she met. Her green eyes were like a sunlit field on a summer's day. But that morning, Siobhan didn't budge. She slept the deep sleep. There was no waking her. Never again.

The nuts and bolts started to loosen.

My cell phone rang. Startled from my memories, I jerked. Fifi barked once and trotted over to her water bowl. I fished the phone out of my pocket and read the faceplate. *Marin Independent Journal.* It was the editor.

A job? I could only hope.

"Hello, sir, how are you?" I asked. I usually answered a call from an editor with only my last name, but this guy was Mr. Social, always asking about my day, my health, or how I was enjoying California. I'd never before met an editor who cared.

After a few generalities, he asked if I'd heard about the drugstore hostage situation.

"Yes, sir, I have. I was actually there when they brought out the suspects."

"I need something quick for the online edition of the paper. I'll pay by the word," he said.

I loved that he still paid by the word rather than the assignment, always a positive for someone with a good thesaurus, but as I listened I realized the word count he was looking for was limited to two hundred and fifty. That would barely fit the facts and barely pay for the gas to deposit the check.

I went back to my laptop and brought up a clean white page. I called Dusty to find out who was the deputy in charge, but after three rings my call went to voicemail. I'd like to think he was busy, but lately my calls were going to voicemail a lot.

I called the Sheriff's Department and asked for the press liaison.

* * *

Two hours later the *IJ* article was written, edited, re-edited, and emailed off. I needed coffee, the real stuff, not the watered-down cup I'd been trying to ignore. Almost noon. Lunch might also be nice. I grabbed my keys and Fifi's leash, planning to kill two errands with one descent down the stairs. Fifi had been facing the door for the last thirty minutes and whining at it for the last five. If I didn't want a wet carpet I needed to move.

I set Fifi down in the parking lot. She trotted over to the tire of a Miata and sniffed it. She turned back to look at me. Whatever my expression said, she decided not to lift her leg. She continued to sniff along the blacktop as I followed. When she reached the grass at the edge, her head came up. My head came up, too, because a distant sound of sirens was growing closer, really fast. The leash pulled in my hand and I looked down to find Fifi heading for the hedges by the carport.

The sirens grew louder still. I counted three. I let the leash out to its full length so Fifi could sniff the bushes and I could still see the road. If the sirens kept coming past the high school, they'd most likely pass the apartment building. I waited, ear to the wind.

Maybe something was going down at the school. I said a quick prayer that it wasn't another high school shooting. Innocent kids cut down was more than I could stomach.

It wasn't the school. Two sheriff's cars and a black-and-white San Rafael police car sped by the drive. I heard what sounded like a sharp sliding stop on gravel after the cars passed. I tapped my pocket, reminding myself I had my car keys.

Dusty ran down the pier and in two leaps was across the plank and onto his boat. What I'd heard was his car sliding to a stop. Something important was going down. I grabbed Fifi under her front legs, not noticing that she was in the process of dousing a dandelion. A trail of pee spewed downward, missing my boots and trickling off to a few drops. Holding her out in front of me, I shook her dry and then sprinted to my car.

With Fifi in the passenger seat, I backed out of the parking spot and drove to the street. Dusty's sheriff's cruiser parked askew blocked the lot's entrance. A second later, Dusty sprinted to his car. He never noticed me. He yanked open the door and hopped in, driving off straight down San Pedro. I looked left, ready to follow, but the *squelch, squelch* of another siren caused me to slam the brakes.

An ambulance rounded the corner and sped past, using its siren as a horn. My tires squealed as I took off after it. The speed limit was thirty-five. By the time I passed the tennis courts I was up to fifty-five. The ambulance sped up as it climbed the hill near the elementary school and again at the bottom of the hill, where it burned through a red light. I fell behind. I slowed enough for a car at the right of the intersection to roll forward and turn left, then I too burned the light.

I kept sight of the flashing lights in the low lands. The ambulance picked up speed as it headed toward the rock quarry. That's when I lost sight of it, right where the road narrowed to one lane. I slowed at the rock quarry's drive to make sure that wasn't where everyone was headed. The very quarry I'd been told was responsible for all the cracks in my walls. From time to time the boat painting on my living room wall would rattle. Dusty said it was from blasting down there.

I sped past and climbed the first hill. The ambulance made a sharp left up on the second hill. I flattened the gas pedal. Near the turn, as I veered into the turn lane, a pair of antlers slipped through the median's high grasses and a deer stepped into the street. I hit the brakes hard. The tires squealed and locked. The back wheels swung out and the car went into a spin.

I may have screamed.

When the car finally came to a stop, I was facing oncoming traffic, but there was none. My heart was beating in my temples. I looked at the deer. It stood frozen in place, ears up. I heard a strangled, gargled sound and turned to see Fifi barf into the passenger's seat.

Really?

I took a deep breath and shook my finger at the deer as if to say "don't move." Turning the steering wheel hard, I cut a path around the buck, making the left turn where the ambulance had disappeared. The neighborhood looked residential. Three police cars and an ambulance should be easy to find.

The Cooler

The subdivision was upscale. A state park, known for its bike trails, stretched beyond the houses to the right and offered a spectacular view. To the left, a group of newer mini-mansions, planted on tiny plots of land, spread down the road. The older homes just looked huge, one story and spread wide. For such large places, they were surprisingly close to the road, with short driveways leading to two-car garages.

I drove downhill and spotted the police cars past the first street to the right. A good thing, too, because Fifi's lumpy brown puke was starting to stink. I lowered the window.

Everyone had gathered in a circular court with three large homes fitted tightly together. Two sheriff's cruisers and a San Rafael police car were parked along the sidewalk. The ambulance blocked one of two driveways leading up to a peach-colored home with two separate garages. The garage that was closed had an A-framed roof, the open one had a flat roof. The rest of the house was a contrast in different angles.

I pulled in behind one of the sheriff's cruisers and rolled down the passenger window. I didn't see Dusty, but a crowd was gathered in front of the open garage. Was there a story here? Could be a carpentry accident, could be a domestic incident, or it could be something that might generate another article for the *Marin Independent Journal*.

I thought of the groceries I needed to buy. Conor was eating through my meager budget. Another paycheck wouldn't hurt. With my fingertips, I lifted Fifi and her leash, which was still attached to her collar, out of the smelly mess.

I tied the leash around the outside passenger mirror. She sat, looking a little dazed. She didn't try to follow me.

A stretcher was in the driveway, some medical equipment piled on top. The two male San Rafael police officers saw me first. They came at me, backs stiff and chins out. I glanced past them, hoping to take in as much as I could before they shoved me back down the sidewalk.

Dusty was squatting next to an open blue-and-white beer cooler, which meant the Sheriff's Department was in charge. Jurisdiction out this way was sketchy; one street could be under the Sheriff's Department and the next could be under the San Rafael Police Department. Once over dinner, Dusty had told me a story about a robbery suspect who'd fled a house on San Rafael turf and crisscrossed between the sheriff's district and the police district by jumping back and forth over a creek behind the homes on each street. Because of the jurisdiction mix-up they never managed to catch the guy.

I focused on Dusty. From my angle, I couldn't tell if he was looking at the contents of the cooler or the man stretched out behind it.

A San Rafael officer clamped onto my arm. "Stop."

He had the darkest eyes I'd ever seen and an odd haircut. His dark hair was short-shaven all around his head except on top where the one-inch strands flopped around.

"Dusty," I called and waved.

The officer hesitated, turning to Dusty. To my surprise, Dusty raised a hand. The officer paused, as confused as I. Did Dusty mean *come on over,* or *let her go,* or any number of other things such a gesture could suggest? One thing it clearly didn't mean was *chase her away.*

I pulled my arm out of the officer's grip and walked up the drive to where the sheriff's deputies were standing with the ambulance attendants.

"Do I need to get a restraining order?" Dusty asked.

My stomach tensed. Not with the kind of fear that comes when someone was holding a gun in your face, but the kind that burns your insides as you wait to hear something you don't want to hear. A few smart replies came to mind, but in the end I said, "I have bills to pay."

His glance flicked down at the person on the garage floor and then back to me. "Do you have your camera?"

"All I've got is the dog and some vomit."

Dusty shuddered and turned back to the crime scene. He reached in his top pocket and took out his cell phone, but I pulled mine out and got the camera app open before he'd turned his on.

I stepped forward to hand my phone to him, but a deputy threw up an arm block to stop me. "Here," I called, "use mine. It has a higher resolution."

Dusty stood and with a blue plastic-gloved hand, he reached for my phone. The deputy took it from me and passed it to him, then the deputy pointed downward and told me to look.

I did. His shoes were well shined.

"Don't go past this line. You can't contaminate the scene before S.I.S. get here," he said in a voice that sounded like a reprimand for an untrained dog.

I expected to see a red line drawn across the drive, but not only was there no line, there was nothing to contaminate, only a joint running the width of the garage where the rough concrete drive met the smooth concrete garage floor.

Dusty walked to the feet end of the man's body. Fine leather shoes, I noted. European. Cost a pretty penny. At the other end, the man's face had the gray pallor of death. A shiny pool of deep red fluid spread to the right of his head. My stomach clenched. My hands flew to my lips and I looked away for an instant. I closed my eyes and took a breath before turning back to the body.

Whatever injury had killed him must have been on the underside of the body since the front of his button-down shirt was spotless. Male. Business attire. Dark pants. White shirt, opened at the neck. Not a carpentry accident.

Dusty squatted. He tipped the blue cooler, waving away what must have been a noxious odor. We all leaned forward, peering inside. Two organic round globs floated in a pale pink liquid that I assumed had once been ice. The rotten stench hit us and we all pulled away, moaning at the same time. Me and one of the deputies leaned in to get a second look. The globs, which looked like a clump of membranes, were clearly some type of body part. A tube-like appendage, about the size of my pinky, was connected to the center of the each dark red mass.

"Anybody know what these might be?" Dusty asked.

I never should have drunk that watered-down coffee. It had soured my empty stomach. Suddenly, I felt the burn as it rose up the back of my throat. I broke away from the crowd and made it to the front lawn before spewing hot liquid from my lips. I heard the chuckles behind me as I wiped my mouth on my sleeve. They could laugh all they wanted. As the only female on the scene, I knew what was in the cooler.

"Do you have the flu?" one of the deputies asked when I turned around. Everyone laughed.

Ha ha.

"How can you tell if your barf is the flu or your wife's cooking?" one of the ambulance attendants asked the group.

"I don't know," someone answered.

I ambled back over to the garage.

"If it's the flu, you'll get better," the attendant said and everyone roared.

Dusty had replaced the cooler in its original position and had stepped away from the body. I met his gaze.

"You okay?" he asked.

"Placentas," I said.

"Excuse me?"

"In the cooler. It's two placentas."

Suddenly, the laughter died. A deputy sucked in his breath.

"No," the ambulance attendant said.

Then, the only sound was the squawk of a blue jay from the tall redwood branch hanging over the roof. Dusty glanced down at the cooler. "You're sure?"

"Oh yeah."

"Damn." He shook his head.

The Scientific Investigative Services van pulled up into the driveway and the deputy behind the steering wheel hit the horn. Everyone automatically took a few steps back from the crime scene.

I looked at Dusty. He waved me away.

The Wait

The S.I.S. deputies took over the investigation while the rest of us stood off to the side in a grassy clump of yard. We watched as they turned over the body and examined the hand rake in the back of the victim's neck.

At the back of the garage was a wooden table with small flower pots, potting soil, and gardening tools strewn about. That was probably where the killer grabbed the rake.

"Looks like you have yourself a murder," I said to Dusty.

"No. I think he planted that rake in the back of his own neck," he said and raised his hand over his head as if to demonstrate. He handed me my phone.

"Funny. Is he married?" If not for the placentas, this might look like a domestic disturbance gone wrong.

"Still running down his history."

I checked my phone for the photos of the crime scene. They weren't there. "You deleted the photos."

"You didn't think I was going to let you keep them do you?"

"What if they don't show up whenever you sent them? The originals are gone."

"You think I'm an idiot, don't you. I checked. They're there."

Dusty's tone was getting tense. I shoved the cell back in my pocket and turned back to the garage.

It wasn't only the placentas that raised questions. On a metal table near the door to the house was a tall white metal canister that looked like a portable cryogenic storage container. It had been tagged, but no one had yet opened it.

I pointed to it. "I once did an article on home insemination. They use those things to store sperm."

Dusty shook his head and rolled his eyes heavenward. "Good to know."

"I'm just saying…"

One beer cooler with placentas and a cryogenic canister with who-knew-what inside. This wasn't an ordinary murder. That was why Dusty had cursed. This case was going to take a while to solve.

Excitement tingled at the back of my neck. This one was a puzzle and I loved puzzles.

"Dusty," I said, ready to point out the obvious.

He held both hands up as a barrier. "You want the story. I know, but don't start. Go home. When I'm done here, I'll call you with whatever we're ready to tell the press. We probably won't mention the placentas right off the bat so keep that nugget to yourself. Are we clear?"

"Okey dokey. If you *do* call with information, I won't write an article mentioning the placentas, but if you blow me off again, the placentas are a go."

His brow furrowed and his lips tightened. He probably wanted to threaten me, but I had him. And he knew it. If we were no longer friends, I didn't owe him anything.

"I'll wait for your call," I said and walked across the yard to untie Fifi.

* * *

The afternoon sun had broken through the fog. I closed the front blinds to kill the glare on the laptop. I felt pretty confident that Dusty would call and not because I had him by the short and curlies. Just in case, I prepared two versions of what I'd seen out in that garage. Next, I phoned Debra Kirkland, my contact at the *San Francisco Chronicle*. This was a big story. I'd send one version to the *Marin Independent Journal* and another to *The Chronicle* depending on what Dusty gave me to work with.

Two paychecks plus the short piece from this morning's robbery. Rent would be paid next month without more of my advance money. If Dusty would let me follow the investigation, I foresaw this case generating several more stories. Respect had flickered across Dusty's face when I'd identified the contents of the cooler so I couldn't see him cutting me out, but with his recent hot-and-cold behavior, nothing was for sure. I had to be prepared to snoop around the case without him if need be—I'd done it before. Didn't relish doing it again, but I would.

I searched the kitchen for a pail, remembering that I'd seen one somewhere. When I couldn't find it, I filled a large saucepan with warm water and grabbed the roll of paper towels. Fifi hadn't left the sofa since we'd come home. I headed for the door with the saucepan, but she didn't so much as lift an eyebrow. Guess she didn't want to watch me clean the mess she'd left in my front seat.

The car smelled worse. The vomit was crusted over and half-baked from what little afternoon sun we'd had. Kneeling on the blacktop and leaning into the passenger's side, I scraped and scrubbed. The wind was picking up and as the passenger door blew back and forth against my back, I felt the chill of fog moving back in.

With a fistful of paper towels, I was drying the last wipe-down when Conor's pickup bounced into the parking lot. A little too fast, he skidded into the slot next to my driver's door. The brakes squealed. He clearly didn't see me as he staggered across the lot and up the stairs.

Drunk!

I tossed the dirty water from the pan into the bushes, picked up the soiled paper towels, and followed him up to the apartment. The door was ajar. He hadn't bothered to close it. What if Fifi got out? Wait—was that a bad thing?

"Conor!"

A moan came from the guestroom. I stomped into the hallway and found him sprawled across the air mattress, eyes closed, tongue hanging between his lips.

Great.

Another few minutes, he'd be snoring. I closed the guestroom door and walked into the main room. Fifi was still curled on the sofa.

In my pocket, my phone vibrated, then rang. Dusty.

"I wanted to get back to you. I'm headed back to the station now. We've a print on the cooler. If you can wait another few hours I may have a suspect's name for you."

"Are you kidding? When I left, I saw a television crew headed out there. In another few hours—"

"They picked it up on the scanners. I can email you what everyone else has now, but I'll have more for *you* once we run this fingerprint through the system."

That was generous. "Thanks." Made me think of the old Dusty, but I wasn't naive enough to think my threat had nothing to do with it. "I appreciate it. Send me what you've given to the press already and I'll call the two editors I've spoken with and see if they want to hold the article a little longer."

I put away the phone. A steady ebb and flow of snores came from the guestroom. Conor was out for a while. My stomach growled. I'd lunched on the last two Melba toast in the package. And I needed coffee. Actually what I needed was something a lot smoother than coffee—Conor had awakened my thirst—but caffeine would have to do.

"Come on, Fifi, let's go for a walk."

She lifted her head, but didn't make a move. I picked up the leash and shook it, but she still just looked at me. My previous hug combined with the car ride from hell must have had her doubting my sincerity.

The way Conor was going at it he wouldn't be awake for hours. If Fifi wanted to stay, she could stay. Since when was I afraid of being alone? A tight twinge in the gut made me think of Dusty, but I was getting used to the idea that whatever I'd felt behind his kiss was my imagination playing tricks on me. If I kept telling myself that for a few more days, I might actually believe it by the end of the week.

At least, I wasn't mooning over the memory of his crooked smile that popped up whenever we were in sync on a clue or line of questioning. Yeah.

I'd seen that smile today.

The Surprise

Instead of going to the fish shack to shop, I took the long route, up and over the hill to a neighborhood market that had a deli counter and a coffee bar. I sipped a latte while I spoke with both editors on my cell phone. I had until 7 p.m. to get them the suspect's name in order to make the a.m. editions. They'd take what I had already written and add the name to the online stories. It was 4:30 and I needed twenty minutes to walk home. I bought a bag of coffee and headed back toward the apartment.

The wind was whipping around from all directions. I buttoned my jacket and tucked my chin into my chest. At one point a Sheriff's Department cruiser passed by, but I looked up too late to see who was driving. Besides, Dusty had already told me he was heading to the office.

I took my phone out and checked to see if I'd missed a call. I hadn't. I couldn't stop thinking about the cryogenic canister. It could hold almost any type of bio matter, but because of the placentas, I assumed it might be sperm. It made the most sense. Maybe the dead guy had been trying to prove a paternity link. Maybe he'd wanted to check out who was or wasn't a baby-daddy.

A hand rake to the back of the head suggested a "heat of the moment" type of kill. The killer hadn't brought a weapon because he or she wasn't planning on killing. These thoughts brought me back to the idea of a domestic situation. I needed to verify that the dead guy was married and find out if they had children or were planning on having children through in vitro or surrogacy.

Conor was still snoring when I arrived, but Fifi was off the sofa and waiting by the door.

"Ah, now you want to go out."

I set the bag of coffee on the kitchen counter and grabbed Fifi's leash.

Downstairs, she wandered the parking lot while I gently nudged her in the direction of Dusty's boat. The padlock was still in place outside. Just checking.

As the hours passed, I started to fear Dusty was playing me. I ran our conversation through my mind. Would he dare call my bluff? If he did, would I publish what I knew, knowing it would kill any chance of us ever working together again?

I was mad, real mad, but at whom? The stupidity was on me, thinking that a drugged kiss meant something. How many men had I kissed when I was on a bender? If only I could remember.

For all I knew, Dusty had been kissing me good-bye, *au revoir*, because he'd later confessed that he'd accepted he was going to die. He'd prepared himself for it. Another one of his Buddhist beliefs that sounded totally ludicrous. *Meet death peacefully.*

Not me. I planned to meet it with a sword, slashing, stabbing, and fighting till my last breath was drawn.

Or maybe in his drugged mind he thought he was kissing someone else, someone who meant more to him. I was the fool here, letting my imagination build a connection that clearly wasn't there. I wished I could say it was the first time, but in truth, I was a mess when it came to men. I couldn't figure them out.

"Haylee, I miss you," I said to the sky. When it came to relationships, my best friend, Haylee, was the one person I trusted to guide me through the labyrinth. With her now waltzing beyond the pearly gates, I probably should steer clear of the opposite sex.

One-night stands, check. A girl has needs. Emotional entanglements, uncheck. Keep my feelings to myself.

Fifi barked once and I turned in time to see a black-and-white cat scurry through the hedges. Growling and barking and growling again, Fifi took off after the cat and got wedged in the lower branches. She kept barking as I tried to pull her back out, but the leash was too tangled.

"Shut up!"

I still hadn't put down the four-hundred-dollar pet deposit. No one had asked so I'd let it slide.

I hoisted her into my arms and carried her upstairs, threatening to hold her muzzle shut each time she burped out a sound. I put her down on the carpet and locked the door. She faced me and barked one more time as if to challenge me. I took a step toward her and she took off at breakneck speed.

"Fierce devil."

"What's going on?" Conor called.

I ignored him and went to the coffeemaker. The latte was still holding, but I felt a need stirring in my soul. I poured some freshly ground beans into a filter and hit the switch. I tapped the countertop, watching and waiting for the soothing smell to fill the room.

The guestroom door opened and the bathroom door slammed. The sound of water rushed through the pipes. Conor screamed a few vulgar words and I cracked up laughing. The shower needed about six minutes to warm to a decent temperature. He was always too impatient or else he forgot and stepped in too soon. You'd think after a month he'd learn, but every day it was the same.

* * *

The latest email from Dusty was on my laptop. I read through the general info sent to all the media outlets:

Victim's Name:	David Chaffe, PhD
Victim's Address:	19 Corsica Place, San Rafael, CA
Address of Crime:	19 Corsica Place, San Rafael, CA
Cause of Death:	TBD
Case Listing:	Homicide
Investigating Detective:	Lieutenant Dusty Arkansas, Marin County Sheriff's Office

Two more paragraphs gave a sketchy description of the crime scene and the current direction of the investigation. Nothing about a wife or ex-wife. Also missing was any mention of either the cooler or the canister.

I clicked open my article and added the names of the victim and investigating detective. The rest of the details I already had written in my articles, as well as a better description of the crime scene. So far I hadn't written about the placentas and I was pretty sure I wouldn't, even if Dusty let me down. I wasn't ready to slit the throat of our friendship just yet.

Fifi jumped off the sofa, barking as if her life depended on it. She ran ferociously to the door, as if ready to tear off someone's leg. A second later, someone pounded on the door. I saved my article, closed the laptop, and managed to reach Fifi as the second series of thumps vibrated the wood. After being stalked by a serial killer, I'd grown skittish about opening the door. Dusty had once talked about putting in a peep hole, but that was another in a long list of things he'd said he'd do and hadn't.

I took a deep breath and threw open the door.

"Can't you at least ask 'who is it' before opening?" Dusty said, standing in the doorway. Two uniformed deputies, both of whom had been at the crime scene earlier, stood behind him.

Fifi kept barking.

"May we come in?" Dusty asked.

I picked up Fifi and stepped aside. "As you like."

He dashed past me toward the kitchen. "Where's your husband?"

"Ex! Ex-husband. And who cares? Have you brought me the name of a suspect?"

He rushed passed me again, this time heading for the bedrooms. He glanced left into Conor's room, then right into mine as if Conor would be in there. Then he focused on the closed bathroom door. The water was still running. Conor was whistling a slow Irish ballad.

Dusty pointed his thumb at the closed door and the two deputies stepped past me and joined him in the hallway.

Fifi barked once. "What's going on?" I asked.

"You'll have your name in a second," Dusty said, holding up three fingers. He counted off to the deputies who had their weapons ready. "Three, two, go."

Dusty turned the doorknob and threw open the bathroom door. "Hands up!"

It looked like something out of a bad television show, three men with weapons charging a naked man.

I stroked the top of Fifi's head. "I don't frigging believe this."

They yanked Conor from the shower. He slipped and the deputy with the broad back jerked forward to catch him, blocking my view of the room.

"On your knees!" Dusty yelled.

32

"On your knees!" Broad Back yelled, his voice echoing off the tiled walls.

"What the fuck?" Conor said.

"Now! Knees!"

Feet scuffled over the tiles.

"Boys, I'm naked as a newborn."

"You're also hard of hearing," the other deputy said.

"Ouch!" Conor cried. "Damn."

I put Fifi down and charged the bathroom, shoving into the tiny space filled by too much testosterone. "What's going on?" I tried to squeeze between the two deputies. Conor was on his knees with his hands on his head, warm mist swirling around him. Dusty towered over him. "The man's in his birthday suit," I said. "Clearly, he doesn't have a weapon. Let him get dressed, or do you plan on dragging him out of here dripping wet?"

Dusty's head came up, his gaze laser sharp. "Briana, get out!"

I leaned forward, almost touching Broad Back's shoulders. "You're better than this."

Dusty's jaw tightened, but he reached for the towel rack and wrenched a towel free. "Now leave, or I'll arrest you for obstruction."

Together the deputies shoved me out. One of them hung back in the doorway, giving the others room to move. I waited in the cool hallway, hands on my hips and thoughts in a wild spiral. What had Conor done to ignite this level of police brutality? He was generally a pretty mellow sort of guy.

When the deputies finally cleared the bathroom, Conor stood between them with his hands cuffed behind his back and a brown towel wrapped around his waist. Dusty and I locked gazes; neither of us spoke. Honestly, I was too angry; I didn't know what his excuse was and frankly, I didn't care.

"Which room is his?" Broad Back asked me.

I nodded left and he took off. He came back carrying the tee shirt and jeans Conor had been wearing earlier. Knowing Conor, they'd been in a pile by his bed.

The second deputy unlocked the handcuffs. Conor moaned and rubbed his wrists. Broad Back shoved the clothes into Conor's chest, forcing him to grab them. "Dress," Broad Back said at the same time.

"Can you shut the dog up or do I have to shoot it?" Dusty asked.

With everything else that was going on, I hadn't noticed that Fifi was about four feet behind me and barking her head off. I picked her up and carried her to the kitchen. I grabbed a handful of crunchy nuggets and dropped them in her food bowl before I put her down. She followed me to the door, which I slid shut in her face. She barked again, but it was muffled behind the wooden door.

Conor had his tee shirt and pants on. His moppy hair was soaked and dripping down on his tee shirt. Dusty was reading him his Miranda rights from a laminated card.

"He has a right to know why he's being arrested," I said when Dusty had finished.

"For the murder of Dr. David Chaffe," he said without missing a beat.

"I don't even know a Dr. Chaffe," Conor said.

"He probably doesn't," I said to Dusty.

"A couple of years ago, you were arrested for car theft. Your prints are in the system."

"I didn't steal that car. Eddie was drunk," Conor said.

"Eddie?" I shook my head and turned my gaze back to Dusty. "He didn't steal the car. Eddie was drunk when he lent it to him and didn't remember. The next day he reported it stolen. Conor was released, all charges dropped. His prints shouldn't be in the system."

"Talk to your lawyer. Point is, they're in and they're a match for the print we found in Chaffe's garage."

"The one on the cooler, you mean?"

"What cooler?" Conor asked.

Broad Back had found Conor's high-top tennis shoes and was motioning for Conor to put them on. Fifi's muted barks filled the silence. Dusty didn't seem to notice; at least, he wasn't fingering his trigger.

"Briana, do something," Conor finally said, his eyebrows teepee-ed in a begging expression. The second deputy cuffed him again.

My mind was a jumble. "He didn't kill anyone," I said.

Dusty nodded to the door. "Evidence says otherwise."

"What evidence? A fingerprint. Ask him about it."

"I plan to. There's also the question of this." Dusty held out an envelope filled with cash.

"That's mine. You don't have a search warrant," Conor said.

"It was on the bed," Broad Back said to Dusty.

"Plain view seizure." Dusty removed a white paper from his top pocket and handed it to me.

State of California—County of Marin
SEARCH WARRANT AND AFFIDAVIT

"And yes, I have a warrant," he said as I read. "I'll need his computer and cell phone. It's listed there." He pointed to a paragraph.

"I don't have a computer," Conor said.

"He doesn't," I said and almost mentioned that he sometimes used my laptop. Luckily, the brain cells kicked in just in time, because there was no way they were taking my laptop. "He goes to the library to use theirs."

The second deputy joined us, holding Conor's cell phone. "Beside the bed," he said.

I hadn't noticed him leave to search Conor's room.

Dusty held out an evidence bag and the deputy dropped the phone inside. "Fingerprint, money, new in town. I've a lot of questions for your hubby and you can write whatever you want." He leaned into my face with an icy stare.

I closed my eyes in an effort to focus.

"Let's go," he said.

"Wait. I need to talk to him."

"He's going to interrogation first. I'll give you a call after that," he said, "but mostly likely, we'll turn him over to the jail afterwards."

Then they were gone. The door snapped shut.

Fifi burped out one last bark.

The Jail

Dusty called an hour later. Conor's interrogation had gone as expected and he'd been taken over to the jail for processing.

"It's a slow night," he said. "He'll be processed quickly. I've gotten him an arraignment for day after tomorrow in case anything comes to light that might prove him innocent before then, but I'm not holding my breath. If you want to see him, I can arrange it, but give it another two hours."

I went back to my articles. I'd yet to put in Conor's name as a suspect, but if I didn't someone else would. It was a simple matter of having a contact in the Sheriff's Department and what journalist didn't have one?

I reminded myself that I needed the money for rent. And someone was going to have to pay for Conor's lawyer. The editors were waiting on the name I'd promised to deliver, and time was almost up. But in my heart, it felt treasonous. I hit SEND on both articles saying only that the Sheriff's Department were questioning a person of interest. That would be a flashing neon sign for the other journalists to call their sources.

Let them. I had to get Conor out of jail.

* * *

From the outside, the Sheriff's Department's jail looked like a WWII bomb bunker, built into the side of a hill. One could easily walk right by and not notice it. I opened the glass door and walked down the red floor of the empty corridor. The phrase Dead Man Walking came to mind.

At the end was a single elevator. Signs on the wall directed all visitors to the floor above. Once inside the elevator, I didn't have a choice. It was either get out or go up one floor. Simple enough.

Upstairs, the doors opened onto another corridor, this one banked by blue plastic chairs. At the end was a line of four people waiting to speak with a woman behind a glass window. Logic told me to get in line.

Every so often I shuffled forward and others filed in behind me. With only two people left before me and maybe four behind, a billowing cloud of rank body odor over took me. The woman in front of me turned around to look.

"It's not me," I said, answering her harsh glare.

She glanced over my shoulder and I turned, too. A scruffy-looking man with a day-old beard and clothes smeared with oily grime stood last in line. He cleared phlegm from his throat and for a minute, I thought he might spit it out on the vinyl flooring.

I shifted my glace to the bulletin board and read the operation permits and a poster about the Inmate Package Program that allowed people to order supplies like toothpaste, body lotion, or Ramen noodle for the inmates. After ten more minutes, it was my turn at the window, but the woman behind the glass answered a phone call instead.

The sign next to me told me to wait to be called. The one on the glass window thanked me for my patience, not knowing that I didn't have any. My boot tapped the floor.

The woman on the phone laughed, mentioned something about food, and laughed again. Behind her was a monitor flicking through views of different corridors somewhere in the building. Most were empty. Next to the phone was a magazine, the back cover showing a half-naked man with water rolling down his buff chest. A perfume ad.

She was now giving the caller details of her weekend plans. I bit the inside of my cheek.

Finally, she put down the phone, gave me a sour look, and motioned me to the glass. On a ledge beneath the glass was another magazine, MANLY FOOD LIST, written in bold yellow type.

Scary.

"Name?" she said.

"Mine?"

"Inmate's."

"Conor Nolan."

She typed it into a keypad. "He's still being processed. Your name?"

"Briana Kaleigh. Is Detective Arkansas still here?"

She glanced back at the monitor on her desk. "He's left. Are you wearing anything metal?"

"Don't think so."

She pointed to a paper taped to the wall. "No cell phones, no metal, no handbags beyond this point. One set of keys, only." The paper on the wall said the same exact words.

She nodded to the blue plastic chairs. "I'll call you when he's ready."

"Do I have time to put my stuff in my car?"

She nodded. "Next."

I took the elevator back down and walked to my car. The lot had emptied out and I decided to move the car closer to the door.

My thoughts were still on spin cycle as to what was going on. I entertained the thought that this was Dusty's way of getting back at me for threatening to reveal the contents of the cooler in my article, but an arrest? That was a little far to go, even for him.

People working in law enforcement saw a lot of bad shit. It sometimes warped their sense of humor, as anyone who has ever been involved with a cop can tell you. I wondered if this was some sort of joke. Dusty knew how much I wanted Conor to leave. Maybe he was trying to scare him away.

But booked for murder? Could Dusty take a joke that far?

Back upstairs, I took a seat across the corridor from the smelly bearded guy. He coughed and cleared his throat of phlegm again.

I gagged. I cast my glance to my lap and my thoughts to the problem at hand. What was Conor's motive? That fingerprint couldn't be his. He didn't know the victim. Did he? I went over his movements of the last month, which were pretty limited. He'd mostly stayed close to the apartment, waiting for the mysterious call, even though he had a cell phone and could have taken the call from anywhere.

Earlier, he'd come home drunk; maybe someone had lifted a print from the bar when he wasn't looking and transferred it. That seemed a little too cloak and dagger, the kind of stuff spy novels are made of, but I still made a mental note to ask Dusty to check for the possibility of a transferred print.

Lawyer? Did I need to find Conor an attorney? At this point, I would assume so. Where could I get a reference? Probably not from Dusty, if this was all for real, and I had to start believing it was. I was waiting to see an inmate. It doesn't get more real than that.

I rewound through the events of the day and evening, developing an argument against Conor's guilt. I might not know much, but I knew Conor wasn't a murderer.

Roughly thirty minutes later, the desk clerk called my name. "You can go up now," she said, handing me a badge with one-dash-four printed on it. "Go through the metal detector and take the right elevator to the third floor. He'll meet you in the visiting room one-dash-four. Swipe the card to get in."

When I reached the room, Conor wasn't there. I started to leave, but the door's lock clicked behind me. My mouth went dry as I realized I was locked in.

The room was about six feet by nine feet with a half-wooden-and-half-glass wall breaking it into two parts—my side and Conor's side. The metal framing the glass window was painted bright green and the walls were painted beige. I pulled out the only piece of furniture on my side, a gray plastic chair, and sat at the window. My foot started to tap.

On the other side of the glass was a wooden door with a glass pane. Though the pane, I saw several rooms with similar doors marked 30 through 40. Conor came out of room 38 and looked around. His glance shot my way and he started walking toward the visiting room. He was wearing slate blue scrubs.

The door buzzed open and he stepped in. He had a matching gray chair, but he didn't sit. He gestured to his clothing, then he jerked down the front of his pants. He was wearing hot pink underwear.

I wasn't in the mood to laugh, but it was a sight.

He sat and picked up the handset on his side of the wall. I picked up mine.

"Can you believe this? Pink. They think it's funny. Tee shirt, underpants, socks, all pink."

"The least of your problems," I snapped. "What have you gotten yourself into this time? The woman downstairs told me that I only have a few minutes so if there's anything you want to tell me you better do it now. I don't know if they'll let me visit again."

"Of course they will. You're still my wife."

I wanted to smack him. Instead, I hit the glass.

He jerked back. "I have a confession to make."

My gut contracted. "Oh, Lord." Not what I wanted to hear. Holding the receiver between my palms, I clutched my hands to my chest the way I'd seen Mrs. Macklin do a hundred times. Had he really done this? Did I not know him at all? I closed my eyes, made the sign of the trinity with the receiver and braced myself for what he had to say.

"I went to Haylee's funeral looking for you. I thought you'd be in pieces, thought you'd need me to hold you together. But that was—"

My eyes flew open. He was pushed back in the chair as if he thought I'd reach through the pane and strangle him. If only.

"What does this have to do with the dead guy in the garage?" I asked.

"Will you shut up and let me speak for once?"

"Geez."

"Like I said, you weren't in pieces—"

"Shows what you know."

He threw a hand out to his side. "Really? Can I just get a word in?"

"Okay, I'll shut up." I made a zipping motion across my lips, wondering if we'd get to the dead guy in the garage before the guard threw me out.

"You had it together, I mean, more than I expected. Your newfound strength irritated me. It made me mad. You clearly didn't need me anymore. Not the way you used to. Your best friend had died and you didn't need anyone to help you cope. It wasn't like when we lost…when we lost…"

"Siobhan."

He crossed his arms and took a deep breath as if bracing against the sound of her name. "You'd changed," he said, releasing his arms and putting the handset back to his ear.

So much about Haylee's death that he didn't know. During the month he'd been crashing in my guest room, we hadn't mentioned it, not once. He didn't know how I'd fought to keep my sanity every minute of every day so I could find her killer for her mother. I'd made a promise to Mrs. Macklin. He also didn't know I'd had a frightening night where I'd almost started drinking again. A night where I lost all sense of time and place. I thanked Dusty for pulling me out of that dark pit. If he hadn't arrived when he had, I don't know where I'd be today.

I tuned back in to Conor's monologue.

"…so I left without signing the divorce papers. I wanted to make you pay."

"Pay for what?"

"For not needing me. I always felt you needed Haylee more than me, but once she was gone…I just thought… Anyway after I cooled off I thought I should give us another try. We were good together once."

"We were kids. Innocents."

"We were good. Don't take that away from me, too."

"We were codependent, Conor. If it hadn't been Siobhan's death, it would have been something else. We were good as long as everything around us was good. You and I together, we could never make the hard decisions. In the name of happiness, we encouraged each other's weaknesses."

I wanted to stand. I needed to move, but the guard's instructions were to stay seated. I didn't want to get thrown out before Conor told me why his fingerprints were on that cooler.

"So all this time there really wasn't a job. You came here to get back with me?" I asked, trying to keep my voice even. As I spoke, my thoughts flashed back on some of the advances he'd made over the past month and I knew he was telling the truth.

"Yes. There was a job. I came across it on the Internet. I was looking for jobs in this area. I knew I wouldn't have a chance if I couldn't show you I could be responsible. I thought once we spent some time together, you'd see…well, it doesn't matter. It didn't happen."

"How did you get the job?"

"I contacted the ad, said I was going to be in Marin for a while and was looking for temporary work. It was a courier job and I was hoping the guy would offer me more work if I did good, but he didn't."

"Whoa. What exactly did the ad say? Do you have a copy of it?"

"Courier needed to transport fragile cargo from San Jose to San Rafael. Mrs. Macklin had told me you'd moved to San Rafael. She sent me your address right after you left D.C."

"And how much were you paid to move this cargo?"

"The first few exchanges took place over the Internet, interviews, references, everything. I gave Mrs. Macklin's name as a reference and my last boss in Texas. I know the company called them both because they told me. After I got the job and signed the contract, the guy told me that I'd receive two thousand dollars on the day of the delivery. When I got the call with the pickup and delivery addresses, one thousand would be deposited in my bank account and another thousand after the delivery." He shook his head. "I figured worst case, they'd screw me out of the second thousand. But even a thousand bucks was still pretty darn good for a few hours travel."

Always the optimist. "Okay, I saw your note this morning," I said. "I assume this was the call you got."

"Yeah, the pickup and delivery addresses. So first thing I do is check my bank account. The first grand was there."

"How could it be in your account if the police found it in your room?"

"Not so fast. Back up. After I got the job, like on the very same day that I was driving up here from Texas, I get another call."

"From whom?"

"Don't know his name, but he knew about the delivery job. Said he worked for the same company and he wanted to add something to the delivery. The guy called me several times. I think he wanted to get a feel for me. He said he'd pay me another two thousand to deliver a cooler at the same drop point.

"The guy was the real fidgety kind. Kept reminding me I had to keep the cooler cold. Told me several times that I should have some ice with me when I picked up the load and make sure the ice didn't melt. All that kind of stuff."

Back on track. "Okay, you picked up the cooler in San Jose today and brought it where?"

"I picked up three boxes with two things in each, things that looked like a large thermoses. Remember the kind we used to take in our school lunches? But bigger." He stretched his hands two feet apart. "Six of those thermoses and the blue beer cooler. The ice in the cooler was pretty melted so I dumped in more."

"Where did you make the pickup? Have you given the address to the police?"

"Of course. I'm not an idiot. I picked everything up at the same location. A private hangar at the San Jose airport."

"Okay. Your fingerprint was found on the beer cooler because you put ice in it. That makes sense."

"Yeah, I know. The beer cooler was the special thing, the delivery the guy was paying me extra for. It looked like it had something dissected inside. Maybe a skinned animal."

A what? Was he joking?

"So I go to this company in San Rafael to make the delivery. When I get to the loading dock, two men in white jumpsuits unloaded the larger boxes and this guy in a suit came out and took the beer cooler right away. He handed me that envelope of cash and left."

"Wait! You met with this man at the company. You didn't go to a house?"

"No. No houses."

"What did the guy look like?"

"Business suit. Grayish hair, cut not too short, but not long either. Medium height."

"White, black, Hispanic?"

"White. He didn't say anything at the dock, but he was obviously the man who I'd talked to on the phone. He took the cooler, looked inside, and handed me the envelope. End of story."

"Until he's found dead," I said, starting to get the picture.

The man he'd described sounded like the dead guy. Not good that Conor had met with him, not with his fingerprints found at the scene. Time of death was clearly after Conor returned because the cooler was there. His contact in San Jose couldn't alibi him out. "Wait. Who did you meet in San Jose?"

"Two Mexican guys. I don't think they spoke English. They helped put the boxes in the truck and went back over to the plane, an older Kodiak."

"Can you describe them for a sketch artist?"

"I guess, but not sure how much I remember."

"Sounds like the man in the business suit might be the vic. He was found dead in a garage with the blue cooler and a cryogenic canister, probably one of the things you thought looked like a thermos."

"Are you shitting me?"

"Why do you think you're here? They have your fingerprint on the cooler."

"I thought it was about that stolen car."

"Keep up, Conor. That was ages ago, but that's how they got a fingerprint match. You're arrested for murder. Dusty read you the charges."

Conor looked dazed. "That's why they were asking about the cooler and the plane and the bar in San Francisco. I'm confused."

"That makes two of us. Wait what bar?"

"After I got paid I wanted to celebrate. Found an Irish bar and made a few friends."

"Yeah, I bet you did. Do you still have the address of where you delivered the boxes?"

He glanced away as if thinking. "It's on a paper in my truck. Looked like a warehouse. Nothing fancy."

Step one would be to find out what kind of company needed cryogenic canisters and placentas. Step two—

"Are you listening?" Conor snapped. "You have to."

"What?" I asked. "Sorry, my mind was someplace else. What did you say?"

"I said you have to help me. You know me. You know I didn't kill anyone. I'll sign anything you want, but, Briana, you have to get me out of here. You're all I have."

"I'll talk to Dusty."

He shook his head then lowered the handset to the ledge.

"I will. I promise."

He scowled and raised it back to his ear. "Did you ever stop to think that your boyfriend might be behind all this? He'd love to see me shut away."

"He's not my boyfriend! And no, I didn't think that. He's one of the good ones. Geez. What's with you two? They found your print. That's why you're here. Dusty was only doing his job."

Conor huffed. "I see the way he looks at you. Oh, don't look so surprised. I've caught you watching his boat from the kitchen window."

"We've been through some things. Some bad things."

He shook his head and huffed again. "Right. I promise you, that detective won't lift a finger to get me out of here. I need your help"

I heard something in the dour way he said "detective," plus Dusty had alluded to an uncomfortable conversation between the two. "Did you say something to Dusty?" And there it was. The head tilt that announced his guilt like a bullhorn. "Oh no, what did you say?"

The door behind me opened and a woman in a skirt suit came in with a guard.

"Ms. Kaleigh," the guard said, "you need to leave now."

The woman in the suit set a large leather briefcase on the floor.

I stood. "Who are you?" I asked.

"Who are you?" she asked right back.

"I'm his, his… ahhh, I'm his wife," I said, more rudely than expected.

"I work with the District Attorney," she said.

"He wants a lawyer."

"That's not what he said earlier. I believe you are leaving."

The guard slipped a hand around my arm to guide me out.

I raised the handset to my mouth and yelled, "Conor, you want a lawyer. Don't say anything."

"Get her out," the woman said.

The guard tore the handset from my grip and pulled me toward the door. "You have to leave now," he said again, hardly straining against my force as I fought to stay put.

My feet slid over the smooth vinyl floor as the guard, now with one large hand planted in my back, shoved me out the door.

"Conor, I'll get you a lawyer. Don't say anything."

"I'd like a lawyer," I thought I heard as the door clicked shut between us. The guard released me and I straightened up, pulling my shirt back down.

He shook his head.

"He's innocent. In more ways than one," I said and headed for the elevator.

The Date

Dusk lingered in the blue-gray sky, although it was well past nine p.m. when I pulled into the apartment parking lot. Fifi was whining as I unlocked the door. In my rush to get to the jail, I'd forgotten to take her out. She jumped up on my legs twice then backed away and sat, pom-pom tail ticking like a metronome.

"Guess you need to go out," I said, as if she could answer me. I grabbed the leash and picked her up. She didn't try to lick me.

Downstairs, all was quiet. It always was after a visit from the police, making me wonder about my neighbors. Six weeks ago, after Dusty disappeared, the police had camped out in my parking lot for almost a full day. For a week afterwards, I didn't see a single neighbor.

The fog was way out on the horizon, but there was a chill in the air. The grassy area where the boaters grilled their catch and the homeless begged for leftovers was empty. A crescent moon hung over the water, not yet bright enough to form a reflection.

I led Fifi to the bushes, which she sniffed and then ignored. She ran off in the opposite direction until the leash locked and jerked her to a stop. She was doing that a lot this evening. Maybe she missed Conor. He liked to lie on the floor and play with her and her squeaky giraffe. Far as I could tell, she liked it too.

She headed over to the concrete barrier near the boats. I hustled but was not going to run. The faint whisper of Latin music drifted down the opposite hill, but a rhythm more recognizable was coming from Dusty's boat. Despite the chill, all his portholes were open, as was the front of his boat. He had the music loud enough that I heard clearly the words to *Shakedown Street*.

At least he wasn't meditating. He played a pingy-zingy sort of music for that. I needed to talk to him and now was as good a time as any. I tied Fifi's leash around a small birch tree and let out the lead. She'd have plenty of room to roam.

I crossed over to the pier. The boat's interior was brightly lit and I thought I heard conversation coming from below. I was halfway across the plank to his boat when I heard a woman laugh.

I paused.

The plank was only ten inches wide so I didn't pause long. Turning around wasn't an option—I'd flunked out of ballet school. I needed to go forward in order to turn around. On the last step before the deck, the plank moaned. I leaped off in an effort to be quiet. Faulty logic. My boots smacked the deck.

I was about to head back across the plank when Dusty appeared in the doorway. In one hand he held a beer bottle by its neck. "What's up?" he asked. He glanced behind him and then stepped up the last step so that he filled the opening.

"I, um, oh what the heck." I took a step toward him. "Sorry to bother you, but I have to talk to you about Conor."

With stiff movements, he came through the doorway and onto the deck. He was wearing khakis and a peach-colored golf shirt. The color gave a nice glow to his skin. He lowered the bottle to his side. "Now's not a good time. We'll talk tomorrow."

"Conor's not a murderer."

"You don't know that."

"I was married to the man. I had his child. I *do* know that."

"What's going on?" asked a woman silhouetted in the doorway behind him. Backlit, I couldn't see her face, but something familiar struck me. Guess Dusty hadn't been watching TV.

She stepped outside and not only did I recognize her, I realized that she was the woman Dusty had waved to at the drugstore this morning. This was the first time I'd seen her looking like an actual female. She was wearing an off-the-shoulder sundress with a thick shawl tucked strategically to show a nice amount of cleavage.

"Agent Clark," I said, my mouth dry and something like cement settling in my stomach. We'd met back when Dusty had been kidnapped. She worked for the FBI and was rumored to be sweet on Dusty.

A sentiment he clearly reciprocated.

I glanced back at him. He looked down at his beer bottle.

"Sorry to bother you," I managed to get out as my face grew warm. I crossed the plank faster than I thought possible.

"We'll talk tomorrow," Dusty called.

"Yep." I kept walking, but waved behind my head. With wet cheeks, I wasn't about to turn around. "Have a nice evening."

* * *

I lit a cigarette. Stood still, smoking it down to the filter, then I stubbed it out. I piddled around for the next hour—washing dishes, vacuuming—unable to concentrate while my grocery list of things to do grew longer. I booted the laptop. I had to find Conor a lawyer, but my mind kept going back to Agent Clark's heaving breasts. More than once I went to the bathroom to look at my own a-little-more-than-boy-size chest. That was not true. I had nice breasts. Not too small, not too big.

Funny thing was I didn't remember Agent Clark being so well endowed in her nondescript blue suit. Maybe she'd had on a pushup bra. I grabbed my breasts and shoved them upwards. Yuk…not attractive. And…ouch.

On a scale of one-to-ten my kiss with Dusty shouldn't have made the grade. He'd been tied up for days and his lips had been dry and cracked, he smelled worse than a sewer, and we were in a horse stall with the stink of horse poo all around us. Not a romantic moment and yet, I couldn't get the memory out of my mind. When his lips touched mine, I was overcome by a sensation of pure love. Honestly, I'd never been kissed like that. Ever. Every kiss always held some level of desire or need. Not Dusty's. It was as if he were giving me a gift.

And now he'd taken it back.

I went to the laptop. I had to find a lawyer, but who could I ask for recommendations? Normally, that would be Dusty, but not tonight. I searched Marin criminal lawyers and came up with lots of websites and a few organizations.

That colorless dress Clark had been wearing wasn't very nice. It was sort of like a sack. Except for the exposed breasts, it wasn't flattering at all.

I emailed the editor of the *Marin Independent Journal.* Surely, he'd know the best lawyers in the county.

Had this been their first date or had Dusty been seeing her all month? Could that explain his weird behavior? Maybe Conor had nothing to do with it. Why would Dusty be weird about dating Clark? Because he'd kissed ME!

I went to the back window. His boat was still open and lit. I could almost hear the music wafting through the portholes. Music? What time was it? There was a noise ordinance. I could report the music. And what would that serve? Kill the romantic vibe. Make them have to deal with the local police instead of each other.

Back at the laptop, I found an email from the editor with three recommendations. He was excited that I had an "in" on this case. He wanted to sign an exclusive contract for my articles, but I wasn't ready to think about that now. I began looking up the three names the editor had sent me.

All were prominent local lawyers with impressive lists of credentials and previous cases. It was quite late when I decided on one. I walked to the kitchen and looked out the window. Dusty's boat was dark. There was no moon to speak of so I couldn't tell if it was locked up.

* * *

I awoke with a hangover. Not from drinking, but one heavy with the regrets of things I'd done and wished I hadn't. With an alcoholic hangover those things were dulled by a haze, making any embarrassment or regrets seem unimportant. Should an embarrassing memory seep in, one always had the familiar alcohol excuse. *I was drunk.* Everyone knows a drunk isn't responsible for his or, in this case, her actions.

This morning I awoke cringing from embarrassment. Without the alcoholic curtain between my thoughts and feelings, I wanted to blame someone. But anyway I turned it, the foolishness was all mine. I had to take responsibility for the fantasy—the kiss, the attraction I thought we shared—and my delusion made me angry.

I shuffled around the apartment. Luckily, I had other things to worry about than my lapse in reality. Conor had forty-eight hours to find an attorney before his arraignment. A public defender was always a possibility, but they were often overworked and looked for the easiest solution, such as a plea bargain. Conor had just earned four thousand dollars, even if two thousand was in evidence, and I was pretty sure I could get more from his family back east if needed. The Irish always stuck up for their own. Especially against the authorities.

Eight a.m., coffee mug in hand, I called the Law Offices of Gerri Runyan. Her online reviews were noteworthy and a few things written about her cases impressed me more than the other two lawyers. Her first glowing recommendation was that she'd graduated from Harvard Law School. It wasn't the prestige that interested me, but that she was from the East Coast. Hopefully, she, I, and Conor would speak the same language. None of those homegrown philosophies or Quantum, Buddhist, or brouhaha beliefs about how "things happen for a reason." I wanted someone solid; someone Conor could depend on.

Her second recommendation was that she'd won a good percentage of her cases. Most lawyers won't take a case unless they feel sure they can win, so I had to convince her that this case could be won. And third, her fee scale wasn't exorbitant. It wasn't cheap, either, but when your life is on the line, you can't shop in the bargain basement.

My only hesitation was the address listed on her website. The other two lawyers had offices near the courthouse, but the address listed for Gerri Runyan was over in central San Rafael. I knew the place from my first visit to California, an industrial area with lots of body shops and masonry stores.

"My ex-husb...ah, my...husband has been arrested for murder and I was wondering if I could speak with Ms. Runyan about representation?" Phone to ear, I walked through the kitchen and looked out over Dusty's boat. Was he alone this morning?

"Does your husband currently have representation?" the woman asked.

Was this an assistant or had I detected a slight Boston accent? "No," I said and listened more carefully for a sign that this was Ms. Runyan.

"Has he been arraigned?"

There it was, the open "a" sound that always gave away a Bostonian. "No. He was arrested late last night. I was told his arraignment is tomorrow morning."

"Let me check my calendar."

Stravinsky's *Rite of Spring* filled my ear. The exterior lock on Dusty's door caught a fleck of light. The lock meant he was already gone. Probably getting an early start on collecting evidence to hang Conor.

The music ended with a click and the woman came back on the line. "I can see you at ten-fifteen. You have the address?"

"Suite three-oh-eight?"

"Yes." A slight chuckle as we disconnected.

Weird. I wrote down directions from my computer search and then lit a cigarette, my third one. I filled Fifi's bowl with chow and she was at my feet before I could put it down. I emptied and rinsed the coffee pot and started a fresh one. All these everyday things helped clear my mind.

I'd just sat at the table to start making notes for my meeting with the lawyer when someone knocked hard at my door. Fifi shot out of the kitchen at breakneck speed and skidded to a stop before crashing into the door. She barked and barked, each burst of urgency pushing her back on her hind legs. Only one person made her that crazy.

I opened the door.

Dusty held out a coffee cup and a white waxed bag. "Breakfast."

Usually, this was my way of apologizing, although Dusty drank juice, not coffee, because he was weird about caffeine frying his brain. I had a snide remark about that.

"Which one of your personalities bought me breakfast?" I asked, accepting the coffee.

He followed me across the room and put the bag on the table next to my laptop. "Cronuts," he said, pointing at it. "A cross between croissants and donuts."

"You should be buying them for your girlfriend, or should I say lover?"

"We were just hanging…I'm not here to talk about her. I'm here to tell you about your husband."

"Ex-husband."

"Have any papers been filed? No. Funny, that's what he told me, too. Since you're comfortable deluding yourself about your marital status, did you ever stop to think that you're also deluding yourself about his guilt?"

"Conor's guilt has never crossed my mind," I lied. I didn't think he'd killed anyone, but he had a magical way of finding trouble. Last night, I'd thought long and hard as to what kind of trouble those canisters contained. "What was in the cryogenic canisters?"

He stiffened. "So we're done with the civilities, back to work?"

He'd made it painfully clear at the drugstore yesterday that there would be no more civilities between us. I'd written his temper off, but after seeing him with Clark last night, well, I wasn't a fool twice.

He was not my friend or colleague. He'd helped me out, I'd helped him out, but whatever I'd been feeling for the last month was *my* problem.

Rather than answer him, I took a sip of coffee and turned away, a tornado of emotions tearing through my insides. I didn't want him to see my doubt…my anger…my shame.

"Suit yourself," he said. "Besides the fingerprint, we caught up with the men who flew in the biomaterials. They work for a medical research firm out of Mexico. Both identified Conor as the man who picked up the medical products."

Fifi wiggled between my legs and looked up at me. This was new. Was she possibly worried about me?

"Besides the placentas, what were the products?" I asked without facing him.

After a few minutes of silence I turned around. "If you don't tell me, Conor's lawyer will."

"The cryogenic containers held vials of cord blood."

"Cord blood? Why...? Stem cells?"

"Just cord blood cells. The company where Conor delivered them, Primordium Labs, stores cord blood."

"Glad you mentioned Primordium. Did those lab people confirm that Conor delivered the materials? Thus the fingerprint."

Dusty walked to the sofa and sat. Fifi trotted over to him, standing just out of kicking distance, and barked. Dusty shaped his hand like a gun and pointed it at her. She ran back to me.

"The two men from the loading dock confirmed that Conor delivered three boxes of medical material. All in good condition. But they also said Conor got into a disagreement with one of the lab techs when he came down to inspect the boxes. That lab tech happens to be our victim."

I went to the front window and opened the blinds. Another foggy morning, gray and hopeless. "The vic was a lab tech?"

"Not really. The victim, Dr. Chaffe, actually ran the lab. Had a team of four techs."

"Did they say what the *disagreement* was about?" I asked, watching my downstairs neighbor walk to his car.

"All they heard was Conor say something along the lines of 'what about my money?' These guys never saw the blue beer cooler."

"That doesn't make sense."

"Yes, it does. Conor's lying. Open your eyes."

My neighbor pulled out of the parking lot. Three cars were left downstairs; one was mine.

"There's more," Dusty said. "Conor's alibi for the T.O.D., the Irish pub in the city. Bartender says he arrived later than what Conor gave us. He had enough time to kill Dr. Chaffe, then drive to the city and get loaded."

I finished the coffee, but what I really wanted was a cigarette. I never smoked around Dusty because it bothered him and it bothered me to bother him. I had to get over that. I had to move on. Helping Conor was the best way to make that happen.

"So you've never had a case where the evidence pointed to the wrong person? It's called a frame-up. Conor told me on the day you met him you threatened to 'run him out of town'. Maybe you're behind the frame."

Dusty was on his feet, shaking an open hand at me, and gritting his teeth. His growl was deeper than Fifi's. "Did he also tell you what *he* said to make me say that? No. Briana, this guy isn't the guy you think he is. You have this stubborn faith in people and I applaud that, but in this case, it's blinding you to his faults. I've done my research. Except for the car theft, Conor has never been arrested, but he's been involved with shady people, people the FBI have on file."

Billy Black. That was the name that came to mind. He ran the upper Eastern Seaboard arm of the Irish Brotherhood. He had Mafia ties both here and abroad and Conor had worked for him but only as a longshoreman.

Then there was the mess that had taken Conor to Texas. I knew less about that. Conor had said the police were looking into some of his business associates so he needed to lie low. He'd always wanted to see Texas.

Conor dreamed of making a "big score," but he lacked the insensitivity to be ruthless. He was a softy who would stop at the side of the road to pick up an injured squirrel and take it to a vet, never thinking that he might catch rabies.

His tunnel vision had always frustrated me. As a journalist, I knew how his innocence could take a wrong turn. Now, it finally had.

"And motive? What would that be?" I asked.

"I think the two thousand we found in his room would do it. A guy like him, two thousand is worth killing over."

"A guy like him. Seriously? Let me tell you about a *guy* like him. He has the biggest heart of anyone I've ever known. Granted, he's a sandwich short of a picnic, but I've literally seen him give a homeless man the coat off his back on a cold Boston night. He wouldn't kill a spider for two thousand."

I went to the kitchen and tossed the coffee cup. I needed a moment.

"We're clearly on opposite sides of this," I said when I came back in. "But I still have some of that stubborn faith in you, too. Once I find proof of Conor's innocence, I expect you to take an impartial look at it."

With a loud slap, Dusty hit his hands together, interlaced the fingers, and shook them at me. He opened his mouth as if to speak, then closed it.

"You know your way to the door," I said. "I have work to do." I dropped down into the chair and opened my laptop. When the door clicked softly shut, I dropped my forehead to the cool tabletop and tried to breathe.

The Lawyer

This had to be a mistake. I parked in front of the address for Gerri Runyan's suite. I pulled out my phone and looked up the address again in case I'd written it down wrong. To the left was a veterinary hospital and to the right, a body shop. If I'd written it down incorrectly, I must have reversed a number or two because there wasn't anything nearby that looked remotely like a lawyer's office.

I compared the number on my phone against that on the building with the sign that read: MARIN SELF STORAGE UNITS. It matched. I turned off the engine, got out, and went in through a door with a sign that read: LEAVE IT WITH US.

What did I want to leave? Conor? Dusty? This case? The kiss? Ah, there it was again. That stupid kiss. The man had been drugged out of his mind. He thought he was dying. Forget it! It meant nothing.

A bald-headed man in a white turtleneck shirt sat behind a counter covered in pine veneer.

"I'm looking for three-oh-eight," I said.

He stroked his scraggy beard. "Three...oh...eight," he said, pointing to a door in the back corner. "Through that door, down two rows and turn right. Keep walking and you'll see it on the left."

I stepped over a large furry dog and went to the door. It slammed shut behind me as I stepped into the long empty corridor. An overhead light popped on. My thoughts were reeling in all directions. Was this a practical joke? Was this a scavenger hunt? Was I about to find a treasure chest that would lead me to the mysterious lawyer? Or was this a huge error on my part, one that I'd laugh about later?

Remember the Boston lawyer I tried to hire for you?

I passed the first row and saw only locked storage cages. The air was cool and dry. I turned at the second row and passed boxes that looked to be about six feet wide and ten feet high. The deeper into the unit I went, the wider the storage boxes became. On the left, I found box three-oh-eight not suite three-oh-eight.

A pair of metal double doors was spread wide open, blocking the entrances of the units on either side. Inside, against the left wall, was a low set of shelves with lots of books shoved in every which way. A printer and a fax machine were on top. On the opposite wall were two tan metal filing cabinets. A wooden executive desk, made of walnut, sat center of the storage box. Behind the desk, a woman in a turquoise-green pantsuit stood, talking into a cell phone. When she saw me she gestured wildly for me to come in. She pointed to a leather chair near the desk without breaking her conversation.

I hesitated. This setup was too unconventional even for me. Did I really want to hire a lawyer who worked out of a storage unit? She gestured again, giving me a stern look at the same time.

I stepped inside, noticing the handwoven rug protruding from under the desk. Otherwise, the floor was concrete. I sat and glanced around, noticing other details such as the two diplomas hanging above the filing cabinets and the desk lamp with a daylight bulb. It gave off enough light to make me think there was a skylight. I looked up. No skylight.

A stack of folders had slid sideways on the desk and were close to slipping off the edge. Compelled, I pushed them away from the edge. My movement caught Ms. Runyan's attention and she pointed to the phone and shook her head.

"Listen, I have a client and I need to make some money, especially if you're going to add two more posts to the rail," she said. "Don't do anything before we talk." She shook her head and puckered her lips as if she didn't believe what she was hearing. "Fine. I'll be by later."

She tossed the cell to her desk and made a face at me as if I'd heard the whole conversation. "Contractors. They're enough to make you go out and buy a gun."

"Interesting office," I said, still sure I'd made a colossal mistake by staying.

She sat behind the desk, rolling the chair in close. "Two hundred a month and that includes air-conditioning and electricity. I was renting an office for four thousand and it wasn't much bigger. I can pass my savings on to my clients and still afford to live in this overpriced county where some asinine contractor thinks he can rip me off because of a building violation."

"Uh-huh."

"Criminals don't pay much."

"I'd think there would be all kinds of white collar crime in Marin."

"Oh, there is, but they don't hire locally, they go hire some fancy L.A. lawyer or bribe some official and are never heard from again. I get the gang crime." She picked up a folder from her desk and waved it. "Or the car thieves who don't actually live in the county." She put the folder down and picked up another one. "Or the guys out of work after twenty years left to rob homes to feed their families. This is an expensive place to live."

"You don't have to tell me."

"I'm here…" she pursed her lips, "maybe two, three hours a day at most. It's all mobile now. What should impress you is the savings I can pass along, not my real estate."

She glanced out over my shoulder, pointed with the folder still in her hand. "There's an insurance company four boxes down." She tilted her head as if to direct me. "And that box over there is used only as a mailing address. Can't be anything legal that I can think of. Every couple of weeks, I slide a business card under the door. Figure I'll get a call one of these days."

Her phone jingled and she picked it up, looked at the faceplate, and put it back down. She tapped a set of manicured nails on the desktop. "Tell me about your husband's arrest."

"Ex…," I said, unable to stop myself.

"Details."

I took an index card from my handbag and slid it across the desk. "That's the case number."

She pulled her laptop over in front of her and typed something on the keyboard. I watched her eyes scan the page. "I've heard about this," she said. "Out in Peacock Gap. Nice homes."

"He didn't do it."

"Prove it," she said, shoving the laptop to the side.

Forty minutes. That was how long it took for me to convince Gerri Runyan to take Conor's case. I signed a contract with her and wrote a thousand-dollar retainer check from Conor's checking account.

"I'd like to hire an investigator," she said. "I have someone I usually work with. He's very thorough."

"I understand that's standard procedure, but most sleuthing these days is done on the computer. In an effort to keep costs down, I'd like to volunteer my services. I'm an investigative reporter and I probably use a lot of the same online services that your investigator uses."

She clipped Conor's check to the outside of an empty manila folder. "My problem with that is your impartiality."

"I believe in Conor's innocence and, you're right, I will be biased, but if I come across any single thing that puts my belief in doubt, I will pass it on to you. You have my word. If at any time, you feel another investigator would do a better job, I'll step down."

When Mercedeses fly.

The Lab

Primordium Labs was in northern San Rafael, past the
Civic Center and Sheriff's Department. I followed the
frontage road along a string of odd storefronts, past Jeff's
Café, an air-conditioning repair shop, and Woofington's
Doggie Daycare. Now, there was an idea.

Doggie Daycare. If I was going to prove Conor's
innocence, I needed my days free to go where I needed to go.
I'd been wondering who I could leave Fifi with. One person I
thought of was Bob, a friend of Dusty's who didn't work
regular hours and oddly was one of the few people Fifi liked,
but with Dusty working against me, I'd ruled Bob out.
Doggie daycare might be the ticket. Fifi would hate me. She
wasn't what one would call social. Maybe there was a fix for
that; she could get training. They could teach her to sit, do
tricks, or play maracas.

She did like music. Haylee had taught her to bark to *Mary
Had a Little Lamb*. Bark only, not bark out the melody like a
clever dog would do.

I pictured Fifi with a red maraca between her teeth and
almost missed my turn, but my GPS told me a second time to
turn right, and then scolded me the third time. I drove
through what looked like an office park. The first block of
homogenous brick buildings gave way to more original
designs. A pseudo-adobe style was a common theme. Many
buildings had signs out front. Siemens. Verizon. UPS. Bail
Bondsman. But others had no signage at all. That was the
case with Primordium Labs. The front parking lot was full of
cars so I suspected I was at the right address. Besides, my

GPS told me I was and electronics, unlike ex-husbands, never lie.

The building was a two-story peach-painted stucco structure. Panels of flat gray rocks, the kind we'd used as kids to skip over the Charles River, covered the front façade. The glass door was tinted gray and on each side were large picture windows, also tinted. I couldn't see inside.

I drove out of the parking lot and around the building. The side walls were covered in the same pebbly panels as the front. There were no windows. At the back were two red industrial garage doors, one closed, the other rolled open. Strips of wide, clear plastic hung top to ground over the entrance of the open garage. I assumed this was the loading area where Conor had made his delivery.

I drove back around and parked in the front lot. The address was stenciled on the tinted glass door, small and just above the handle. The door was locked so I reached for the buzzer, but the door clicked open before I hit the button.

Inside was freezing, the air-conditioning way too high. The layout was tasteful and minimalist. The walls at each end of the office were paneled redwood with a door in the center of each panel. The carpeting was pale gray and high quality. To one side of the reception area was a rust-colored sectional sofa. A low hum filled the air, but there was no machinery visible.

"May I help you?" asked a well-dressed woman, standing behind the long, narrow reception desk of polished redwood. A swirly "S" of designer track lighting held crystal bulbs above her head.

At one end of the desk was a small monitor showing an industrial film about storing cord blood. I assumed that was what the film was about, but I couldn't be sure since the sound was muted. There was the classic image of a family, husband, wife and two children, one a boy the other a girl. Then a cut to the mother with a big pregnant belly in a hospital bed, beads of sweat on her brow, family circled around the bed. Next came a close-up of hands working in a lab setting, also vials, glass tubes, and a centrifuge in the frame.

"Are you here to inquire about our storage facility?" the woman asked, tearing my attention from the screen.

I flashed my old District Dispatch press pass. "I was wondering if I could get a tour of your facility."

When she smiled her teeth were so white they appeared to glow. "That would need to be set up with our publicity liaison."

"Could I speak with that person?"

"I'm afraid we've lost a member of our team recently and she's gone to be with the family."

That was a nice way of saying, *our lab director got bludgeoned with a hand rake yesterday.*

She picked up a pen and scribbled something on an orange Post-it. She tore the note off the pad and offered it to me. "Her name is Nara Hibbert. This is her extension. If you'd like to call, she should be back tomorrow."

Seeing I wasn't going to get more, I thanked her and left.

Next, I drove over to the jail, but was told Conor was with his lawyer and no more visitors were allowed.

With the wheels of justice rolling, I could think of only one other thing I wanted to do. So I returned to the apartment, where I grabbed my gun and snatched up Fifi. I drove us out to China Camp, a state park that was a little east of the crime scene. I parked in one of the reserved barbeque areas and got out.

This side of the park was deserted during the week. From what I'd seen, barbequers and picnickers used it only on weekends. A system of bike trails and hiking trails that were active all week was across the road, but I'd driven out to this spot a few times to escape Conor and knew it to be isolated.

A sign warned me away, noting that this area had to be reserved through the park. It listed a phone number for me to do just that. The sign also stated the fine I'd receive if I disobeyed. A few years back, California had gone broke and one way the state had decided to recoup money was to close some of its state parks. China Camp was on the list, although it had yet to be closed, thanks to a few serious environmental campaigns. Even so, it was a long shot that there was more than one ranger still on the payroll and the odds that he or she would come across me in all this wilderness was slim.

I went to a metal trash container and looked for something I could use for target practice. A Diet Coke can fit the bill. I carried it over to one of the two picnic tables, Fifi trailing behind me. I set the can on the edge of the table and backed away, counting off sixty steps. Behind the table, the land dropped off straight down into the bay. No risk of hitting a stray hiker because no one could reach this point without a boat. And I checked; there were no boats. Daylight silhouetted the Coke can against the bay's open landscape. We were totally alone.

Fifi stretched out on the warm asphalt. I raised the gun, balanced, and fired. Fifi leaped up and barked once. I was rusty. I aimed and pulled the trigger again and again. Fifi barked at each shot. It took three shots before I hit the can, but when I did, it flew off the table and down the cliff. A detail I hadn't planned for.

I went back to the trash bin and dug around in the debris. I carried three more cans to the table and centered them better, hoping that the propulsion wouldn't send them so far afield. I went back to where Fifi was curled up licking her paw and turned to aim.

The gold-colored can reminded me of Dusty's bald head when the sun hit it. Sometimes sprouts of new growth would twinkle with the light. I squeezed the trigger. The sound exploded against the silence. The can popped and flew backwards off the table.

Fifi barked.

The red can, taller and thinner than the others, reminded me of Conor, who always stood out from the crowd, a characteristic I'd once found charming, but lately just annoyed me. When was he going to grow up and take responsibility? I fired. The can flew into the air. Dark liquid spewed from the opening before the can disappeared beneath the table.

Fifi barked.

I looked down at her and she sprawled backwards on the warm asphalt, offering up her belly for the pleasure of a scratch. *Right.* The last can was silver, the color of her rhinestone collar. I took aim at the can and didn't miss.

Fifi jumped up and barked.

In three shots I'd cleared the table. A serene sensation washed over me and I almost smiled. *I still had it.* Then the strangest thing happened.

I dropped down beside Fifi and my eyes filled with tears. Something deep inside opened up and I began to wail. I crumpled and let the misery flow.

The Wife

On the way back from China Camp, I decided to swing by the crime scene once more. I'm not sure why; I was pretty sure the house would be deserted, but it was nearby and I had time. To my surprise, there was a silver Audi parked in the driveway.

I remembered the receptionist saying that the publicity liaison was with the family, which told me there was a family. Maybe I'd meet the publicity liaison, too.

The garage was closed and crime scene tape stretched across the width, blocking the door from opening without breaking the seal. Technically, the house wasn't part of the crime scene so someone could be inside, but I didn't see Dusty allowing that.

A shadow passed behind the sheer curtains on the front of the house. Someone was inside. Maybe the wife. Dusty might have allowed a family member to come pick up belongings. I parked at the curb, took Fifi out, and tied her to the passenger side mirror. I went to the door.

An Asian woman, about my height, opened the door just far enough to stick her head out. Her shiny, black hair hung down past her shoulders and matched a pair a thick-rimmed glasses in color. "Yes?"

"Are you Ms. Chaffe?" I asked.

The woman looked at me with distrust, but said nothing.

"My name is Briana Kaleigh and I'm a journalist—"

She started to shut the door, but I got my foot in fast. I get that a lot. "What I meant to say is my husband has been unjustly arrested for killing your husband and I'd like to ask you some questions in the hopes of finding who really did this."

She pulled the door back and stepped forward to block me. "You have to go. I'm only here to pick up a few things. I don't have long."

"I understand. I know the detective working the case. We've worked together several times. I'm sure it would be okay with him if I asked you a few questions about your husband's work."

"I spoke to detectives yesterday."

Of course she had, and if Dusty knew I was here, he wouldn't be too happy. As my father was fond of saying, *you gotta do what you gotta do*.

Forgetting my foot, she started to close the door again until it bounced off my boot.

"Please, move," she ordered. "I'm in a hurry."

"You may not believe me, but I know my husband didn't murder yours. Until the real murderer is caught, you, too, could be in danger."

That got her attention. She stopped kicking at my boot and took a breath.

"Please. I won't take long." I shifted forward, putting more weight on my foot as if I was about to enter. "For your own safety."

She didn't move at first. Her faraway look made me think that she was processing what I'd said. Finally, she took a step back, not really opening the door, but allowing me to. I stepped inside.

An ebony grand piano was the first thing I noticed. It filled a good part of the living room. Red velvet-covered chairs were set out in rows of four as if for a concert. On the walls were several four-by-five gold-framed photographs of the inside of various concert halls, each labeled by name and place. The one closest to me was in Milan.

Ms. Chaffe led me past the chairs and piano, down a corridor, and into a personal office. On the floor were two cardboard boxes half filled with files. The room was dark. Textbooks lined two walls and other books were stacked in piles against the bookshelves. The massive executive desk was old wood, its chair, a more modern black leather, backed up to the only window in the room. The window was without curtains and gave a view on to a lush garden of blooming zinnias.

"I'm gathering some of David's work," she said. "We have to talk while I work."

"Ms. Chaffe, did your—"

"Don't call me that."

"I'm sorry, you aren't Ms. Chaffe?" I glanced around the room for a personal photo.

"Yes," she said. "Yes, I am. I meant, call me…Ir—. Call me Bathilde."

That sounded German, something she clearly wasn't. Her speech was as Californian as any I've met. "Ah, I'm Briana."

She went to the desk and squatted by an open bottom drawer that was half full of files. She flicked rapidly through them.

"Do you know why your husband had brought home a cooler of placentas and cord blood in a cryogenic container?"

Her busy little fingers paused only an instant, then went back to work. "He often brought his work home," she said, pulling out a handful of files and laying them on the carpet. "As you can see."

"What kind of work was that?"

"He was testing," she said and went silent. She pulled another set of files and gathered all the files in her hand. She stood and kicked the drawer closed, then dropped the files into one of the boxes.

"I'm sorry…what did you say? He was testing what?"

She went to one of the bookshelves and rapidly scanned the book titles on the top shelf. She paused. "I didn't mean testing. He was in charge of stem cell research. He mostly worked with differentiated cells, first manipulating them and then painting them on scaffolds, studying which ones might be used to create a viable blood flow."

That made no sense to me, but I persisted. "Why did he need placentas?"

She didn't answer as she continued to scan the bookshelves. I repeated the question.

She yanked two books out of the bookshelf and dropped them in the box on top of the files. She pulled out the next two books in the set and dropped them in, too. "Maybe he was going to see if he could reproduce them somehow. Yes, that must be it."

"Why would someone want to kill him?"

She stopped scanning the books and turned to me. "I was told there was an argument about money. Your husband needed to be paid."

"And he *was* paid, so there was no reason he would have killed Dr. Chaffe. Had your husband been worried about anything in the past week? Perhaps acting different in some way?"

She paused again, looking at me yet past me. Finally, she shook her head, but I felt there was something more she wanted to say.

"Anything that you remember could help. It doesn't matter if you think it's insignificant."

"There's nothing. Can you help me carry these to my car?"

She closed up the box with the books and then the other one, which was only half full. She picked up the lighter box and handed it to me without waiting for an answer. She picked up the heavier box and led me out of the room.

We went out by the front door and she checked the knob to make sure it was locked. My time with her was drawing to an end, and I had nothing.

"Could any of his colleagues tell me more about his work?" I asked, watching her shove a gym bag across the trunk of the Audi while balancing the box on the bumper's edge.

She put the box in and turned to take the one from me. "He worked fairly independently at the lab. Each technician has their own project. If you want to talk with someone you should talk with the CEO, Vincent Kerner."

She slammed the trunk shut. "Is that all? I need to go?"

"Inside, I felt like there was something you wanted to tell me."

She glanced over my shoulder. "Is that your dog?"

Fifi, still tied to the outside mirror, lay in the grass licking her paw. I heard the click as the car door opened. Ms. Chaffe slammed the Audi's door and the engine came to life. I stepped away from the trunk, half afraid she'd back over me if I didn't.

She backed out, never once glancing my way.

I walked over to Fifi and she rolled to her back offering up her belly.

"Are you serious?"

Something was bothering me, but I couldn't put a finger on it. Maybe I was just irritated because I hadn't managed to get a single lead. Spouses were usually more helpful. They always had opinions that they wanted to share. Mrs. Chaffe was a closed-mouth wife, a rarity in my work.

As I untied the leash, I did a mental walk-though of the house, past the red velvet chairs, past the piano, down the corridor, and into the office. No personal photographs. Not necessarily unusual; he was a scientist, probably not the sentimental type. The wife spoke and looked like a scientist too, maybe explaining the scarcity of personal decoration.

Nothing in the house suggested children were a part of the mix. So who played the piano? And what about the beautiful garden? Which one of the brainiacs was a weekend landscaper? How well could the wife hurl a hand rake?

The Arraignment

The following morning I was in court by eight, although Conor's case wasn't called until eight-forty. He was still dressed in the slate blue scrubs that had been issued by the jail and I imagined the neon pink undies underneath.

"Not guilty," Conor said, when asked by the judge to plead.

The judge moved on to the question of bail and the D.A. argued against it. Gerri Runyan had told me she would. Next, Ms. Runyan stood and gave the pertinent information for bail: Conor's clean record, no passport (which I wasn't sure was true), wants to clear his name, etc.

The judge shot her down pretty quickly, which I also expected. This was a murder case, after all, but Ms. Runyan had another play. She mentioned me, his wife, who was willing to house the defendant, and said he could be monitored by an ankle device. I wasn't too keen on this idea, but Conor was too innocent for jail, even one that looked like a college dormitory.

Ms. Runyan had warned me that this was a long shot, so I wasn't too surprised when the judge also refused to let Conor out on bail, monitor or not. Conor turned to me and shrugged. He didn't look upset. Maybe the jail's meals were better than mine.

I jotted a note in my notepad since I was covering the arraignment for the Marin Independent Journal. When I looked up, the bailiff was already leading Conor out of the courtroom. Ms. Runyan headed down the aisle and I jumped up to follow her.

"Is that it?" I asked.

She turned slowly, her irritation noted in the way she lowered her chin before speaking. "I told you not to expect bail."

"I know, but what about pointing out that the only evidence is circumstantial?"

"I'll do that at the motions hearing in a couple of weeks, but what I really need to do is go over that evidence with a fine-tooth comb and I still haven't received all of it. Maybe you could pressure the D.A. to send it over," she said, raising her eyebrows to punctuate the sarcasm.

For an instant, I actually contemplated asking Dusty, then remembered that I was no longer his favorite pet.

"Is there anything you'd really like me to do?"

She gestured to my notepad. "Put a positive spin on that article you're writing."

* * *

I spent the afternoon on the laptop, researching why people stored cord blood. When I'd given birth to Siobhan, no one had asked me if I'd wanted to keep my cord blood and I certainly hadn't thought to ask, but evidently, today, there was a whole industry built around harvesting and storing stem cells from blood leading from the placenta.

The value of these cord blood cells was that they were unassigned. What did that mean? I found a second article that was less technical. Unassigned cells were cells not designated to any specific function such as growing a kidney or an ear. Because they had no specific function they could be assigned a function in the lab. The theory was that because these cells came from the original host's body, once they were used to create a new organ and this organ placed back in that same body, there would be minimal rejection.

Rejection of an organ was the biggest risk in any transplant, thanks to our bodies' natural immune barrier. Kind of like spitting out a fly when it flew into one's mouth, our bodies being the mouth.

These unassigned cells also had the least amount of antibodies. A second plus. The more the antibodies, the bigger the chance of rejection.

According to another article, all this was speculation because for now, cord blood was only stem cells for blood and so far could only be used in blood diseases such as leukemia. They worked great for bone marrow transplants, but the reality of growing organs with blood stem cells was a long, long way off.

Despite this reality, companies harvesting and storing cord blood for a fee touted that all was possible. New organs, new limbs, cancer cures. One online caption read: SAVING ONE CHILD AT A TIME. Enough to make me break out the tissues until I saw the prices.

First came the cost to harvest. Harvesting involved removing the blood from the umbilical cord with a syringe; purifying out the white blood cells; placing the remaining cells in a plastic vial with a preservative; and then snap freezing the vial in liquid nitrogen. Second came the cost to store these vials for the life of the host in the hopes that if your child one day was urgently ill, this blood would save his or her life.

Great marketing. What parent wouldn't do anything to save her child?

I thought of Siobhan. SIDS. Sleep snatched her without warning. If someone had told me saving my child's cord blood might one day save her life, would I have done it? Damn straight.

But the truth was cord blood wasn't a cure for SIDS and wouldn't have saved her. It wasn't a cure for many illnesses and it wouldn't save most of the children whose parents were paying for the belief that they had cheated death. Death comes. A shadow in the night. A wind beneath the tires. A hush in a hospital ward. Death comes.

With unsure hands, I lit a cigarette and walked to the coffee pot. Although I wanted a strong drink, I was going to settle for coffee. I grabbed the coffee bag from the cabinet and switched my thoughts away from dead children.

Dr. Chaffe had two placentas in a cooler, no cords attached that I saw. He also had a canister, so one might believe the stem cells had already been harvested. Why did he have them at home? And who would kill him for it?

I switched on the coffeemaker and went back to the laptop. It was five p.m. My article about Conor's arraignment had gone live an hour earlier on the Marin IJ website. Out of habit, I read it for typos, although it had been uploaded rather than typed in. It didn't say anything of interest because there was little to say except that the defendant in the murder case of Dr. Chaffe had pleaded not guilty and that the flimsy evidence against him might support his claim.

I'd mentioned Ms. Chaffe as being upset by her husband's death. In my opinion that was more false than true, but who was I to judge how people grieved? She'd been bothered, for sure, and she'd talked to me, which meant she was interested in finding the real killer, but she was far from the brokenhearted, teary-eyed widow. I'd seen more sentiment when my nephew's pet turtle got run over by the vacuum.

Dusty wasn't going to be happy that I'd interviewed Ms. Chaffe, but he had to understand I wasn't going to go quietly into the night, not with Conor's freedom at stake.

Why did I worry what Dusty would think?

"Come on, Fifi, let's go outside." I grabbed her leash. The walls of the apartment were starting to close in on me. I didn't want to think any longer about Dusty or stem cells or death. I picked up Fifi and hooked her leash to the ugly rhinestone collar that reminded me of Haylee and her silly affection for this animal. Fifi tried to lick my chin, but I managed to dodge her snake of a tongue.

"Don't piss me off, or you'll walk down the stairs on your own four legs, you lazy ball of fluff."

The parking lot was completely full, cars in every spot and one parked along the side. Was someone having a party? On a Thursday?

I glanced back at the building. A party might clear my brain. But did I really want to be around alcohol? I led Fifi past the parking lot and over to the green space where three columns of smoke rose from three different barbeques. My stomach growled. I wondered how wilted the salad was in my fridge. Was there anything in the freezer that I could put on wilted salad leaves? When I looked down, I found Fifi staring up at me. Was she wondering if we had any dog food left?

"Maybe we could share," I said.

She turned away and trotted toward one of the barbequers.

It was either beg, or go to the store.

I wasn't feeling social so the store it was.

The Imposter

When I got back from the grocery run, someone had taken my parking space and the lot was still full. I pulled back onto the road and turned into the harbor parking area, taking one of the last three slots. I got out and hoisted the heavy paper bag onto my hip and locked the car. Some time ago, Marin had passed a law banning single-use carry-out plastic bags and was now getting around to enforcing it. I'd had to pay a nickel for the paper bag and that irked me more than the two-twenty I'd paid for a single can of dog food.

As I headed back toward the apartment, the door of a black Sentra opened in front of me and out stepped Dusty.

"Why are you sitting in your car?" I asked, pausing only to be civil.

"Listening to the Giants game."

He reached to help me with the grocery bag, but I pulled it tighter to me. "You don't have a radio in your boat?" I started for the apartment, trying not to picture Agent Clark and her bare décolleté.

Décolleté. A nicer word than cleavage. Leave it to the French.

Dusty hustled up beside me. "I just got here. I was waiting for an inning change before going inside. Then I saw you and I had a question."

I stopped walking.

"What's wrong?" he asked.

"Nothing. Ask your question so you can get back to your game and I can feed that hungry breast…I mean…beast! waiting upstairs."

He stepped back, probably surprised by my abruptness. It surprised me, too. I wasn't trying to be a bitch, but my emotions had been off kilter since seeing him with Agent Clark.

"I only meant that you're busy, I'm busy, ah, what can I do for you?" A weak apology as far as apologies go, but it was all I could muster, seeing that he was wearing a new pair of slacks and a lime green polo shirt that looked good against his slightly tanned skin. Trying to impress a certain someone, no doubt.

One hand moved to his hip in a defiant stance. "I read your article in the IJ and saw that you'd spoken with Ms. Chaffe."

I started walking again, anger tightening my muscles. "Look, I'm not going to stop investigating just because you're lead detective. Conor's freedom is on the line and I've promised to help him."

"I understand but—"

I didn't let him interrupt. He wasn't going to tell me who I could and couldn't interview. "So yes, I spoke with Mrs. Chaffe. I also went by Primordium. And I plan to go back tomorrow for a tour with that Nara Hibbert person. You can't stop me. As far as you're concerned, I'm a journalist doing a job. I won't get in your way unless I uncover something I think you need for your investigation of my innocent..."

"Husband."

"Fine! Husband! As long as he's incarcerated, he won't sign the divorce papers, so for my sake I want him freed as soon as possible. Plus, he's innocent."

I was walking so fast I was almost running. Dusty was falling behind, not because he couldn't keep up, he had one stride to my two, but maybe because the venom wafting off me frightened him.

"I'm just a little curious how you managed to speak with Mrs. Chaffe since she's only returning this evening from Hamburg."

I stopped, shifted the bag to my other side. "Hamburg?"

"She's a concert pianist. Her contractual agreements wouldn't allow her to leave before this morning. I have a deputy picking her up as we speak."

"Is her name Bathilde?"

"That's right. Bathilde Chaffe. How did you contact her?"

"We have a problem, Houston."

Dusty's chin dropped to his chest. He shook his head. "That doesn't sound good, doesn't sound good at all."

"Would you happen to have a picture of her?"

"I've seen one of her concert brochures. Tall, blond, German looking, nice—"

I held up a palm. "Enough. Not the same woman who told me she was Bathilde." I shoved the bag of groceries at him. He'd offered before. "Let's go upstairs."

Fifi was curled up on the sofa and barely raised her head as I came through the door, but the minute Dusty stepped in, she was leaping and barking and nipping at his heels.

My brave protector.

"Can I step on her?" he asked.

I took the bag from his hands so he'd be free to caress her. *Fat chance.* "Not today, you're here in an official capacity."

He flicked his hand at Fifi's snout. "I don't like the way that you're getting attached to that vermin."

Well, I didn't like who he was dating. "Speaking of vermin…" I shut my mouth, deciding this wasn't the moment.

While I carried the bag into the kitchen, he sat on the stool by the dining table.

"Why official capacity?" he asked.

I unloaded a package of frozen berries and a head of lettuce onto the counter. "Looks like I have information for you."

He huffed, then yelled at Fifi, who was alternating between barking and snapping at his leg. "Briana, one day this withholding information is going to land you in jail."

"Speaking of withholding...how long have you been dating Agent Clark?"

"What? Are you kidding me? We're just friends."

If a nod could be sarcastic, mine was. I'd seen the way she'd dressed and it wasn't to meet a friend. But I wasn't sure I wanted to hear the details. "I didn't know I had information until you described Mrs. Chaffe."

"Go on."

I emptied the rest of the bag on the counter. "Yesterday, I happened to notice a car in the victim's drive so I knocked on the door. A woman answered, an Asian woman with great hair. She told me she was Bathilde."

Was that true, or had I assumed she was the victim's wife?

"What else did she say?"

I thought about my answer as I folded the paper bag and carried the lettuce, tomatoes, and juice to the fridge. I didn't want to be cagy, but I didn't want to say anything that would get me in trouble either. "She was busy, said she had a short time to move out what she needed. I figured you'd let her collect a few things."

"Not me or any of my people that I know of. Did you see a suitcase? Was she packing clothes?"

I joined him at the table and sat in the only chair. I really needed to buy another one. Maybe with the money I was making on these articles. I was already formulating a new one on the mysterious woman. "Actually, and now I see this is important, she was loading files and books into boxes from what looked like Dr. Chaffe's office. She asked me to help carry them to her car."

Dusty snorted and that set Fifi off on another barking jag.

"Fifi, stop!" I said.

She tilted her head and silently trotted over to her empty food dish.

"Who do you think the woman was and how did she get in the house?" I asked as his cell phone played a tune that sounded like something one would hear in Dracula's dungeon.

"Work," he said before getting up and answering the call.

He walked to the other side of the room in an effort to keep me from hearing, but the urgency in his voice pricked up my ears. I glanced out the front window, pretending I wasn't listening. The sun was low, close to dropping below the horizon.

"Ten minutes," Dusty said.

I turned and watched him slip the phone in his pocket. He looked at me and appeared to hesitate.

"Guess you'll want this story," he said. "Grab your camera."

I was moving before he finished his sentence. I snatched my keys and cell phone from the kitchen counter, and grabbed the camera bag from the corner on my way to the door. "What's going on?" I asked, locking the door behind us.

"Fire at Primordium. Take your own car, it's going to be a long night." He passed me and took the stairs two at a time.

I ran after him, but he was already pulling out of the lot by the time I reached my car. So much for his Giants game.

The Fire

The office park was a flurry of activity. I left my car five streets away and had to run four blocks to reach the official police blockade. Fire engines filled every street around Primordium, but most of the focus was at the back by the loading dock.

Broad, orange-red flames rose high in the sky above the other buildings. A thick black tower of smoke spread east toward the hills.

I shoved through the crowd. Two TV reporters with microphones were interviewing bystanders, but as I listened I realized most were gawkers, having seen the flames from the highway. They'd stopped only to see what was going on. I elbowed my way forward. A man in a straw hat mentioned an explosion, but I couldn't tell if he was talking about one explosion or several.

A moment later I had my answer.

A loud boom filled the air, shaking the ground beneath my feet. The crowd simultaneously swayed away from the sound. Stillness filled the void, and then the voices slowly returned. Someone whistled. A few laughed. One woman with long brown hair stood frozen, her jaw hanging open.

I held my camera high and aimed into the crowd to capture the reactions. After taking a few more shots, I shoved my way to the yellow tape stretched between four wooden sawhorses. It closed off the road to Primordium's loading dock. Two San Rafael police officers stood guard at each end of the blockade. No one was getting down the road, not that anyone wanted to after that blast.

Another set of sirens roared up and I counted the incoming trucks, three plus an ambulance. The new arrivals made it a three-alarm fire. The explosions probably had something to do with that.

While the new trucks tried to wedge in on the already clogged roads, another boom shattered the chaos and a flash of flames reared upward. The police officers, guarding the perimeter, nervously checked over their shoulders several times even though they were a good block away from the danger. I clicked off a dozen more shots.

Stars were popping out across the darkening sky, making the flames appear more menacing. The smoke was almost invisible against the night. I watched several firemen set up two banks of lights. Halogen spots from several fire engines were aimed at the building.

I laid my camera in my bag, at the ready should I need it, and pulled out my cell phone to text the editor of the Marin Independent Journal and let him know I had an exclusive so he wouldn't send anyone else. Hopefully, since Dusty had freely told me about the breaking story, he'd give me more information down the line. Earlier, he'd seemed friendlier and less combative than the past weeks.

Sex with Clark must be relaxing him.

Don't go there.

I hit SEND on the text and looked up ahead for Dusty. When I'd pulled in, I hadn't seen his car and I didn't see him in the melee of firemen, police officers, and sheriff's deputies. With so many trucks and emergency personnel, I couldn't tell what was going on. From time to time, water arced from the hoses, but I couldn't see how much of the building was gone. I was too far away.

A San Rafael officer rushed down the road to her colleagues who were holding back the crowd. She spoke to the two at the right and when she was finished, she crossed behind the tape to the officers on the opposite side. They all nodded before she rushed back up the street. Probably didn't use radios or cell phones because they didn't want anyone else picking up the conversation.

Someone was claiming he had though. A man behind me was proclaiming that the explosions were over and after another couple of minutes, to be sure, the firemen would enter the building to try to contain the flames. From the ohs and ahs, the crowd was hooked on his every word, but I paid him little attention.

The chemicals burning inside could be toxic to the firefighters. They'd need to contact the staff to know exactly what was burning. No one was going in any time soon.

I listened to his pronouncements a few more minutes before I cut in. "Where are you getting your information?" I asked.

"That's what the officer said to those guys at the end. I can read lips."

Huh? "Did she say anything else?" I asked. How could they possible know for sure that the explosions were over?

"She did, but I couldn't get it all."

"Oh, an unreliable witness." I glanced at the television reporter, inching closer to speak with Mr. Lipreader.

I turned back toward the flames. It was a hot fire, the size of the flames and reddish-orange color told me that. Another siren, this one from an ambulance, passing behind the crowd.

Was someone hurt or was it a precaution? I texted Dusty and waited.

And waited.

Behind me Mr. Lipreader was telling the crowd that it was believed the fire started when a Bunsen burner ignited a flammable liquid. He said the explosions were probably the propane tanks used for the burners.

I'd once seen a propane tank explode during a safety demonstration. First of all, the tank had a release valve to feed off pressure and gas as it heated. Propane gas would accelerate the blaze, but not to the level that I was seeing here. There had to be a larger accelerant. Also, the explosion of a propane tank, the smaller ones used in labs, wasn't comparable to the ground-rocking explosion I'd felt tonight.

Maybe if the whole basement was propane, but I was sure that wasn't the case.

"The fire spread too quickly for the sprinklers," Lipreader said.

"Whose lips are you reading this time?" I asked.

He held up a cell phone. "It's on Twitter."

"Oh, good! Hard facts." And about as reliable as a lipreader.

I texted Dusty again, this time asking if he knew what caused the fire. It was a little too convenient for a fire to break out in a lab two days after the head of said lab was murdered. Too con-ve-nient.

Especially since I knew Conor didn't kill Chaffe.

All at once a flurry of activity ahead pulled everyone's attention. Even Mr. Lipreader fell silent, but it was impossible to see what was going on through the parked trucks and bustling personnel.

"Look! What did I tell you," Mr. Lipreader said, and the crowd responded with a slight shift forward, pressing me against the yellow tape.

"Please step back," the officer to my right said, gesturing menacingly with his hand.

The man behind me didn't want to back up so I stepped on his foot.

"Excuse me, sorry. Sorry. Are you okay?" I asked, then turned my back on him before he could reply. I texted Dusty a third time asking what was going on.

Ahead, there was more movement, firemen running every way and shouting, but I couldn't hear anything that might be a clue. Although Primordium was almost a block away, it was lit up like the Ice Capades from all the spotlights.

I took a few more pictures, then checked my phone. Dusty had left a text.

Where are U?

I texted back my location and looked down the road. Firemen were everywhere and the officers had moved out of the road to give them access. Maybe Lipreader was right. Maybe they were ready to enter the building. Almost forty minutes had passed since the last explosion.

Dusty's familiar form burst through the crowd of emergency personnel. He had on a bright yellow-orange rain jacket, similar to what the firemen wore. He ran around the back of one of the trucks, heading my way.

I knew better than to feel hopeful, but he'd brought me along. Maybe he was coming to share information. Maybe we were headed back towards some type of friendship. I raised my hand and waved so he'd see me within the packed mass of humanity.

He waved back. I took out my camera and waited for him to reach me, hoping against hope that he'd take me closer to the action. When he was about six yards away, I ducked under the tape to meet him. Two San Rafael police officers were at my side immediately, one from each end of the barricade.

"I'm with him," I said, pointing at Dusty.

Dusty wasn't wearing a uniform and neither officer knew him so he had to produce his badge, which he did with an absentminded flash at both men. He took me by the arm and led me to the edge of the barricade.

This wasn't good. We were headed away from the fire.

"Do they know what caused it?" I asked. "Was anyone in the building? What's causing the explosions?"

"Bri—"

"Why the ambulances? Anyone hurt?"

He covered my mouth with his hand. "Briana, I have to tell you something."

He dropped his hand.

Why the drama? "I'm listening." Everyone in my life was so dramatic.

"You need to get over to Marin General. Your husband's been hurt."

"Conor?"

"Unless you have other husbands I don't know about."

"But isn't he still in custody?"

"I just got the call. He's been hurt and he's been taken to the hospital. Do you remember where it is?" he asked.

Of course I remembered where it was. I'd driven there every day while Dusty was recuperating from being kidnapped and almost killed. How could he ask such a thing? I was deflecting. Focus.

"Where's your car?" he asked.

I glanced around, question after question running through my head. Dusty took my arm again and led me past the officers, past the tape, past the crowd, and out onto the service road.

"Do you remember where you parked?"

I looked around again, nodded, and pointed up the road. "What happened?"

He led me in the direction of my car. "I don't have any details, but you need to get over there. I'll call you when I finish here."

* * *

A sheriff's deputy was posted outside Conor's room. The deputy let me in. Another deputy was standing beside Conor's bed while a woman in pale blue scrubs attended to Conor's face.

"Omigod, omigod, omigod." I dropped my camera case and rushed to his side. Conor didn't have a lot upstairs, but the two things he did have, the things that allowed him to cruise through all his bad luck, were a big heart and the sweet face of an angel.

The deputy moved to block my path. "Ma'am, step back. Ma'am, away from the bed."

I wanted to punch him. Instead, I rose up on tippy toes and put my face to his and yelled so loud the woman stopped working on Conor. "How did this happen!"

The deputy seemed to realize that he was dealing with a crazy and leaned away, or maybe my smoky smell gave him pause.

The deputy outside opened the door and stepped in. "Everything okay in here?"

With teeth gritted, I spoke slowly to the deputy blocking me from the bed. "Please, move away. I want to see what you've done to my husband."

The deputy clearly didn't know what to do—fight the crazy or acquiesce. He glanced at the other deputy, who must have given him a sign because he took a sidestep allowing me access to the bed.

Conor's face was swollen beyond recognition. It looked as if someone had taken a baseball bat to it. His wild hair had been shaved back off his temple, where a nasty opening oozed. Both eyelids were violet and swollen shut. His lip and left cheek were a bloody mess.

"Briana," he said and let out a low whine.

I reached for his hand and squeezed. "How bad is it?" I asked the woman in scrubs.

"Not as bad as it looks," she said softly. "We're waiting on x-rays, but his right arm is probably broken. As are two ribs, but we'll have to wait and see. He'll need stitches here." She pointed to the gash in his head. "And maybe two or three here." She pointed to his lower lip.

She wiped away the blood on his cheek.

All the air was suddenly sucked out of me. I collapsed forward, burying my face in Conor's hand. The deputy caught me around the waist as I gave in to my sobs and my legs went slack.

"He doesn't deserve this," I mumbled. "He didn't do anything but try to earn some cash."

Even as I formed the words another dialog was running in my head. I wondered if the Irish Brotherhood could do something. At least get Conor out on bail. It was wrong to think of approaching them. Their services didn't come for free. But it was my duty to take care of Conor and I was desperate.

The Beating

As the nurse had said, the x-rays showed that Conor's right arm was broken. The doctor said he'd probably tried to ward off blows. He also had two cracked ribs and a total of fourteen stitches: eight in his temple, four in his lower lip, and two on his nostril. No vital organs were damaged, although the doctor noticed from one of his secondary tests there was the beginning of cirrhosis in his liver.

No surprise there.

I stayed at the hospital most of the night while they stitched him up and set his arm. I waited until he was in a painless sleep before driving back to the apartment.

Fifi was whining at the door. I unlocked it, picked her up, and carried her downstairs. I figured I'd find a puddle somewhere inside, but who could blame her? I'd been gone a long time. Doggie Daycare was looking like more of a necessity than an option.

I set her down in the grass, too tired to care that I'd forgotten her leash. If she wanted to run off, she was on her own. I was beyond tired; my legs were moving of their own volition and my mind was already snoring.

Still, I had enough energy to glance over at Dusty's boat. Habit. The padlock was locked on the outside. He wasn't home yet, or maybe he was sleeping at his girlfriend's place. I was so tired that *that* thought barely stung. I didn't care about anything except finding a soft spot to curl up and close my eyes.

Fifi finished her business and trotted over to me.

"Let's go," I said, picking her up.

* * *

My head had barely hit the pillow, or so it seemed, when a loud banging on the door woke me. Peeking through one eye because the other one was still asleep, I managed to unlock the deadbolt and open the door, only to be blinded by a burst of sunlight. Before I threw my arm up to block my eye, I caught a glimpse of Dusty holding something in his hand.

He pushed past me and I slammed the door. When I turned around he was facing the dining table, his back to me.

"Do you *know* what time it is?" I asked.

"Could you put some clothes on?"

I glanced down. I'd removed most of my clothing to sleep. I still had on my socks. And I smelled like smoke. Automatically, my arms crossed my body as if to hide something, but nothing vital got covered. I took off for the bedroom.

My jeans were inside out and spread across the floor. The whole room smelled like a bonfire. I picked them up and put them on, not wanting to stink up a clean pair before I'd showered. I pressed the button of my cell to check the time. 6:30 a.m. I'd gotten to bed after four.

"Do you know what time it is?" I asked again, stomping back into the main room.

Dusty cautiously peeked around, as if I might have returned with no clothes. Once he was satisfied that I was decent, he held an 8x10 photo out to me.

"Is this the woman you saw at the Chaffe house?"

"Seriously!"

He shoved the photo at me a second time. "I haven't had any sleep either," he snapped. "This is important. Take it and tell me if you've seen this woman."

I snatched the photo from him and walked over to the blinds. Slowly, I inched them open to let in a little daylight.

The woman in the picture was Asian, long dark hair, and she was wearing a cotton button-up shirt with what looked like a white lab coat over it. She was smiling. The last time I'd seen her she hadn't smiled, but I'd assumed she was a grieving widow.

I handed the photo back to Dusty. He was still dressed in the same clothes he'd been wearing last night and he reeked. "That's the fake wife. Who is she?"

"A lab tech who worked for the deceased. She's missing, as is everyone else who worked at Primordium except the receptionist."

"Any bodies recovered?"

"Not a one. But it was a hot fire. Now, they're sifting for bone."

"Geez." I opened the blinds all the way. "I need coffee."

I headed to the kitchen in search of a jumpstart for my brain. The missing workers meant something, but I couldn't focus.

"Could I get half a cup?" Dusty said, stopping me in my tracks.

Dusty didn't do caffeine. I spun around to make sure I heard right.

"It's been a long night."

"Right." I continued to the kitchen. "No excuses needed around here."

He joined me as I loaded the machine with ground coffee. He went to the cabinet and took out two mugs. "You smell," he said, drawing up next to me.

I turned to face him. We were close enough to touch, but we didn't. "You're no pocket full of posies, yourself."

We chuckled and he patted me on the back. A nice friendly...pat. That made me laugh more. How ludicrous we'd become.

I switched the machine on and watched him walk out, his shoulders heavy as if he were carrying the weight of the world. He sat at the dining table, and rubbed his face in his hands.

"I didn't get the exclusive on the fire," I said, joining him.

"Arson. That much I can tell you. An accelerant, but the biggest problem was the dynamite."

"Whoa. Is that what caused the explosions?"

"Yep."

"I thought it might have been the cryogenic containers."

"They were a problem. A few exploded but nothing serious for the firefighters. The chief said they were lucky that so few contained gas."

"I assume you've spoken with the receptionist."

"Flake." He rubbed the nubs pushing up on his bald head. "I shouldn't say that. She did what she was hired to do."

"Which was?"

"She never went into the building. She had a key to the front door and one to a lounge off the right of the reception area. She was to call the CEO to meet with any potential clients. He'd come out and take the clients on a tour and finish in a conference room next to the lounge."

"Strange. She's never seen the building she works in?"

"She had a tour when she was hired. That's it. She was told she'd lose her job if she went into the other parts of the building. She was told it was a health hazard since they stored bio-sensitive material."

"Is that true?"

Dusty huffed and I realized it was a stupid question. Of course it wasn't true, not if they gave clients a tour whenever needed.

"Yeah, I see, so why the secrecy?" I asked. "Wait!" I slid around on the stool and drew my laptop over. "I was supposed to talk with a...wait, where is the file? Here. Nara Hibbert. This is her phone number." I turned the laptop to him and pointed at Hibbert's phone number. "She's the publicity liaison. I was supposed to set up an appointment with her to learn more about Primordium Labs."

Dusty took out his cell phone and pad. He looked up a note in the pad and punched in a number. The toasty aroma of roasted coffee beans sent me back to the kitchen. As I filled my mug I listened to Dusty's call. I poured him a bit more than half a mug. I stayed by the coffee machine, arranging the sugar and flour jars on the counter, hoping he wouldn't notice that I was listening.

"Get me an address for both," he said and disconnected.

I offered him the coffee mug as he came through the doorway. "Sugar?"

He shook his head and took the mug, gulping it down. He handed the empty mug back to me. "I have to run. We need to check the airlines as well as follow up on other leads."

"When are you seeing the fire marshal?"

"In Marin, we have a fire investigator. I'm meeting with him at two this afternoon. Hope I can squeeze in a nap before then. Thanks for the coffee."

Fifi nipped at his heels as he headed to the door.

The Daycare

The sandy beach beneath me is warm. A spray from the waves cools my skin, and the roar of the breakers echoes in my ears. Without warning, an eel leaps from the surf, locks onto my cheek and sucks. I dig my nails into the wet, slick creature and tug, finally yanking it away, clinging to its…fur?

I opened my eyes. Fifi's snout hung next to my face. Groaning, I rolled toward the back of the sofa. Sunshine filled the living room, soaking my skin in sweat.

I struggled to my feet. Fifi leaped off the cushion and scampered into the kitchen at whiplash speed. After Dusty's morning visit, I'd fallen asleep. The time on my cell phone read 11:48. Fifi had missed breakfast, after having had dinner at four a.m. I was surprised she'd let me sleep as long as she had.

"I'm coming. Stop whining."

Once Fifi was scarfing down her chow, I stripped off my smelly clothes and stepped into the shower. The smoky odor flourished under the warm spray, but little by little the soap cleansed it from my skin and hair. Now, I had to figure out how to get the stink out of the apartment. Doing laundry would help, but I hated to wash clothes if I didn't have a full load. Basically, I hated doing laundry.

I needed to go by the hospital and see how Conor was doing. I also needed to investigate last night's fire, not just for the paycheck, but because it surely had something to do with Chaffe's murder. Only an idiot would think otherwise. The arson part didn't surprise me, but something Dusty said about so few canisters containing gas did.

Online I'd read that Primordium "hosted"—their word, not mine—over a hundred families. I would assume those families had at least one canister each of cord blood stem cells. Had Primordium lied to make their services more enticing? Maybe they "hosted" many less families, or was there a reason so few canisters contained gas? Maybe gas was only needed until the canisters were placed in cooling chambers. I'd need to do more research on the process.

As I finished dressing, Fifi danced around my feet. The pee-pee waltz. She needed to go out and she needed a walk, both of which had to be added to my to-do list.

"I'll take you with me."

She ran for the front door as if she'd understood. I grabbed my camera bag and loaded it with my notes, my camera, and an extra battery. I was searching for where I'd left my phone when it rang. Sometimes things just work out.

"Conor's being moved back to the jail in about thirty minutes," Gerri Runyan said.

"He's hurt. They can't move him back yet!"

"He'll be placed in administrative hold."

"What does that mean? He can't take another beating."

"Administrative is their word for isolation. He wants to see you."

"I want to see him. What did he say happened?"

"He's not talking. Another reason it would be good if you came to speak with him. See what you can get out of him. I want to know. The deputies want to know. There are rumors."

"What do you mean, rumors?"

"Talk to your husband, then come by my office."

I calculated the time. I couldn't speak with Conor until he was back in the jail. Thirty minutes to get him checked out of the hospital—give or take—plus travel, another thirty. Plus however long it would take to get him signed into his isolation—say another forty minutes. I threw the phone in the camera case and picked up the dog. That left me almost two hours to run by what was left of Primordium. Maybe the fire investigator would be there.

* * *

Two fire trucks were on hand at the office park, but both looked unoccupied and unused. The firemen were probably still sifting through rubble. Two small crowds were gathered on two sides of Primordium. Some sort of protest. People were yelling and waving anti-stem cell banners.

They organized quickly enough.

Fifi stayed close, which was unlike her. Usually she'd run ahead until her leash jerked her to a stop just so she could search out any dog lovers before I caught up. The shouting must have frightened her. I had to admit, it was a little aggressive.

I led her around the periphery of a Bible-singing group where each person was dressed in black pants, a white shirt, and a black blazer or vest. I made the sign of the cross to ward off their evil-looking juju.

We stepped off the curb and into the street to get around the next group of women waving handmade banners that read things like: ONLY GOD CAN HEAL; FOCUS ON FAMILY NOT CELLS; STEM CELL RESEARCH IS UNETHICAL.

I took out my camera and framed a shot when suddenly Fifi was between my legs, vibrating like a Cuisinart. A black German Shepherd with a big belly and a shiny black-and-brown coat was growling and snapping at my ankles.

A woman in a tie-dyed tee shirt dropped her sign and grabbed the German Shepherd's collar. That made the dog growl and lunge again for my ankles.

"Whoa!" I slid an inch away. With Fifi between my legs, I couldn't go far. I shoved my camera back in the camera bag.

"Don't worry," said the woman tugging on the collar. "She won't hurt you. She's all bark."

I looked at the bared fangs inches away from my leg and the word "denial" came to mind.

"I'm not all bark. If those teeth get any closer to my leg I *will* hurt her."

The woman's jaw dropped. She uttered something that I didn't pay attention to because the dog lunged for Fifi. I slammed the camera bag downward and was about to clock the German Shepherd on its snarling snout when the woman jerked the dog back, turning it away from me and leading it down the sidewalk.

I bent and picked up Fifi. "You were about to become a crime scene." Trembling, she leaned into my chest.

The San Rafael Police had set up two manned barricades, one near the parked fire trucks on the road of Primordium's burnt-out loading dock, the other at the front of Primordium where most of the protesting was being held. I squatted and set Fifi down. She leaped back into my lap before I could stand.

"I have work to do."

She batted her lashes at me while giving me a forlorn eye stare.

I could get information that might clear Conor, or at the very least give me fodder for another article, or I could protect Fifi, but with so many people and dogs around, I couldn't do both. But I had an idea.

I turned around and headed for the main service road. We walked south, the opposite direction from where I'd parked. Two blocks later I found the sign I was looking for.

WOOFINGTON'S DOGGIE DAYCARE.

A bell tinkled as I carried Fifi inside.

"Why, hello. Who is this beautiful young lady?" said the woman standing behind a lectern-like structure by the door. She walked around and held out hands with long thin fingers tipped in burnt orange and blue polish.

Fifi, who normally welcomed a stranger's caress, pulled back and pushed into my breasts. Something about the doggy smell of the place must have warned her that I was up to no good.

I put Fifi on the floor, catching sight of the woman's bare feet beneath the flowing gauze pants. Her toenails matched her fingernails. She stooped and reached to stroke Fifi, who again pressed up against me. But the woman was not to be put off.

I wondered how she knew Fifi was a she not a he, but Fifi's hot pink polish and rhinestone collar probably gave that away.

After a caress or two and a quick ear scratching, which warmed Fifi to her, the woman stood, shoved her brown waist-length hair over her shoulder, and held out a hand to me. "I'm Willow. What can I do for you today?"

"I need to work, and this one"—I nodded to Fifi, who had moved away from me and was sniffing the bottom of the lectern as if she was going to lift a leg any minute—"needs company. I saw your sign and thought daycare was a perfect solution, if it isn't too expensive."

Willow stepped back around the lectern. "I think you'll find our rates are reasonable and we offer lots of different services, from daycare, grooming, and specialized diet programs to overnight stays in a suite or ultra-suite."

"What's the difference between a suite and ultra-suite?"

"Our suites have made-to-fit bedding and brightly painted walls with tempered glass doors. The ultra-suites have raised beds and a flat-screen television playing appropriate programing."

Like...*Scooby-Doo* or *Beverly Hills Chihuahua*?

I smiled and tried to stop myself from mentally listing every doggie movie ever made. *Turner and Hooch, Beethoven, Bingo, Bolt.* A lot of B-named dogs.

Two dogs wandered in from what looked like a grooming room. One was a yellow Labrador and the other some type of mutt with bristly gray fur. Fifi's back stiffened when she saw them. The mutt spotted her and pulled up short. Its back arched like a cat and it took a step away, walking the long way around the room to get to Willow, who cooed its name.

The Labrador, who was just a puppy, bounded up to Fifi, with friendly eyes and what might be considered a smile on its muzzle. It stretched out a long pink tongue to lick Fifi's nose.

Fifi snapped and growled or growled and snapped; it happened too quickly to know which came first. The Lab cried out in pain or fear and lurched away, its paws sliding on the linoleum in four directions, sending the poor thing belly down on the floor.

Willow was there before I could blink.

"Now what's this?" she said as if to scold Fifi.

Fifi stood her ground.

Slowly, Willow's gaze raised to meet mine, making me feel as if the whole incident had been my fault.

"She's better with people."

Willow lifted the Lab into her arms. It was half her size. "This is Tucker. He's the most lovable guest we have. Are you okay, sweet Tucker?" She inspected his snout, then kissed it. She kissed his ear, then put him down on the floor.

She turned back to Fifi. "No more of that, Missy." She walked to the lectern. "Our daycare offers supervised playgroups, or for an extra fee, we provide private strolls. There's a splash pool available if your dog likes watersports. Did you bring her dinner or would you like us to provide it?"

Watersports? Dinner? "Ah, you...I guess."

She smiled down at Fifi, who was still eyeing Tucker like he was a juicy rack of lamb. He'd backed into a corner near the mutt. "Good. Today is pan-seared salmon. And don't worry, all our kibble is grain-free."

I had no idea what that meant.

"I'm sure your...what did you say her name is?"

"Fifi."

Willow's smiling lips pinched together in a question and then returned to a teeth-baring broad smile. "Fifi."

"She's French," I said before I could stop myself. *French poodle—get it.*

"What about grooming?"

Fifi had only been with me six or so weeks. I'd yet to figure out the grooming schedule and pricing, although her inheritance was supposed to cover it.

"What do you offer? And how much?"

"Basic grooming for a client her size is thirty, or forty-five dollars if you want her to have the oatmeal or plum shampoo and conditioner. There's the flea-and-tick bath for twenty-five. I highly recommend that because the fleas this year are atrocious. After that, we have a series of specialty treatments."

"How special?"

She handed me a Woofington's brochure with the treatments and the prices. "We have the Paws and Ahs, which is an ear-cleaning, nail-trimming and filing treatment. That Winning Smile, which is an ear-cleaning, teeth-brushing treatment. The Blueberry Facial. The Anal Gland Expression. Of course, we also offer the controversial Woof Supremacy, which is shaving off the coat for summer. We don't recommend it, but it's your decision."

I flipped the brochure over for the daycare prices. "How much to leave her here for a few hours?"

"With or without suite?"

"Without."

"Splash pool?"

"Without."

"Bottled water or faucet?"

For heaven's sake, she licks her butt. "Faucet is fine."

"Fifteen for the day, including dinner."

I glanced at Fifi. She bared her teeth at Tucker. His eyes drooped, his mouth hung. He noticed my attention turned his way and with what looked like a hopeful reprieve, he lurched out of his sitting spot and landed on all fours.

Fifi barked. Tucker glanced her way and took off galloping through the back doorway and was gone.

"We also have training classes available," Willow said, no longer smiling.

The Fire Inspector

I was late to the party, as the saying goes, and rather than concentrate on the fire inspector's words, I was chewing my lip and wondering why neither the Marin IJ nor the Chronicle editor had told me that the inspector was giving a press conference today. I'd stopped by with only the hope of speaking with one of the men shifting through the rubble. Good thing I had.

Earlier, I'd learned from a Marin County message board that fire investigators from several county departments had been called in to shift through Primordium's debris for evidence.

The group of reporters gathered for the press conference were flanked by three San Rafael police officers. A fire chief and another fireman, both with skin as smooth as porcelain, stood on the curb and slightly above the crowd. Another set of officers stood with them. Both firemen had the gentlest eyes I'd ever seen; ones that could melt someone's heart. I caught myself glancing for wedding bands. Both wore one. The chief and fireman fidgeted as the fire inspector continued with the details of the fire. From time to time they gave each other a look as if to say, "What are we doing here?"

The protest raged on behind us. The snide remarks were loud enough to be heard over the inspector's discourse although we were well inside the police barricade.

I caught sight of another IJ reporter typing into his tablet as the inspector answered questions from the crowd of maybe twenty.

"...from the strategic placement of dynamite we know the person or persons who did this were professionals," the inspector said. Was there such a thing as an ugly fireman? The inspector was a tall, lean man with pale blue eyes, wide lips, and a hint of military in his posture.

"Meaning a fireman?" asked a woman in the crowd.

A slight gasp from the press or maybe it was just me.

The inspector shook his head and gave her a piercing stare that could slice through steel pipes. "Meaning this is a person who has set fires before." He paused, ignoring the next question, but still staring at the woman.

I threw my hand in the air and waved it in an arc over my head. "What can you tell us about the dynamite used?"

He was still ignoring questions so I called mine out again along with several other reporters volleying for attention.

Finally he tore his eyes away from the woman who'd irritated him and glanced back over the crowd. "Obviously more testing is needed, but from specimens recovered it looks as if the dynamite was homemade." He looked back at the woman who had suggested a fireman did this. "Again pointing to a professional arsonist. Nitroglycerin is highly unstable."

"Why was dynamite used?" the IJ reporter asked.

"There could be several reasons, to localize damage or to make sure the accelerant stayed lit, in this case gasoline. But more likely, to take out the sprinkler system, which would have helped us contain the fire sooner. The sprinkler systems in these buildings are kept up to code and are the first line of defense in an interior fire such as this."

"Anyone taking responsibility for the fire?" asked a man behind me.

The inspector's chin came up. His eyes shifted subtly to the protesters. Anyone not paying attention would have missed the gesture, but reporters paid attention. Several heads turned toward the waving signs.

"No one has taken responsibility."

And no one would. Whoever started this fire was tied into Chaffe's death. I was certain of that. Proving it was going to be the problem.

I raised my hand again, realizing what had bothered me last night. The fire inspector nodded to me. "Primordium's website boasts that they host hundreds of families. I assume that means cord blood in hundreds of canisters with liquid nitrogen. With so much liquid nitrogen being released, why was the fire so hot?"

The inspector looked at the fire chief to his left. He leaned in and mumbled something then he turned back to answer. "The fire burned hot because of the dynamite. That's all I can tell you at this time."

"Did the canisters with the cord blood survive?" asked the woman next to me.

Her question brought on a shout of slogans from the protesters. The inspector didn't answer right away, but waited for the row of officers to quiet the rowdy crowd.

"Not much survived," he said. "We are still going through the debris."

"Back to the canisters," I said, "how—"

"That's it for questions," the fire chief said, nodding to the inspector. "We have a lot more work to do and will give you our findings tomorrow. Thanks for coming out."

I stood still while those around me dispersed. I watched the handsome fire chief, fireman, and inspector walk back into the building that had once been Primordium. The top floor had collapsed, leaving the burned black stucco walls of the first floor. The loading area was gone. The firemen had completely torn down the back wall of the building.

I couldn't shake the feeling that the clue to Chaffe's death and Conor's release was in that building. All I could do now was wait to see what evidence turned up.

The Excuse

In the main jail's hallway, Gerri Runyan stood before me, taller by a head. She had both hands on her hips and looked as determined as a Giants' pitcher. "You better find out if these rumors are true. It will help direct his case."

"I'll talk to him, but he's more stubborn than a telemarketer. Can I see him now?"

She picked her handbag and a slim leather briefcase off the row of plastic chairs. She opened the case and pulled out a yellow sheet of paper, torn from a legal pad. "Here are a few things I need investigated. I'd appreciate it if you could have the information for me by the day's end. As his wife you may know some of the answers, but I don't want opinions, I want file numbers, docket numbers, everything in the system that the prosecutor can find."

I glanced at the list of questions. Number three was Conor's arrest for car theft. An arrest that was supposedly expunged from his record. I'd make sure it was removed this time. I thought of the phone calls I'd need to make. I wondered if I could use Dusty's database, then remembered Dusty was more likely to help a crack whore find a dealer than he was to help me with this case. Agent Clark's off-the-shoulder sundress popped into my mind. I squeezed my eyelids closed.

"If this is all, I'd like to see Conor."

Gerri gestured with an open palm to the line of visitors waiting for a turn at the desk.

"I'll email you what I find," I said, waving the page as I walked away.

Twenty minutes later I was upstairs, waiting for Conor in a different visiting room from my last visit. This room was on the opposite side of the corridor from the general visiting rooms, but it looked the same except it was painted turquoise-blue instead of green. I assumed the hallway behind it led back to the isolation cells.

Conor looked through the window of the door on his side. His bruised, stitched, and bandaged face tried to smile when he spotted me. His red-ringed eyes told a different story. What had I done at Haylee's funeral to make him think I wanted to give our relationship a second chance? Maybe if I'd been clearer, he'd still be in Texas, safely enjoying one beer too many in some dive bar.

He opened the door and came straight to the doubled-glass panes that separated his side from mine. He flattened a hand against it. His need for comfort broke my heart. I pressed my hand to his; the cold surface felt as thick as a cinderblock.

His broken arm lay in a beige sling tied around his neck. The large cut on his temple was bandaged in gauze that covered most of his head. His lip and nose were purple and swollen, black stitches protruding. The red scrubs he wore reflected on his pale skin, making him look as if he had a permanent blush.

"Sit," I said, gesturing to the chair.

He lowered himself down and picked up the handset. "Get me out of here, Briana." He spoke slowly because of his swollen lip. He reached and rubbed the stitches with his index finger.

"Who did this to you?"

He looked down and shook his head.

"You're being framed for murder. Gerri says it's rumored that someone was paid to do this to you. Is that true?"

He raised his head and looked at me, his pain constricting my throat as if it had hands around my neck.

"So what? Get me out of here."

"Conor."

"I'm not a rat."

"It's not like that. Someone is setting you up. This is about prejudicing the judge. The current evidence against you is circumstantial. But when you go before the grand jury, all beat up and stitched up, you're going to look like a thug, maybe even a killer. It'll sway the court. Someone out there wants to push their agenda. Someone wants you to go down for Chaffe's murder." I scooted closer to the glass. "Please, tell me what happened."

He gave me nothing but a cold, long stare. My heart ached. He was sticking to the brotherhood code. It made no sense.

"This is a frame-up. It's not worth an act of loyalty."

Still nothing.

"The company you were a courier for burned down last night. Around the same time that someone was using you as a punching bag." I paused to let the words sink in. "Just tell me and I won't tell anyone else. I'll use the information to help get you out." Not sure how I would do that, but I needed to find the right words to make him trust me.

I'd never seen him so closed down, so distant. It was as if I were looking at a stranger.

"Did someone threaten to hurt me?" I asked. Half of Marin now considered us husband and wife. Threatening a family member was pretty common. "You know I can take care of myself, right?"

Nothing. This was about more than a brotherhood code. He didn't know any of these people so he wasn't being a rat. A strange sensation crept up my neck. What else could frighten him into silence? If not me, was there someone else's welfare that someone could hold over him? I couldn't think of anyone. So was he afraid for himself? Made more sense. Was he still in danger? Who had control of him in here?

I leaped off the seat, my heart pounding. "Not a guard!"

His head came up.

I slowly lowered myself back down on the chair. *One-miss-iss-ippi, two-miss-iss-ippi, three-miss-iss-ippi.* I kept counting until all the emotion was burned off me. I had to keep calm if I was going to get him to talk. And I needed him to talk. If a guard had been paid to do this, then the threat was still present.

"You know these rooms are soundproof. No one can hear us. Did a guard do this?"

After a slight hesitation, he shook his head.

Our brains needed time to formulate a lie. One sign that someone was lying was a pause before answering.

"Don't you see what that means? Someone paid that guard and you have to ask yourself, why?"

"I got in a fight. I lost. Now get me out of here."

"What would you have to fight about? You don't—"

He leaned forward. "Briana, stop! Focus. I need your help."

* * *

I rushed back to the apartment to type out two articles. I wanted to get mine to the Marin IJ before, or about the same time that the other IJ reporter turned in his. Mine was more in-depth because I was linking the fire to the recent murder of a lab tech and the fact that the only suspect was incarcerated at the time of the fire. The second article I'd send to the San Francisco Chronicle. They may have had a reporter at the press conference. I don't know their reporters by sight.

The articles were already written in my head. I just had to type them out and read them aloud to make sure my musings made sense. I finished a little before four p.m. I left messages with both editors to expect the pieces. I could go pick up Fifi, but she wouldn't have had time to digest her dinner, which was served around four-fifteen, so instead, I pulled out Gerri Runyan's list and read over the information she was looking for.

I opened a page on the laptop and started listing the information that I didn't need to research. Address. Date of birth. Parents. Criminal history. That one I'd have to research. I couldn't depend on Conor to tell the truth, but I was sure he'd never been arrested for anything other than the car incident and that needed to be removed from his record. To clear that, I'd have to file a request in Massachusetts. I saved the file I was working on and went to the Internet to research how to erase that criminal record. If I filed the papers before Conor's visit to the grand jury, it would become common knowledge that it was an error that never should have come to light. It would help him look less of a criminal.

The next time I looked at the clock, it was a little after five and I needed to pick up Fifi. I pulled out my checkbook and wrote a check to Woofington's and stuck it in my back pocket. Fifi's leash was still in the car.

The Adonis

The narrow parking lot of Woofington's was almost full. A man and woman stood at the door as if waiting to go inside.

"Is this a line?" I asked the man in front of me.

He turned, smiling, not just with his mouth, but with his stunning sapphire eyes, his chiseled cheeks, his dark eyebrows. Even the wisp of brown curl on his forehead beamed. My knees turned to jelly, and for the first time in my life, I thought I might swoon. If Adonis was the god of beauty, this guy was certainly a brother.

"Willow doesn't like too many people inside at a time," he said through a perfectly formed set of lips.

His skin glowed with vitality.

"Oh." *Breathe*.

The door opened and a woman led a collie out on a leash. She smiled at Adonis. The woman waiting in front of him went in, leaving the two of us standing alone. He glanced around, unable to find a place for his gaze, or maybe my leering was making him nervous. Today was a day for good-looking men.

"Are you a fireman?" I said before I could stop myself.

He shook his head. "I'm an analyst."

His voice was almost as alluring as his face. I must have managed to look away because I noticed he was wearing a sport coat over an Oxford shirt with the first two buttons unbuttoned. Not a fireman. What was I thinking?

"What do you analyze?"

He glanced down at the sidewalk, then up. "Statistics mostly. Sometimes projections. Very boring stuff."

"You don't look very boring." *Omigod, did I really say that?* One day I would learn to think first.

He glanced down again but more in my direction.

"Maybe we can get a coffee sometime," he said, looking at me with those sparkling eyes. "I'll tell you all about it and see if I can put you sleep."

"I love a challenge. You're on." I could think of a way he could put me to sleep and it had nothing to do with talking.

The door opened and out came two ladies. One was carrying the mutt that had been afraid of Fifi, and the other had a brown Chihuahua in her arms.

Two out, two in. Adonis held the door for me. The yellow Lab I'd seen earlier was waiting in the doorway between the main room and what looked like a grooming room. When he saw Adonis, he bounded across the floor, his wide paws making a slapping sound as he came. I stepped out of his path so as not to be knocked over.

"Hey, boy, how are you? Did you miss me?" Adonis petted and rubbed the dog's coat as the dog circled and leaped at him. "Down now, stay down."

I took another step away to give their reunion more space. Willow scooted around the lectern to pet the dog, too.

"Ohhhh, Tucker," she cooed. She smiled up at Adonis and stepped so close to him I thought she was going to do an eye exam. "He's such a good dog."

Too much sloppy sweetness for me. I skirted the group and walked toward the grooming area. I peeked inside and at the far end Fifi sat on a furry leopard-spotted cushion. Her head popped up.

I shook the leash in her direction. She stood, stretched her front legs, yawned, and stretched her back legs. Clearly, eager to leave. She cocked her head at me.

"You can stay," I said and left the doorway.

The click of her nails on the linoleum trailed after me. I stopped and waited. Tucker, wanting to share the love, bounded over to me. I squatted to pat him, but as I did, Fifi lunged and snapped at the Lab.

He drew up short and looked as if he'd been slapped.

"Fifi," I said, more embarrassed than surprised.

Willow rushed to Tucker's rescue, her lips pinched tighter than a Ziplocked bag. She led him back to Adonis. "This one has been giving Tucker a hard time all day," she said.

Adonis wasn't smiling anymore. He and Willow scowled at Fifi.

Fifi lifted her chin. Was she grinning?

"Great," I said, snapping the leash to her collar. I picked her up to carry her safely past Tucker. When I reached the door, I pulled the check from my back pocket and handed it to Willow.

"Thanks," I said. I shifted to look at Adonis. "Tucker's a sweetheart." Without a pause, I jerked open the door and left.

Dropping Fifi in the passenger seat, I sat behind the wheel and watched Adonis lead Tucker to a gray Mercedes. They ran, they stopped, they jumped, they hugged.

Ahhhhh.

A twinge of jealousy tweaked my solar plexus. I wished Adonis would hug me like that.

Finally, Tucker was in the back seat and Adonis pulled out of the lot.

So much for coffee. We didn't even exchange names before Fifi killed our vibe.

I turned to her. She was curled in the passenger seat, her snout resting on her front paws. I was starting to understand why a beautiful woman like Haylee had never dated much.

"You're trying to turn me into an old maid, aren't you?"

She lifted her head, glared at me, and lowered her muzzle back on her paws.

I started the car.

Fifteen minutes later we were back at the apartment. Fifi made a quick tour of the bushes while I fantasized about Adonis asking Willow for my name and number. Having seen the way Willow looked at him, how every woman at the daycare had looked at him, I doubted she'd give it to him.

After Fifi's behavior, did I really think he'd ask? I picked Fifi up to carry her inside. As I crossed the parking lot, either out of habit or because I sensed him, I glanced over at Dusty's boat. He was unlocking the outside padlock; Agent Clark stood beside him.

He opened the door and with a hand centered on her back, he guided her inside and stepped in behind her, not looking over his shoulder, not turning in my direction.

Fifi was suddenly very heavy in my arms. My whole body felt tired from the stress of the past few days. I squinted at the stairs, wondering if I could even make it up to the apartment. But I had to.

* * *

I finished gathering the information on Conor that Gerri Runyan had requested and emailed the file to her. Next, I tried to bring up Primordium's website, looking for the list of employees so I could contact them one by one, but the webpage had been removed. Dusty had said most of the employees were missing. The only one he'd managed to contact was the receptionist. If the webpage was down, someone was still working for the company and I wondered who that was. Luckily, I'd made a screen grab of the employees' page the first time I'd looked at the website. Much of sleuthing was waiting, and I'd planned on reading the page while waiting for Conor, or for Dusty, or for information, et cetera, but I'd been so busy, I'd never gotten around to reading it.

I opened the file and clicked on the screen grab. All the employees had smiling pictures next to their names. At the far left was the receptionist, Susan Gadow, and beneath her name, the publicity liaison, Nara Hibbert, She looked older than I'd expected.

Down the center of the page was a list of scientists. They were broken into two labs. The CEO, Vincent Kerner, was the only name listed under the Antibody Engineering Lab. The deceased, David Chaffe, was the director of the Research Lab. Listed under him was another scientist, Justin Wertz, and an Asian woman, Eri Ikeda; the woman who had pretended to be Chaffe's wife. It was the same photo Dusty had shown me this morning.

The last column listed three lab technicians, two men and a woman.

Nine people altogether, eight if you removed Chaffe. Everyone looked friendly; almost everyone looked smart. The receptionist was beautiful, nice lines, puffy lips, but her expression looked like a person caught in the headlights. One of the male lab techs had hooded eyes, which I rarely equated with smart unless I meant "street smart."

I thought about the loading dock where Conor had made his delivery. Who worked there? Why did a lab need a loading dock? Equipment deliveries. Cryogenic deliveries. Had it been a sterile loading dock? Did such a thing even exist? Why wasn't the receptionist allowed back there? Was something else being delivered? Something illegal?

This circled me back to why Conor had delivered placentas and cord blood to the vic. I had way too many questions and no one to bounce them off of. I had to swallow my pride and accept Dusty's relationship with Clark. I couldn't afford to lose another friend.

The Receptionist

Having had so little sleep the night before I'd thought I'd go unconscious the minute I closed my eyes, but I hadn't. I lay in bed while visions of Conor's bruised face kept me tossing and turning half the night. As dawn broke, what little information I had on the case stirred my thoughts.

Four cups of coffee and two cigarettes later, I'd compiled as much data as I could find on all the Primordium employees: education, previous jobs, previous affiliations, previous and current addresses and phone numbers. I paid yearly fees to several services that gave me access to confidential records, such as criminal backgrounds, educational and family backgrounds, credit cards and credit history. For an extra fee, I could have real-time access to their use. That was the good news. The bad news was that one of those subscriptions, the most expensive and thus the most extensive, was coming due in a week and I didn't have any extra cash.

Fifi was whining and dancing around with a squeaky toy and doing just about everything to keep me from working.

All I'd found on Primordium was that its funding came from a holding company based in Switzerland. Very little information was listed for the holding company. It had opened about two months before Primordium, which raised a big fat red flag, but I'd need to locate the CEO of Primordium to get the rest of my questions answered.

I stood and stretched my arms over my head. Fifi jumped up against my thigh. "I'm taking you back to doggy daycare if you don't let me work."

She ran and grabbed the squeaky toy and brought it back to me.

The ringtone to my phone rang out from deep in the apartment. I rushed to the bedroom to answer it.

"Is it true, yer 'usband's in jail?"

Mrs. Macklin, Haylee's mom and my adoptive one. "How did you know?"

"Conor called me. Yer need to git in touch wi' his family. Yer hear me?"

"I'm taking care of it." I'd thought about calling his dad, but the minute I did, he'd get in contact with Billy Black and the last thing Conor needed right now was an active link to the Irish Brotherhood. "The evidence against Conor is very weak and I think he'll be released soon. I don't want it to look like he has friends who might be under FBI investigation. You understand, don't you? It wouldn't look good for Conor to get a visit or a phone call from anyone unsavory."

She made a humming noise, but she understood me. I needed to push it home.

"I'll call Mr. Nolan if the situation gets worse, but I expect all charges will be dropped soon and Conor can head back to Texas."

"How's Fifi?"

"Driving me crazy. I've enrolled her in daycare and she loves it. She loves being around other dogs."

"Dat doesn't soun' loike her."

"It's true, she loves it." I bared my teeth when Fifi wheezed out a scream from the squeaky thingy.

Conversation turned to her grandkids and her husband's gout. She complained about the pain in her left knee and I realized for the first time that she and her husband were growing old. I'd soon lose them, too.

I was plumb full of cheery thoughts.

When she rang off, I walked around the apartment, slowly making my way to the kitchen and the back window that overlooked Dusty's boat. I'd felt lethargic for the last couple of days. I'd tried to write it off to worry about Conor and lack of sleep, but now with the irrational fear of losing the Macklins pounding in my heart, I recognized the signs. I was headed into the darkness. My resolve would soon wither and when I looked for reasons to drink, it would be difficult to find reasons not to.

I had to do something. The only thing I knew to do was to keep busy, so busy that I didn't have time to think. I headed back to the laptop, leaned over the chair, and hit PRINT, sending the list of employees' info to the printer.

* * *

The first stop was the receptionist's apartment. It was on a tree-lined street in northern San Rafael. I drove by it once without seeing the narrow driveway. I found parking on the street and walked to the complex. Two rows of four apartments separated by the driveway. There were carports for parking and two of them had cars. Apartment B2 was on the right side. I knocked on the door.

The woman who answered didn't look anything like the put-together receptionist I remembered meeting. Her yellow blond hair was in a messy knot on top of her head and she wore no makeup. A pair of square black-rimmed glasses dulled the sparkly eyes that I remembered. She was wearing torn jeans and a shapeless gray sweatshirt. Her feet were bare.

"Susan Gadow?"

"Don't know what you're selling, but I don't have time." She started to close the door.

"I'm here to talk to you about Primordium."

Her hand fell from the door and she backed away as if I'd just pulled a gun on her.

"I don't know anything. Don't hurt me. I'm only the receptionist. Don't hurt me," she said again, backing into the apartment until she had her butt against a wall. She raised her hands as if to ward off a blow.

"Who are you afraid of? Me?" I shook my head. "Ah, no. You've got it wrong. I'm a private detective."

She lowered her hands a bit and cocked her head. "A what?"

"A detective working for a lawyer," I said, only half lying. I was here for myself.

She stepped toward me. "What lawyer?"

"Runyan. Gerri Runyan. She's representing—"

"I don't care," she said and rushed out of the room.

I waited, half-expecting her to return with a loaded shotgun, but from the sounds coming from the back of the apartment she was either having trouble finding the shotgun or she was doing something else entirely while leaving a total stranger standing in her living room.

Something heavy fell to the carpeted floor with a dull thud. She cursed and then another loud thud.

She hadn't told me to leave. Maybe she needed help. I rounded the corner and headed down the hallway. At the end, Susan stood in what looked like a bedroom, her hands on her head. The low mumble of a television came from the same direction.

Her fingers pulled at her hair. "Oh, shut up!" she said, then rushed out of view.

The television went silent and I wondered who she was talking to. I walked into the room. "Susan, if I could ask you a few questions about your employer."

The bed was unmade. Clothes were strewn everywhere. Several romance novels had been tossed across the clothes. The drawer of her bedside table hung open.

Susan was haphazardly stuffing a black duffel bag with clothes from a drawer of a three-drawer dresser. "I don't know where they are. That's what you want to know, right? I don't know."

She nervously glanced between the half-opened drawers and the flat-screen television on top of the dresser.

"Maybe they're with Dr. Chaffe." She dropped the duffel bag to the carpet. She squatted to pick a handful of shirts off the rug.

Her earlier fear of me was starting to make sense. "You think they're all dead?" I asked.

"They're gone, aren't they? And I'm not going to be next," she said, zipping the duffel bag.

"Why would someone want to hurt you?"

"Why would someone burn down Primordium? Why would they all disappear? All we did was help people." She picked up three paperbacks from the ones tossed across the bed. Two were trashy romance novels, the third was Jane Austen's *Mansfield Park*. "Have you read any of these?"

"Austen writes the best romance. Always has, always will."

She tossed the other two on the bed and stuffed *Mansfield Park* in a pocket of the duffel bag. "I gotta go."

She tried to shove past me, but I blocked her path by stepping in the doorway. "Maybe something illegal was going on. Think about it. Did you ever see anything that you'd categorize as sketchy?"

She dropped the duffel bag on the carpet. Her hands went to her hips. "Sketchy. You want sketchy. What about terrorism? That's sketchy. Bio warfare. That's sketchy. What about zombies? That's—"

"Wait! Are you saying Primordium was involved in terrorism? In bio warfare?"

"I'm saying they could be involved in all kinds of stuff. I wasn't allowed past the first floor. Don't you think that's weird?"

"I do."

"We used to get all kinds of medical magazines. Really technical stuff and I read this one called, *An Argument for Zombies*. It talked about brain chemistry and a lot of weird stuff that I didn't really understand, but it was written by a smart scientist for other smart scientists who are creating body parts out of cells. Maybe they were creating zombies."

Whoa, was that the sound of the ocean whistling through her ears?

"Susan." I suddenly felt the need to speak slowly as if speaking with a child. "You must have handled the incoming calls. Was there anyone who called often?"

She shook her head and picked up the duffel bag. "Everyone had their own cell phones. The only calls that came in the main line were people wanting information about storing the cord blood. I need to go. They might be looking for me."

"Who?"

Using the duffel bag, she shoved me against the doorframe and pushed past me. "Whoever burned down the building."

The duffel bag scraped the wall as she rushed down the hallway.

I started after her. "Wait. No one wants to hurt you. You weren't allowed in the building. Wait! At least leave me a contact number."

She stopped at the front door. "The others didn't know anything either. Lock up when you leave."

My cell phone rang. It was the editor from the IJ.

"What's up?" I said into the phone, watching Susan make her getaway in a beat-up white compact car.

"Hello, Briana," the editor said. "I liked the article you sent us yesterday, nice angle linking it to the suspect in holding."

Trying to free my ex-husband in the court of public opinion, I thought, but instead I said, "Glad you liked it, sir."

"I'd like to rerun it perhaps as an add-on to another article. Do you have any ideas?"

"How about a more in-depth description of Primordium. I just finished speaking with their receptionist." Unfortunately she'd told me squat.

"Can you get it to me by three?"

"I'm on it." I pulled Susan's door closed and checked that it was locked. I probably should have made a coffee before I left; I was running low on caffeine. I tried the locked handle again. Too late.

The Aspirin

I stopped for a burrito on my way back to the apartment. During summer school, a food truck hustling Mexican food to the high school students was always parked in front of the school, but today being Saturday, the truck was noticeably missing. I had to park in the overcrowded parking lot of the strip mall and wait in a ten-minute line for a beef-and-bean burrito. By the time I paid for the thing, I wasn't hungry.

My head was starting to pound so I ordered a latté from the café next door and drank it as I searched for where I'd parked.

Back at the apartment I put the burrito on the cabinet out of Fifi's reach and went straight to my laptop. The IJ editor wanted a new article in two hours. That was just about how long it would take me to organize my thoughts and get them down. I pulled up the file on Primordium.

All these employees were missing.

I pulled out my cell and called Dusty. He answered on the first ring.

"I'm working on a piece about Primordium for the IJ," I said.

"No comment," he said before I could tell him why I'd called.

"I'm not asking for a comment, I'm asking for permission," I said.

"And if I say no?"

"Geez, you're testy." For a guy who's getting sex, I wanted to add, but knew better. "Will you just listen? I'll be mentioning the employees and I thought about adding that the Sheriff's Department would like to interview certain individuals, I could even mention them by name, if you'd like. Or I could say something general about the Sheriff's Department is trying to locate all the employees. Who knows, maybe a neighbor or friend will give up someone's location."

The line was silent for a minute. On my end, I was wondering if I'd proposed a good idea or if Dusty was going to be mad that I mentioned it at all. He was so hard to read lately.

"Can't see any harm," he finally said. "But don't mention any names. Say something like the Sheriff's Department is trying to locate the lab workers for clarification on flammable substances used on the second floor."

"The fire inspector said they didn't use flammable substances. He said the fire was set."

Dusty made a guttural noise. "Your question is about finding the missing lab workers. I'm all for that, but I'm not about to tell the general public why I want to speak to these individuals."

"Oh. Right. So I have your blessing?"

"I wouldn't go that far. No names."

"Thanks." I ended the call and started typing. Now, I had a nice twist to add to the article. The editor would tack on info from yesterday's piece and instill more doubt in the public's mind about Conor's guilt.

Despite the growing ache above my eyes, I stayed glued to the keyboard and managed to get my final draft emailed off ten minutes before deadline. That left the editor time to call with any changes, but the piece was fairly straightforward. I didn't foresee any problems. Adding the Sheriff's Department's contact info always gave a certain legitimacy to a piece.

I stood and stretched. Fifi was asleep on the sofa. I went to the kitchen and nuked the now cold burrito. The smell of warm beef brought Fifi skidding to a halt at my feet. I tore off a piece and dropped it into her bowl.

The financials of Primordium were driving me crazy. With a little help from a priority software, I could usually follow a money source, but I kept coming up nil on Primordium. The holding company, UM Ltd., was a shadow on the web. I couldn't find out who or what it was or who it belonged to. It was rare not to find anything.

There were those who could do a better search, and I mentally ran down the list of who I knew. When I'd worked in D.C. I'd had my CIA and FBI connections, but I'd burned those bridges during my drunk and disorderly days. When I was busted down to photographer, I never saw a reason to make amends. Now I did, but was pretty sure it was too late.

Oh, but what about Dusty's new squeeze, Agent Clark? She was FBI.

I swallowed and massaged my temples. Clark. Psss. She wouldn't throw me a line if I was drowning. But what would she do for Dusty? With Primordium's fire, he had to be having doubts about Conor's guilt. Maybe he'd start listening to me if I could bring him some evidence.

What evidence? I had nothing.

I stuffed the last chunk of burrito in my mouth and wiped my hands on my jeans. I grabbed my phone and texted Dusty.

Ask Girlfriend to look into UM Ltd.
Holding co. owns Primordium.

I sent it then typed:

My lead.

Just a friendly reminder whose lead got him the information. Hopefully, he'd be equally friendly and remember to share.

My head was pounding. I hoped I wasn't coming down with something. I needed to follow up on this fire and the disappearance of employees. The circumstantial evidence against Conor was looking more and more suspect.

Chaffe's murder. The fire. The beating. I needed to find a link, but first, I needed to find some aspirin.

* * *

I left Fifi asleep and drove to the drugstore. People in Marin took their dogs everywhere, but I was still uncomfortable taking her into stores and restaurants, mostly because I was afraid she'd attack other dogs. Nothing like a dog fight to cure a headache.

When I was drinking I lived on aspirin. I took them for breakfast, for lunch, and then switched them out for whiskey sometime in the afternoon. When I stopped drinking, I stopped taking aspirin. I hadn't bought any in over a year and was amazed as I stood in the aisle, staring at all the different brands. Some were combined with Vitamin C. Some were combined with ingredients to relax me. I didn't want to be relaxed. I thrived on teeth-grinding, jaw-clenching adrenalin, a state that was hard to maintain without an intravenous flow of caffeine.

I grabbed a brand I recognized and read the label. No caffeine, but it looked pure enough with only one ingredient I didn't know.

I carried it to the pharmacy counter, but the clerk was helping a woman with a crying infant at the drive-thru window. The child's screams made me want to tear open the box and down every last pill. Instead, I massaged my temples with my thumbs.

When the clerk switched off the intercom, he turned to me, scrunched his nose and pursed his lips. I watched the woman drive away.

The clerk let out a long low exhale. "Poor kid," he said, walking over to the counter.

"Poor mom." I held out the aspirin box. "Can you tell me what this is?" I pointed at the mysterious ingredient. Out of the corner of my eye, I saw the next drive-thru customer pull up to the window. A strange stir of familiarity caused me to turn and look.

The car was a silver Audi. The driver, an Asian female. Her hair was shorter, bobbed with bangs, and she wasn't wearing glasses. But I thought I recognized the profile. I stepped out of her line of sight. This was surreal. An hour ago I was profiling this woman for my article.

"Forget the aspirin," I said to the clerk. "Help the woman at the window and I'll decide."

He pursed his lips again, looking more confused than irritated, and walked over to the window. He flipped on the intercom. "May I help you?"

I wanted to get a better look at the driver, but I didn't want her to see me. Instead, I closed my eyes and focused on her voice. If this was the scientist who'd pretended to be Chaffe's wife, then contrary to what the receptionist believed, all the scientists weren't dead. Her name was Eri, but for the life of me, I couldn't remember her last name even though I'd typed it a mere hour ago. I listened. Her voice was amplified through the intercom. Was she the same woman? I thought back to the moment when I'd watched her load the boxes in Chaffe's home. I couldn't be sure, but the gray Audi... It couldn't be a coincidence.

I fished in my handbag for my cell phone, but realized I'd left it connected to my radio in the car. The car. I had to follow her and see where she was hiding out. I tossed the aspirin box to the counter and took off down an aisle.

With all the coddling I had to do, I'd barely gotten my car's engine started when the Audi passed me, heading for the exit. I backed out, almost hitting a homeless man staggering across the lot. He screamed at me. I gestured him away and watched the Audi turn right onto Third Street.

A blue SUV pulled into the drugstore parking lot from a side exit and blocked my escape down Third. I waited for it to get around the small lot and I whipped around its bumper. The light turned red as I pulled up to the exit. I hit the brakes and a solid line of cars zoomed past me down Third. The Audi was barely visible. There wasn't space between cars to make a right on red, but I pulled out anyway. I heard the screech of brakes and the car I'd cut off laid on the horn. I switched lanes to get a better view. The car I'd cut off sped up beside me. The driver flipped me off.

I waved.

Dusty. I had to alert him.

I grabbed my cell phone off the dash and pulled off the cable connecting it to the radio. With one eye on the Audi and one on the phone I punched the two for Dusty's pre-programed number. I swerved right and had to drop the phone to get control of the car. As it happened, I came close to sideswiping the guy who'd flipped me off. His horn sounded again. I waved and snatched up the phone.

As I put the phone to my ear, the guy hit the horn again. With the Audi in sight, I glanced at the irritated driver. Giving him my attention was sure to calm him down. It worked. He eased off the horn so he could make several hand gestures, only one of which I understood. It was pretty universal.

Voicemail. "Dusty!" I said after the beep. "I have the fake wife. The Asian scientist from Primordium. I'm following her silver Audi west on Third Street."

The light at E Street turned yellow. I hit the gas pedal hard, making it through the intersection as the light turned red. The cars in front of me were stopped so I slammed the brakes, skidding a few inches. A Ford Explorer blocked my view of the Audi, but it hadn't turned or changed lanes so I was trusting that it was a few cars ahead.

I'd heard a siren in the background of my thoughts, but had ignored it. Now, a police cruiser was beside me with its lights flashing.

"Oh, shit." I waved the cell phone at him. "Police." I said, but my window was up and he couldn't hear me. It's against the law to drive and talk in California.

Just then the Audi turned right onto a side street. I signaled and moved back into the right lane. The police cruiser moved over too. With its lights flashing and siren blaring, most of the traffic had dropped behind. The angry motorist was probably back there enjoying the sight.

I rolled down my window. The police officer was gesturing for me to pull over. I pointed up the road, several times. He lowered his window.

"Pull over."

"I can't."

"You better."

"You need to follow me," I said, and put on my signal. The next right was the one the Audi had taken. H Street. I swung right and the cruiser cut a lane and followed, lights still flashing. He'd turned off the siren and in my rearview, I saw he was speaking, probably to his dispatcher.

I don't know if it was the adrenalin of the chase or the fear of being stopped by the cop, but my teeth started chattering as if the temperature had dropped below zero.

Four streets up I caught sight of the Audi turning left. I stuck my arm out the window and motioned the officer to follow. Hopefully, that would let him know I wasn't running away. I had visions of being surrounded by San Rafael cruisers any minute.

Every street had a stop sign and I came to a complete stop before proceeding. It felt like an eternity before I reached the fourth street where I'd last seen the Audi. I gestured again to the officer as I turned left onto a residential tree-lined street. The houses here were older than I'd seen in San Rafael. Some were rundown, but others had beautiful gardens and trimmed lawns.

I looked for the Audi. She had to be hiding out here. The cruiser pulled up beside me again.

"Police matter!" I yelled and pointed up the road, not at anything in particular.

"You're not the police," he yelled and again waved me over.

With parked cars on each side there was little room to maneuver. I dropped back, then realizing he might cut me off, I sped back up beside him. My cell phone rang, Dusty's name on the faceplate.

I held it up for the officer to see. "No, but this is."

The officer pointed a gun at me. "So is this, now pull over!"

With one hand on the steering wheel and another on my phone, I mentally made the sign of the trinity and prayed the cop wouldn't hit a pothole. I pictured the headline: Journalist Killed for Cell Phone Call.

I raised the phone to my ear. "Dusty, I've lost sight of the Audi because a San Rafael cop is about to shoot me." All this I said loud enough for the officer to hear.

"I'll try to reach his dispatcher. Hold a sec," Dusty said.

I waved the cell phone at the officer. "Back off." I didn't have enough room to watch my driving and look for the Audi. I tried to watch the road and not the gun.

The cruiser's radio crackled. The cop lowered his weapon.

Dusty was back on the line. "Where are you?"

To my surprise, the cruiser slowed and dropped behind me. Dusty must have gotten through.

I moved to the center of the road so I could see the driveways. Scanning side to side, I gave Dusty my location and sped up. I didn't see it, but I heard it.

The booming sound of a garage door hitting a hard surface. Luckily, I had the windows down.

I stopped and looked for a brick or concrete drive. Almost every house had one. I thought the sound had come from the right. I killed the engine and got out of the car. The officer was beside me.

"Did you hear a garage door close?" I asked, my heart pounding.

He glanced over the roof of my car. "Not sure."

I tried to catch my breath. "What should we do?"

"I know what I'm going to do. I'm writing up your ticket and I hope you have a good lawyer. Illegal turn. Talking on a cell phone. Running a red light."

"It was yellow!"

"Running four stop signs. And last but not least, resisting a police stop."

"I stopped at every one of those stupid signs. And it was a call to the police! They are looking for the woman I was following."

"Yeah, right. Show me your license."

He was determined not to play nice. "Show me yours," I snapped.

His hands were on my shoulders faster than Fifi on roast beef. He whipped me around and against my car, hands held behind my back.

"What…"

Two sirens screamed down the street. A black Sentra with a blue flashing light on the dashboard slid to a stop behind my car, missing it by inches.

"Really!" I yelled and tried to break free from the officer's grip.

The officer shoved me tighter against the car, bracing me with his thigh. The second car, a black and white San Rafael cruiser, stopped farther back.

Dusty leaped out of the Sentra. "Put that away," he said to the officer. "I know she's annoying, but not worth a lawsuit."

I glanced over my shoulder and saw a pair of handcuffs and a yellow Taser in the officer's hands. *Ouch.*

"Oh, if it isn't Deputy Vishnu," the officer said, hooking the Taser to his belt.

"That's Hindu, I'm Buddhist. And while you're trying to find your navel, could you let her go?"

"I'm arresting her."

"Do you have to? She a material witness."

The officer dropped his hold on me and I turned to face the two of them. The officer was about the same height as Dusty, but had thinner, narrow shoulders. A tag over his right breast read: WATKINS.

"How about five traffic violations?"

Dusty let out a low whistle. "Only five?"

The two male officers from the cruiser joined us. One was young and sort of looked like Billy Bob Thornton, the other had a crewcut and thick thighs.

"I stopped at every frickin' stop sign, every one."

"Where did she go?"

He meant the scientist. I glanced around, totally clueless. "I lost her here because of Watkins crowding me. I'm pretty sure I heard a garage door slamming shut."

"Slamming, not rolling?"

"Slamming."

"You see where the Audi went?" Dusty asked Watkins.

"Honestly, I thought this one was a nutcase."

"I get that." Dusty glanced at the houses. "Right side? Left side?"

I shook my head. "I thought right, but I couldn't say."

"I really don't want to go door to door." He looped his thumb on his belt and glanced down at his feet.

I figured he was trying to think of a solution, but I couldn't see one. "One of the other neighbors might know her," I said, thinking out loud.

He nodded. The radio in one of the cruisers squawked. Watkins walked over to his car.

"Guess that's what we'll do," Dusty said to the other officers. He took out his phone and showed both men something on it. I peeked over Crewcut's shoulder and saw that it was a picture of the scientist that I'd been following.

"Her hair is shorter than the picture and she has bangs," I said.

Both officers went to work pulling up her picture on their phones.

"I've got to go," called Watkins from his car. "Chief said these two are all you can have right now. He can maybe send you someone else in an hour, if needed."

Dusty waved him off. "These two will do, thanks."

"Want me to help?" I asked.

"I want you to get in your car and wait. I heard about your race down Third Street. It's a miracle no one was hurt."

"I didn't race! I was trying to keep an eye on the Audi."

"Car! Now!"

He joined the other two officers and I heard him giving them instructions as they crossed the street.

The Scientist

I sat on the hood of my car, watching Dusty and the two San Rafael officers go door to door. The officer who looked like Billy Bob stood for a long time on a front porch talking with a woman wearing a blue housedress and fuzzy red slippers. She pointed across the street. Officer Billy Bob turned toward where she gestured. I figured he'd hit pay dirt.

Dusty stood watching the San Rafael officer speak with the woman for a minute or two, then he headed my way. I knew from past experience that he hated canvassing a neighborhood almost as much as he hated chickens. He'd grown up on a chicken farm.

"Looks like a live one," I said as Dusty stopped beside the car.

He nodded, but kept his eyes on the officer.

Time ticked by, neither of us feeling the need to speak. Officer Crewcut had reached the end of the road and was sauntering back in our direction. The woman on the porch looked over at us before going back inside her house. Officer Billy Bob started down the sidewalk.

I took out my cell phone to check the hour. Dinnertime. By now, Fifi would be clawing at the door.

"You don't need to hang around," Dusty said.

I nodded. He'd probably arrest the scientist, at the very least take her in for questioning, and there was no way he'd let me sit in. "Did you ask your girlfriend to look into who owns Primordium?"

"She's not my girlfriend."

"Right. So who owns Primordium?"

"She'll get back to me."

"Will you share with your friendly neighborhood journalist?"

"If I can."

"You always can."

He ignored me and walked over to join the other two officers as they drew near. "You have something?" he asked Billy Bob.

The officer pointed across the street to a green-painted house with coral-colored shutters. In every window across the front, the shades were drawn. The driveway was empty. The lawn, overgrown with weeds. It looked deserted.

"According to the neighbor," he said, "Ms. Ikeda's the daughter of the woman who lives in that house."

"No one answered the door when I knocked," Crewcut said.

Officer Billy Bob said something I didn't hear.

I slid quietly off the hood and crept up behind Dusty.

"One way or another she's coming with us," he said. "Let's go." He caught sight of me and nodded to my car. "You can go. Your car is blocking the road."

"So is yours."

"Where's that Taser?"

Crewcut's hand went for the one on his belt.

I shuffled back toward my car. "Can't you take a joke?" I kept walking, but I wasn't going anywhere if I didn't have to.

I turned the key and the engine didn't catch. As if it would on the first try.

Dusty glanced over his shoulder.

I held my hands up in frustration, but didn't know if he could see them. The three of them approached the green house. Dusty drew his gun and gestured Crewcut around the back. Dusty and Billy Bob approached the front door. Billy Bob knocked and stepped to the side next to Dusty.

I doubted Ms. Ikeda, Eri, was going to shoot at them, but what did I know? Why was she in hiding? For all her innocent image, she could have killed her boss and burned down Primordium.

I slid out of the car. Dusty was too busy to notice little ole me.

When nothing happened, Dusty pressed his ear to the door. He motioned Billy Bob around the opposite side of the house. The officer peered into windows along the front before disappearing around the corner.

It looked as if Dusty tried the door, but I couldn't be sure. He walked to the garage and put his hand on the outside handle as if to lift the door. It didn't budge. Oh, right, the Audi. If it was inside, we'd know it was the right house. Too bad the garage didn't have any windows.

The front door opened and Crewcut stepped out, his hand clasped to the Asian scientist's upper arm. She was wearing jeans and a yellow shirt. She was also screaming at Crewcut, her voice high enough to shatter glass.

Crewcut called to Dusty, "She was watching through the window."

The scientist squirmed in the officer's grip. "Don't hurt me. Please! I don't know anything!"

"Calm down. We've been looking for you," Dusty said.

"Please! Please, my mother is ill. She needs me."

"Stop resisting," Crewcut said.

"Don't hurt me!"

A man stepped out on the porch of the house next door, probably attracted by the scientist's screams.

Her fear seemed overblown, reminding me of the way the receptionist had reacted to me this morning. She'd thought I was there to hurt her, too.

I ran across the yard as Billy Bob came around the house.

"My mother! Please!" the scientist said again, pulling against Crewcut's grasp.

"Eri!" I called. Hopefully, she would remember me.

"I told you to leave." Dusty raised up a hand as if to hold me back.

He'd need that Taser to stop me now. "You have a big misunderstanding here," I said.

Eri's mouth went to Crewcut's hand. He yelped and shoved her head away with his free hand.

Dusty was still focused on me. "What are you talking—" he started to say.

I walked right up to the bottom of the steps where Crewcut and Eri stood. "These are the police. They aren't here to hurt you," I said to Eri. "They want to ask you some questions about your employer."

She stopped twisting. She looked at me and I saw the recognition settle her. She looked at Dusty, then at Crewcut.

"They're the police," I said again, giving time for it to soak in.

There was a pause where no one spoke, as if everyone was trying to adjust to the situation.

"It's okay," I said to Eri.

"We need you to come down to the station with us," Dusty said more softly.

"I can't leave my mother. She's very sick," Eri said, wiping the tears from her cheeks.

"I can have someone sent over to watch her," Dusty said.

"Can't you question her here?" I asked.

Eri nodded. "I can't leave my mother."

Dusty scowled at me. He huffed and pulled me down from the step. "I guess I can get some recording equipment sent over."

"Everything okay over there?" called the man from his porch next door.

"Everything is fine." Dusty said. He waved his badge in the direction of the other house, but was looking at Eri. "Please go inside," he said to the man.

"I don't know what I can tell you," Eri said. "I don't know anything except that we were sent an email yesterday morning and told to leave town."

"Whoa," I said, looking at Dusty

He reached for his cell phone. "Okay, not another word until I get some recording equipment over here."

Officer Billy Bob pulled me aside. "I think you should go now."

"No!" Eri called.

We both looked at her.

"I remember you. You're a journalist, right?"

I nodded.

"I want you here. A witness to what I say, in case…"

"In case of what?" Dusty asked. He ended his call and put the phone in his pocket. "We can't have this conversation made public," he said to her.

Panic filled Eri's face. Her eyes were moving rapidly side to side. She was either thinking through her options or panicking. I didn't know which.

"I'll keep it off the record," I said. I wanted to hear what she had to say. It could help Conor.

Dusty shook his head. "What are you worried about?" he asked Eri.

"Sometimes the police twist what people say. I want her as my witness." She stood taller, her chin out, her voice stronger. Her fear completely vanquished.

I'd never seen a transformation happen so quickly.

Dusty huffed. "Journalists are more likely to twist your words than we are. We just want the facts."

"If she goes, I won't talk to you." Eri jerked her arm free of Crewcut's grip. "Don't come in again without a warrant." She stepped through the doorway and slammed the door.

Dusty turned to me. "Now look what you've done."

The Interview

Reluctantly, Dusty allowed me to stay and Eri agreed to speak with him. A uniformed deputy arrived from the Sheriff's Department with recording equipment. While the deputy set up microphones and a camera in the living room, Dusty dismissed the two San Rafael officers. Guess he didn't think Eri would try to make a run for it. I didn't think Eri would leave either because I'd helped her carry food back to her bedridden mom. The woman was bone-thin and her skin had an unhealthy sheen. I didn't ask what was wrong, but I didn't need a medical degree to tell she wasn't long for this world.

The house smelled of illness, a sanitized odor that was anything but clean. The caustic cleaners only managed to mask, not eliminate, the stench of a decaying body. The top of the dresser was a myriad of bottles: pill bottles, vitamin bottles, juice bottles, protein shakes, skin lotions, creams. The trash can was overflowing with used tissues and plastic gloves.

The living room was neat and tidy, but decorated in an austere style that had gone out of fashion in the 1950's. A pale turquoise velour sofa was faded by time, the stretched seams showing the vibrant color it had once been. The deputy set two directional microphones on a sharp-edged mahogany coffee table with centuries of wax buildup.

Other furnishings around the room were sparse, decorated with Asian trinkets. A white vase with blue hand-painted scenes looked old enough to be valuable. Two watercolor paintings hung on the wall, both of birds on a branch, one in spring and one in winter. A Japanese character adorned each painting, probably proclaiming some profound meaning of life, but since I didn't read Japanese I couldn't say. One could be the character for Spring and the other for Winter. How was that for profound?

Dusty came back in from the front yard. "Are we about ready?" he asked the deputy.

"I just need a sound check," the deputy said. He had an accent so slight I barely noticed it. He was dark-haired and tanned, but didn't look Mexican or even South American.

I looked for his name tag, but he wasn't wearing one.

I stuck out my hand in greeting. "I'm Briana. We haven't met."

He grinned. "Ah, but I've heard about you."

What? That was never good. I tensed. "And you are?"

"Matteo."

Italian. No, Spanish. Maybe Portuguese. But his accent wasn't either. "Where is your accent from?"

"What accent?" He switched on a microphone. A loud squeal caused Dusty and me to cover our ears.

Eri ran into the room. "Mother is sleeping!"

The squeal died out. Matteo adjusted a few knobs on his equipment and switched on the second mic. No squeal.

Dusty checked his watch. "Can we get started?"

"Hot date?" I asked without wanting to know the answer. If Eri said anything that might clear Conor, I'd make sure Dusty's evening was only beginning.

"Ms. Ikeda, could you sit on the sofa with me?" Dusty said. "Briana, you stand there behind the mic and *please*, don't say a word, not even a mumble."

Matteo had brought a chair over from the dining table and was sitting next to the camera he'd set up.

I went to the dining table and carried another chair over, placing it directly across from Dusty. He knew better than to think I wouldn't have questions. I knew that he didn't want my voice on the recording, but if I signaled him from here he'd surely see me.

"We're ready," Matteo said, switching on the camera.

Dusty nodded. "Interview with Eri Ikeda."

While he gave the date, time, and his badge number, I looked for a clean sheet in my notebook. Time for a new one. I had three unused pages left.

"Let's start with why you're in hiding," Dusty said.

"I told you," Eri said. She leaned back and crossed her hands in her lap. "We all received an email at work. It said to go into hiding if we wanted to remain safe."

"When did you get this email?"

"The day Primordium burned down."

"Two days ago? Thursday?"

Eri nodded.

"Ms. Ikeda, I need you to vocalize your answers for the recording," he said, gesturing to the mics. "Who was the email from?"

"It wasn't signed."

"It had to be from someone," Dusty said with emphasis.

Eri brought her clenched hands up in front of her heart. She shook her head. "Mine said it was from me. Justin's said it was from him. It was as if our own accounts had generated the email. The subject line said, *urgent*."

Dusty looked down at his notepad. "Why did it say to go into hiding?"

"To be safe. That's all it said."

"Do you have a copy of this email?"

Eri shook her head, then looked at the mics. "It was on my business account. We had to leave all business computers and cell phones at the office."

Conveniently burned to ashes, I thought.

"Did the email say to do that?"

"No. Vince did."

"Vincent Kerner, the CEO?"

Eri nodded. She unclenched her hands and rubbed the palms together. She ran her palms over her lap.

"Let's talk about Kerner," Dusty said.

But I had another question about the email. I waved my hand at Dusty. He looked at me and shook his head. I waved both hands at him.

"Do you know Kerner well?" Dusty asked.

I kicked the coffee table. Both mics jumped.

"Okay. Cut!" Dusty said to Matteo. He scowled at me. "What is it?"

"She said everyone got an email…how does she know everyone got it? The receptionist didn't get it."

"I meant everyone in the lab. Justin saw it first, then me, then Vince. I don't know about downstairs. I never see those people."

"Can I continue now?" Dusty said to me.

"How did Kerner act when he got the email?" I asked. He seemed likely to have sent it.

Eri appeared to be thinking back. Dusty looked from her to me.

"It could be important," I said. "Maybe Kerner sent the email to clear them out."

Dusty scowled and then glanced back at Eri. "How did it play out?" He prompted her. "Justin received the email and what did he do?"

"He said, 'Vince, what's this?' Vince and I read the email over his shoulder and Vince asked me if I got one. I went to my laptop and I had the exact same email. Vince went to his laptop and he had one, too."

"Did Vince seem surprised?" I asked.

"Surprised? No." She pinched her lips closed and shook her head. Her gaze was far away. "He started barking orders. Do this, don't do that. It was as if he was following some imaginary protocol."

"Okay, Matteo, let's turn this on."

"Wait!" I had one more question. "Did either you or Justin ask about why it said to go into hiding?"

"Justin did."

"And?" Dusty asked.

"Vince said to do what the email said and then he told us to leave our laptops and cell phones for the police."

"Why for the police?" Dusty asked.

"I assumed he was going to call the police after we left."

"Is that all?" Dusty said to me.

I smiled a big wide grin. "Thanks."

He gestured for Matteo to restart the recording. "Resuming interview with Dr. Eri Ikeda after bathroom break," Dusty said, looking at me.

His next few questions had to do with Vincent Kerner. How long had she known him? Did she know if he was a shareholder in Primordium? Et cetera.

From her answers, I got the impression that she respected his research, but thought he was a lousy CEO. His research was funded by Marc Upton. I recognized the name, but didn't know where I knew it from. I thought he had something to do with tech, but almost everyone in the Bay Area did. I jotted his name on my pad.

Then, I noticed the questions that Dusty wasn't asking: How long had she worked at Primordium? Who hired her? Had Kerner hired her? These basic questions were part of a first interview. He must have talked to Eri after David Chaffe's death. Standard operating procedure—interview the co-workers. I had to find out what she knew about Chaffe's death.

"We really need to speak with Vincent Kerner," Dusty said. "Do you know of any family or friends we can contact to reach him?"

Eri looked down at her lap and shook her head. "He's not married. We all got the same email. He probably left town. I've been frightened since the lab burned, but I can't leave my mother."

"There's no reason to believe you're in danger," he said. "The email was probably meant to scare you so you wouldn't talk to the police."

Eri left the sofa in one bound. Dusty motioned to Matteo to stop recording. Eri paced the length of the room several times.

She stopped. Her glance froze on me. "If that's what they wanted, then I shouldn't be talking. The email was a threat. First David, then Primordium. I'll be next." She fled the room.

"Leave it to you," Dusty said, gesturing my way.

I stood. "Me? You pointed out the obvious."

He came to stand beside me; his hands went to his hips. Matteo snickered and raised an eyebrow. I glanced at Dusty and realized I was mirroring his position. I dropped my arms and stepped away.

"Shut up," I said to Matteo as I passed his chair.

Dusty looked at us. "What's going on with you two?"

"Matteo's being a jerk. What about the email? Can't you find out who sent it?"

"We can try, but Primordium had their own server and it went up in flames with everything else. I was hoping to find a cell phone or laptop, but Ms. Ikeda says everything was at Primordium. Convenient."

"More like…planned."

He nodded and walked over to the hallway, glancing down it. He turned back to me. "Could you go bring her back? We need to finish this and get her some security."

Security. "You think that's necessary?"

"I do."

By recognizing her at the pharmacy, I'd put her and her mother in mortal danger. I suddenly wished I was anywhere but here.

I wandered down the hallway and peeked into her mother's room. The woman was sleeping peacefully. The door to the next room was almost shut. I knocked. "Eri?"

I heard a sniffle and decided to go in.

Eri was seated at an old-fashioned desk, antique white with brass drawer pulls. With her elbow propped on the desktop, she looked like an adolescent poring over homework.

"Detective Arkansas will get you security. You and your mom will be safe."

She was crying, more silently than before, but the rocking shoulders gave her away.

I was good at being impulsive, not so much with being comforting. I wondered what else to say.

About the time I was turning to fetch Dusty, Eri looked up. "Why would anyone want to hurt us?"

That's what I wanted to know. "Maybe your research."

"It was nothing groundbreaking." She stood, shaking her head. "We weren't close to anything new."

"Why did Chaffe want those placentas?"

Her glance shot upward, her face cleared. "That's it. It has to be."

The Clue

The sofa creaked as Dusty sat back down with Eri. She'd figured something out and I couldn't wait to hear what she had to say.

Dusty gestured to Matteo by circling his index finger. Then he picked up his notepad from the coffee table. "Resuming interview with Ms. Ikeda after a ten-minute break requested by Ms. Ikeda." He leaned back on the sofa. "Is it—"

"Do you think this has anything to do with what Dr. Chaffe was looking into?" she asked, interrupting him.

"Ah, it's a possibility," Dusty said. "If there was something illegal going on, someone may have wanted to cover it up."

"Illegal?" I said.

Dusty shot me a tight-lipped glance. I grabbed my mouth, to show I understood.

He turned his attention back to Eri. "When we spoke Wednesday after the death of your colleague, you said that the lab was receiving cord blood from a hospital in Mexico. You said this cord blood was used for research only, but I have to tell you that the fire inspector found little trace of any kind of blood. Very few canisters, no gas, no blood."

I may have gasped or coughed or laughed or something because Dusty shot me an irritated glance before continuing.

He flipped back a few pages in his notebook. "You told us that the private banking of family cord blood paid for the research in your lab," he said, reading. "Now we know there was no cord blood banking. In your opinion, could this proposed banking have been a front for some other activity?"

Eri's mouth dropped open and her head shook from side to side. "What do you mean there were no canisters? Did you check the vault? And…what about Justin's research? If there was no banking, why was he trying to find a less expensive way to store the cord blood specimens? His research was about increasing our profits."

"Maybe there was a money angle. A lab like yours had to be funded by someone. You've given us one name, a Marc Upton, who sponsors Mr. Kerner's research…do you know anything at all about the owners of Primordium, a UM Limited Holding Company?"

"There had to be canisters. I processed many myself, one just a week ago. Sometimes I went to the hospitals to pick up the placentas and bring them back. Once I spun the white blood cells out, I placed the vials in canisters and put them in the storage vault. Did your firemen go through the vault?"

So much information that didn't make sense. Having missed their first interview after Chaffe's death, I was only getting snippets of that conversation, but what I was getting didn't make sense.

"Primordium. The owner?" Dusty said.

Eri's glance was bouncing from me to Dusty to Matteo, but she wasn't really looking at any of us. Finally, she pulled up her shoulders and answered Dusty with a very controlled voice. "Primordium was on my checks, signed by Vince. I've never heard of this other company. Vince sometimes gave people tours and he said they were donors, but I didn't concern myself with the business side."

"What about Mr. Kerner's research?" Dusty asked. "What did it focus on?"

Kerner's, what about Chaffe's? Why was he curious about the CEO and not the dead guy unless he saw Kerner as a suspect? I waved my hands at Dusty. He glanced at me and shook his head. Using my pen, I scribbled, *I have a question*, on my palm and held it out to him. He shook his head while reading the message.

I kicked the coffee table again. This time one of the mics fell over. Dusty gestured Matteo to stop.

He stood, towering over the table. "If you do that again I'm going to come across this table and strangle you."

Matteo snickered.

Both Dusty and I snapped at him simultaneously. "Shut up!"

"What about Chaffe's research?" I asked.

"Ms. Ikeda already told us about that in an earlier interview."

"I don't know about it and it concerns Conor."

"You'll hear about it at trial." He sat back down on the sofa. "You either let me finish or leave. Your choice."

I looked at Eri. I wanted to know what she knew. I made a zipping motion across my lips and Dusty nodded to Matteo.

Matteo switched on the equipment and grinned at me like a tattletale who'd gotten his way.

"Resuming interview after bathroom break," Dusty said. His index finger found the soft spot of his temple and he gently massaged it. "You mentioned Kerner's research was funded by…" He flipped the page of his notepad. "Upton, Marc Upton. Kerner told us a different story."

"Wait, I know what you're going to say," Eri said. "Upton's a very private person. We're not supposed to know about his funding, but I learned about it one evening when I came to process a new arrival. I saw a check that Vince hadn't had time to deposit. Also another evening, I saw Vince at dinner with the man. I know who he is because he funded the last lab where I worked."

"Where was that?"

"A stem cell research facility in Berkeley. It's closed now."

Dusty made a note. "Okay," he said, flipping to a new page in his pad. "Let's go back to the placentas. That seems to be the first domino."

I perked up. This could be it, the information I needed to free Conor.

Dusty looked at me, pursed his lips and gestured for Matteo to stop recording.

I knew what was coming.

"I think you need to leave for this part," he said to me.

I shook my head. "Eri, you can't be alone without a witness, remember. He'll bully you."

Dusty's eyebrows drew together and for a moment, I thought he might pull out his gun and shoot me.

"I want her to stay," Eri said softly.

"Her presence will compromise another investigation," Dusty said.

"Compromise?" I blurted out. "Aren't we both looking for the truth?"

He gritted his teeth.

"I want her to stay," Eri said again.

"She wants me to stay," I repeated.

Dusty appeared to be reading from his notepad, but I knew he was looking at a blank page and figured he was making a decision. I awaited my fate.

"Can I go check on my mother?" Eri asked after a moment of silence.

"Of course," Dusty said.

Once she'd left the room, Dusty looked at me. "I'll bully her."

"Always a possibility."

"When have I ever bullied a witness?"

"I'm sure it happened lots of times before you had me to calm you down."

That got a smile out of him. "You have been nothing but a pain in my backside since you came to town."

"Yeah, love you, too," I said as a joke, but the silence that followed just made it awkward.

Matteo snickered.

I tilted my head in Matteo's direction. "This guy's annoying," I said, "Can you shoot him?" I needed to change the subject fast. "Fact is, I'm looking for information that will clear Conor. Even if you don't like him, I don't think you're hoping to put an innocent man in jail for the rest of his life. You said that Chaffe's death was the inciting incident in this whole mess. Conor was in jail for everything that followed. And he was beaten by a guard."

"A guard! Who told you that?"

"No one," I said, remembering my promise to Conor. And Conor hadn't actually confirmed it. "But think about it. Why would someone beat him?"

"Ah, in case you haven't noticed, he has a mouth on him that begs to be hit." Dusty ran his hand over the blond stubble on his head. He looked at Matteo, then back at me. "If you stay, I don't want to see any of this in print. If I do, I'll throw you in jail with your husband until the case is closed. And the way things are going, that could be a very, very long time."

His voice sounded tired. I suddenly felt guilty for my bad behavior; he had enough on his plate.

"I won't print anything without your permission."

Eri returned to the sofa with a tissue in her hand. "Mother will need her fruit drink soon. How much longer?"

Dusty looked at me. "I'm going to regret this." He turned to Eri. "A few more questions."

Matteo started recording.

"Resuming interview after requested break," Dusty said, glaring at me. "You stated previously that Dr. Chaffe thought some of the stem cells you were receiving from Mexico weren't good. That was why he'd requested the placentas from the shipment coming in."

"That's right. He wanted to compare the placentas against the stem cells in that same shipment."

Dusty paused, and read from his notepad. "So Dr. Chaffe didn't believe that stem cells from the shipment would match the placentas." he said, looking up.

Eri shifted on the sofa. "No, he didn't. We work with a hospital in Mexico City, retrieving discarded placentas and cord blood. We set up a small lab to process the cord blood before shipment to the US. David set it up himself."

"But why did he believe they wouldn't match?" Dusty asked.

"He'd been suspicious lately. The stem cell samples we were receiving were smaller than normal and arriving too often. Also he didn't believe the hospital was delivering that many babies. He asked a trusted source in the hospital to freeze the last two placentas after the cord blood was extracted and processed."

"Let me interrupt you. What is smaller in this case?"

"When we clamp and cut the umbilical cord from the baby we use a syringe to draw out the blood. When the mother delivers the placenta, we clamp and cut the cord from the placenta and draw out more blood from that end of the cord." Eri used her hands to illustrate. "Next, we spin out the white blood cells. Red blood cells don't have a nucleus and are of no help. We discard them. Now we have about sixty cc's or two ounces. The samples in the last shipment were a little more than thirty cc's."

"Maybe someone was only doing half his job and withdrawing blood from only one side of the umbilical cord," Dusty said.

"That's one possibility. That's why Dr. Chaffe wanted to compare the blood of the placenta to the samples we received. We received a shipment of stem cells for research Sunday night. The last child born at the hospital was Sunday morning. Stem cells from that shipment should match the tissue of the placentas, but when a new shipment was scheduled for Tuesday—so soon after the last—David contacted his source and asked for the last two placentas to be shipped along with the stem cells."

Dusty shook his head. "I'm confused. What would this tell him?"

"One of two things. If his testing showed that the placentas matched the blood coming in Tuesday, then the processing of the cord blood was happening behind schedule and what cells we were receiving were probably contaminated. But if, as he believed, the placentas wouldn't match Tuesday's shipment, then the stem cell samples in that shipment were coming from another source."

"Stolen?" Dusty said.

Eri's gaze dropped to her lap. She shook her head. "No. Not stolen." She paused.

Dusty had to prompt her. "Then where?"

"Corpses."

"Gross," Matteo said, his accent thicker.

"Can you give me more information on that?" Dusty asked, flipping the page in his notepad.

"Stem cells that exist in some tissue like muscle or connective tissue can remain viable for up to several days after death if the body is kept at about thirty-nine degrees. Some researchers believe it can remain viable even longer.

Of course, it's much harder to harvest these cells than cord blood cells and usually yields smaller amounts. It was the smaller vials that alerted David," she said, her voice cracking. "I don't think he had time to test the cells before…you know." She picked up the tissue, new tears gracing her cheeks.

Dusty shifted on the sofa.

Motive for Dr. Chaffe's death was looking quite obvious. Someone didn't want him to test those samples.

"I need to feed mother now."

"One more question," Dusty said. "Who did Chaffe share his suspicions with?"

"Only me and Vince."

The Dinner

I'd almost reached my car when I heard Dusty's voice. I glanced back at Eri's house and saw him heading down the sidewalk toward me. Here it came, his lecture about not printing anything. He would, again, threaten to throw me in jail. But it had been a long day and I wasn't sure I wanted to wait around to listen.

I got in my car and rolled down the window as he stepped up to the driver's door.

"I don't need the third degree," I said. "Heard it already."

"What are you talking about?"

I lowered my head, too tired to fight him. "Go on then."

When he didn't speak I looked up. He appeared confused. "I was thinking we should talk," he finally said. "You brought up some interesting points, I'd like to hear your thoughts."

Oh.

I did have some ideas, but most of them revolved around how to free Conor and I wanted to talk to his lawyer, but couldn't do that until Monday morning. "What do you have in mind?"

"We could grab dinner."

"Dinner! Fifi. I'll be lucky if I have any furniture left." I turned the key, but as usual the motor rumbled and died. "I have to get back and feed her first."

He put a hand on the hood. "Need me to look at that for you?"

I turned the key a second time and the engine came to life. "I'm good."

"Okay." He glanced down the road to his car. "What if I pick up some Chinese and meet you at your apartment?"

"Sounds good. I'll see you there." I made a U-turn and headed home.

Fifi was scratching at the door when I arrived. Her bark echoed through the stairwell between the two apartments. I'd just gone out for some aspirin, but that was almost five hours ago.

The adrenalin from the chase had cured me. I felt fine, although hungry enough to chew off my arm.

Fifi leaped at my legs as I pushed my way into the living room. I grabbed her leash, picked her up, and carried her outside. I'd be lucky if she didn't pee all over me before we got to the grass.

We were climbing back up the stairs when Dusty pulled into the lot below. I left the door ajar for him and lugged Fifi to the kitchen, where I filled her food bowl. I always put a little extra when I felt guilty. I knew it wasn't good for her, but I couldn't help myself. I still carried the promise I'd made to Haylee to take care of the dog. I felt guilty that I resented the promise. I felt guilty that I didn't know what a dog needed. And I didn't like feeling guilty, so I overcompensated.

"I wish you wouldn't leave your door open," Dusty said, putting two white takeout bags on the counter. "This case is full of threats and you have a habit of stirring up the hornets."

I reached in the cabinet for two plates. "I saw you pull in so I left it open for you. Besides, who'd want to kill me?"

He took the plates from me and carried them to the table. "I'm sure there's a long list. For starters, slandering prison guards isn't going to make you friends with the department."

I filled a pitcher with water. "What one person calls slander another might call fact."

Dusty carried the pitcher and the food bags to the table. I followed with glasses and silverware.

He sat on the stool, leaving me the chair. "If you're so sure of yourself, why don't you tell me about it?"

"And if I do and something gets said or something gets done, the next beating might be fatal. Conor's not talking. He's scared. Once he's released, I hope he'll give up a name." I forked some sticky rice onto my plate. The deputies at the jail were part of the Sheriff's Department. "Sounds like someone in the department is taking bribes."

Dusty started loading up his plate with sweet and sour vegetables and rice. "There's always one or two. Correctional officers don't make a healthy living. Most can't afford to live in the county."

He passed me the container of cashew chicken. He was pretty much a vegetarian so he'd bought the chicken for me. I felt a moment of pleasure, but brushed it aside. I had to let go of the fantasy I clearly still harbored. He was with someone else.

"You have to admit, your case against Conor is getting weaker by the day," I said, spooning a pile of cashew chicken over my rice.

He nodded and ate a forkful of vegetables. After swallowing he said, "If someone's using him as a scapegoat, he's better off in jail."

"Patsy."

"What?"

"Back east we call it a patsy. Anyway, I guarantee someone is using him as a patsy, after that beating, I'm not so sure jail is safe for him. As you mentioned, he has a mouth on him and it's gotten him in more than one jam."

"You two must be perfect for each other."

I menacingly shook my fork at him. "Past tense. Once you release him, I'll have my divorce papers and all will be right with the world. Well, mine, at least." I scooped up some rice and chicken. *Yum.*

"Is that so?" He looked at me longer than was comfortable, then he said, "I've got someone I trust looking out for him."

"If you dropped the charges, I think he's ready to leave town. He's had enough."

"I can't do that just yet. Too many unanswered questions."

I scraped more chicken onto my rice. "Such as?"

He pushed a few forkfuls around on his plate. Took a sip of water. I watched his inner turmoil change his facial expressions. He was here because he wanted to bounce ideas off me. In the past, we'd worked well together and he'd probably already bounced ideas off his people and they were still coming up empty.

I needed to give him a starting point. "You have to locate Kerner."

"We've been trying. The man has plenty of resources."

"Enough resources to think he's behind this? One—he knew what Chaffe was looking into. Two—he told Eri to bring Chaffe's work back to the lab. You'll need to confirm that with her, but why else would she have been at Chaffe's house? It wasn't her idea." That was maybe a big assumption but easily verified. "Three—he told everyone to leave Primordium on the day it burned to the ground. I figured that Chaffe's notes also burned."

Dusty's tense shoulders and sharp glance down at his plate validated what I was postulating.

166

"What are you not telling me?" I asked, before bringing another forkful to my lips.

"The fire inspector said there was a heavy fuel load in the center of the building that kept the fire going."

"Heavy fuel load? What would that be?"

"Like paper, books, some furniture," he said.

I put down my fork. "It's no secret the fire was deliberately set, another thing pointing to Kerner. Who else could have emptied the vault in such a short time? It had to be the person planning to destroy the building. It had to be an inside job."

"I don't have the luxury of jumping to conclusions, no matter how obvious Kerner looks. I need proof."

He knew I was right, but wouldn't lower himself to agree with me. I reached for my fork. "Fine. Start by X-ing off those who couldn't have done it. Chaffe, the receptionist, Eri. Have you spoken to Nara Hibbert yet? Do you want any more rice or can I finish it?"

"Another MIA," he said.

That surprised me. "She was a downstairs person. What info would she have?"

He handed me the rice container. "Take the rest, but can you hand me the soy sauce packet?" He bit the corner off the sauce packet and dribbled soy over his remaining vegetables. "Let's forget the *who* for a moment and ask *why*?"

"Stem cells are the hottest research item out there today," I said. "Yes, Kerner was harvesting and storing stem cells for the families, but he knew the odds of anyone ever needing them were close to nil, so he sold them off to researchers. Money is always a good motive. Since the place was torched to hide evidence, I'd go with the money angle."

Dusty stood. He reached for the empty pitcher and went to the kitchen. "I agree with you there, but I've had forensics accountants combing Primordium's bank records and Kerner's bank records and both look on the up-and-up."

"Doesn't mean there's nothing there."

He set the refilled pitcher on the table. "This reminds me of the late eighties when AIDS research was the hot ticket," he said, sitting. "We had labs broken into, research stolen. It was a mess. I remember asking a scientist, 'Aren't you all working together? Don't you all want to find a cure and save these people?' He told me it had nothing to do with saving people. It was all about the money. The first group to find a cure would be richer than a European country. That was the motivating factor."

"Pretty sad."

He poured me another glass of water, then refilled his glass. "I'll say. Back to Primordium. The day Dr. Chaffe was murdered I saw the vault. Like Eri Ikeda said, it was full of canisters. So what happened between Tuesday and Thursday? It had to be about Chaffe's suspicion of the new stem cells they were receiving. What if they were from corpses instead of placentas? According to Ms. Ikeda, a stem cell is a stem cell."

"No. Not at all. Hold on." I grabbed my laptop from the corner table where I'd stashed it. I booted it up next to my plate. "I've done some research," I said, opening the folder of articles. "Stem cells from cord blood can only differentiate into blood cells. They are only used to cure blood illnesses. They aren't the type of stem cells that can create any type of cell, like those needed to create a heart. Those stem cells come from an embryo. This is how companies like Primordium rip off the families who bank cord blood with them."

"Rip off? What do you mean?"

"People hear *stem cells* and think they are the end-all cure for the future. Maybe that's so, but cord blood only creates blood cells and therefore can only cure blood diseases like leukemia or sickle-cell anemia. With me so far? Good. Because of the misinformation about stem cells, companies like Primordium can make money by banking cord blood. It's the new baby-shower gift, harvesting and banking cord blood."

"I gave my sister a stroller," Dusty said, grinning.

"You were smart." I sipped some of water. "Let's say you *do* have a history of a blood disease in the family so you store the cord blood in case Junior contracts the same illness. Most likely you won't be able to use Junior's banked blood because it contains the genetic defect." I make a tossing gesture as if to throw the sample away. "Toss that blood out. Also, as Eri said, the sample removed from a birth is small, enough stem cells to transfuse a small child or baby. If the child is over fifty pounds when the disease shows itself, more cord blood will be needed. Then, the parents will have to go to a public banking facility to get enough blood for a transfusion."

He handed me a fortune cookie. "So Primordium is a private bank, but you're saying public banks also exist?" He broke open his cookie and read the fortune. "'If winter comes can spring be far behind?'"

"Public banks don't charge fees and they function more like public blood banks. Anyone can make a donation," I said, cracking open my cookie. "Private storage banks are stealing viable donations by making unrealistic promises. Families should be donating to public banks, filling up the public stock so if they need stem cells, they'll be there."

I pulled out the message, read it, and tossed it in an empty carton.

"Hey, what did it say?" Dusty asked.

"Something stupid." I put a piece of the cookie in my mouth.

Dusty reached inside the carton and took out the fortune. "'The person you desire feels the same about...you.'" Dusty threw the strip of paper back into the empty carton. "Your love life has more twists and turns than a blackberry bush."

"What love life?"

We finished our cookies in silence, each of us focused on our own thoughts.

I stacked our plates and the empty cartons.

Dusty stood. "You still didn't clear up the difference between stem cells from a dead body versus from the placenta."

"Ok. Think of type one stem cells as those from cord blood. They can only be used to heal blood based diseases. Type two stem cells are the most controversial. They are embryonic and come from a three- to five-day-old embryo. Those protesters marching around Primordium are mostly against that type of stem cell research. As always, embryos are a hot topic. So far, we don't know if Primordium's research went in that direction. We need to find out what Kerner was working on."

Dusty let out a low, long sigh.

"What can I say, all stem cells aren't created equal," I added.

"And the dead bodies?" he asked.

"Whole different set of stem cells. Let's call them type three. They're adult stem cells and are found in different tissues and organs of the body. They're thought to regenerate indefinitely into their originally assigned function—say a ligament into a ligament or a kidney into a kidney—but new research suggests that, as with embryonic stem cells, these, too, can differentiate into other cells and create tissue or organs other than their original assignment. Most of the research you hear about today revolves around these types of stem cells. But if they're coming from corpses, who knows if they are any good."

I carried our plates to the kitchen. Dusty followed with the rest of the trash. "That brings me back to the black market motive," he said.

"What black market motive?"

"When Chaffe died, we were thinking Primordium was dealing in some type of black market. Your husband being one of the couriers."

"Conor wasn't a courier. He was hired as a freelance driver. A one-time trip. Maybe they would have offered him a full-time position if Chaffe hadn't been murdered. But you said your accountants haven't found any evidence of black market sales."

Fifi joined us in the kitchen, looking from person to person for a snack. We both stood with our arms crossed watching her, but thinking of other things.

I broke the silence. "A better question is who would want to stockpile stem cells? The canisters were there on Tuesday. According to the Fire Inspector, they weren't destroyed so someone moved them to a different location. Why? To protect them? This someone knows their value, at least to research, which makes me think of Kerner again. He wouldn't want them destroyed even if he was destroying other evidence."

"The guy's probably in some non-extradition country by now. Let me help you with the dishes."

"No. I'll do them tomorrow morning with the breakfast dishes."

He walked back to the table. "You probably have to walk the mutt again. I'll go with you," he said, sponging down the tabletop.

I looked down at Fifi, who was standing on her hind legs with the other two paws pressed into my knee. "Yeah, okay."

I picked her up and grabbed the leash.

It was close to ten p.m. so we tried to be quiet going down the stairs, as quiet as one could be on metal steps.

"Hey, not by my car," Dusty said.

Whoops. Old habits die hard. I led Fifi to the grassy area between the parking lot and the boat pier. "Your boat looks funny." I walked closer and saw that it was leaning in the mud. There was very little water in the harbor.

"It's a minus tide. This one's extreme, probably because of El Nino."

"What's a minus tide?" I asked. "When the water goes underground?"

He chuckled and glanced over to his boat. "It's when the tide drops below the average low tide level. Not great for the hull. I'll probably have to repaint it if we have many more like this."

Some of the other boats were sitting on stands. We walked around the pier, looking at the waterless harbor.

"I've been thinking about Marc Upton," I said, pulling Fifi away from the edge. She looked like she was about to leap in to the slime. "Did you ask your girlfriend about UM Limited?"

"Please stop calling her my girlfriend."

"Okay. Did you ask your lov-er about UM Limited?" I asked in a low raspy voice.

"Keep it up."

We walked back the way we'd come and I crossed over into the grassy area. Problem was I really wanted an answer, but his relationship with Agent Clark was like a bad cold; annoying, and not much I could do about it except let it run its course.

The CEO

Early the following morning Fifi and I were out walking when I heard the far-off sound of sirens. Fifi stopped. Her ears perked up.

"Twice in one week. Want to check it out?" I asked as if she understood me.

She took off down the sidewalk so fast I almost lost my hold on the leash.

"Hey, slow up," I called, running after her.

We didn't have far to run. The sirens had stopped by the time we reached the boat shop. Cars were backing up around the strip mall. Probably some shopper had fallen. Stores always went overboard on injured shoppers. But how many stores were open this early on a Sunday morning?

Fifi tugged me forward. We cut through an office plaza because a small crowd was gathered at the rear corner of the strip mall. Lots of police cars, now silent but with flashing lights, were blocking the rear access. That was where trucks entered to deliver to the stores. They unloaded at the back along a pier than ran beside San Rafael Creek. An ambulance was parked at the end behind a discount grocery store.

Not a regular area for shoppers, although when the stores were closed it was a nice walk by the creek.

A couple of houseboats were docked at the pier. Maybe someone on one of those had had an accident or taken ill. Then I saw the SIS van parked next to the last building. Scientific Investigations meant a crime. I walked faster.

A gaggle of news crews had put down roots at the point where delivery trucks turned right to reach the loading docks. I picked up Fifi and shoved my way forward to the police tape, which was partly blocked by an ambulance. I inched though the last few spectators until I reached the back edge of the ambulance. I put Fifi down.

Straight ahead on the concrete was a chalk outline of a body. Four numbered markers had been placed for the SIS team.

Dusty was talking to a guy in a blue uniform. This wasn't his jurisdiction. It belonged to the San Rafael police department and they had loads of officers on the scene.

"Dusty!" I called and waved.

He reacted to the sound of his name. When he saw me, he held up a finger, then he turned back to the SIS man he'd been speaking with.

The morning fog hadn't burned off and the wind was whipping around the crime scene, playing havoc with the markers. An SIS guy propped his foot against one to keep it from sliding across the concrete. Another SIS guy replaced the number "2" marker with an orange traffic cone before taking a picture of whatever it was indicating.

I didn't have my camera so I took out my phone and snapped off a few shots before someone opened the ambulance's rear doors wide, blocking my view. I pushed the door farther back so I could see around it and broke the police tape barricade.

"What are you doing?" yelled a San Rafael police officer. He bent to grab the falling tape. "Step back. Now!"

I held my hands up in an *I surrender sort of gesture*. "Sorry. Geez."

Seeing the commotion, Dusty hustled over. "What are you messing with now?"

Fifi barked and lunged for him. He took a step away.

"I couldn't see," I said.

"Back!" the policeman said again before wrapping the tape end around the handle of the ambulance door.

I peeked in the ambulance and on the stretcher was something or probably someone covered by a sheet.

I looked Dusty in the eye. "Tell me it's not Eri Ikeda or someone else from Primordium."

"It's not Eri," he said.

"Ugh, someone else. Who? Another scientist?"

He didn't react.

"The receptionist?" I guessed.

Still nothing

"Kerner!" I asked.

He tilted his head towards the news crews. "Need to notify next of kin," he said in a low tone.

I nodded to let him know that I understood. "Let me know when I can go to print."

There went his number one suspect, or at least, mine. "Anything look similar to Chaffe's murder?" I asked.

He nodded, but didn't say what.

"What can you give me for the IJ?" I was actually being polite instead of rattling off wild guesses to force him into talking.

He glanced over his shoulder. "Drop site."

"Lack of blood?" I asked as confirmation.

"And lividity."

"Arkansas!" someone called.

"Later," he said and rushed away.

He joined a San Rafael officer and an SIS guy. They walked to the edge of the pier and looked down at the water. A houseboat was docked a few feet away. I'd never seen it go out to sea. It was always docked there. Tied up behind the houseboat was a San Rafael police boat. One officer stood onboard, typing one-handedly into a tablet of some kind.

Officer Billy Bob was a few feet away, his cell phone pressed to his ear. "We need to start canvassing the boats," he said to the officer next to him. The officer glanced across the pier and nodded.

Had the body been brought in by boat? There were no deliveries on Sundays so this area behind the stores would be quiet. The stores wouldn't even open for another hour and a half.

I had enough for an article and I wanted to beat the other reporters to press. Hopefully, Dusty would release the name within the hour.

I picked up Fifi and pushed out of the growing crowd of spectators. When we reached the parking lot of the offices next door to the mall, I put her down and started to run for the apartment. Fifi kept up with a steady pace, but by the time I reached home, I was wheezing and coughing so much I could barely climb the stairs. One day I had to stop smoking.

But not today.

* * *

Twenty minutes after I got home, Dusty sent me a text telling me Kerner's name had been made public by a television station. As I reread my article, I made sure that it asked as many questions as I had. I couldn't draw a connection to Chaffe because I didn't know what the association was, but I could imply a connection by simply asking: Was there a link between the murders of two employees of the burned-out Primordium? I mentioned more than once that the only suspect was in jail during the fire and second murder. If this didn't make the prosecutor rethink her case, nothing would.

I sent it to the editor.

Next, I telephoned Gerri Runyan and told her about the new developments. Normally, I would have waited until Monday, but with Kerner's death I felt I should at least give her cell number a try. Maybe she'd see my name and pick up.

When she answered I related all the information of the last twenty-four hours.

"That'll work for us," she said, referring to the email threat against Primordium's scientists. "Will this scientist, Eri, testify in court?"

"She's in hiding. The threat was real. I have more."

"More? This is pretty good."

"Vincent Kerner, the CEO of Primordium is dead. Turn on your TV. The news should be breaking soon. His body was found behind Montecito Shopping Center this morning."

Silence.

"Hello? Are you still there?" I asked.

"Just a minute, I'm getting out of bed to turn on the TV."

"You're in bed?"

"It's Sunday."

"I hope you aren't alone," I added as a joke, but her snicker put me in my place. I was right. Everyone in the world was having sex, but me. I was pathetic. I didn't even have a friend with benefits. With Dusty and Clark together, I wasn't even sure I had a friend. There was always the stoner that lived below me. He'd said "hi" a few times and high he'd been.

Yes, that's what I needed. An addict.

I heard someone in the background say something and then I heard the television burst on and just as quickly the sound was switched off.

"This is great news," Gerri said.

It was good news for Conor, but I couldn't help but think how frightened Eri would be. She'd be sure that she'd be next and she'd be worried for her mom.

"Here it is," Gerri said.

I assumed she'd found the broadcast.

"I'll call the D.A. first thing in the morning," she continued. "I'll have Conor out by noon."

"Dusty, I mean Detective Arkansas, thinks he's safer in jail if someone is trying to set him up."

"Nonsense."

"Yeah, that's what I thought." Dusty didn't like Conor and he wanted him where he could keep an eye on him. "I think I need to look into this Marc Upton, but for a tech titan, he's mysteriously missing from the Internet. There's a medical journal piece and a few old articles, but almost nothing in the last decade."

"Oh, that's interesting. Sorry, something on the TV. Upton, huh, seems I heard he was ill or something. I know a guy that used to work for him. It was a while back, but maybe he can put you in contact with someone else. I'll email you his info later today."

"Thanks," I said and cut the call. She sounded eager to get rid of me, either to crawl back in bed or to turn up the sound on the newscast. Probably the former.

The Accountant

Gerri Runyan's contact was a man named Orion Stevens. He was semi-retired and offered to meet me for coffee Monday morning at an Italian trattoria in Larkspur. I'd been there once and remembered they served the best cappuccino I'd ever tasted.

He was seated at an outdoor table for two, a big mean looking dog curled at his feet.

"Mr. Stevens?" I asked.

He looked up and tugged at his shirt. "Blue enough?"

He'd told me to look for a guy in a blue shirt. I wasn't that naïve. I searched the Internet and found a photo. In the image, he was surprisingly young looking and since he was retired I assumed it was an old picture, but his big white smile and spiky brown hair matched the image perfectly. He looked to be in his early to mid-forties.

"I expected someone older," I said, taking a seat opposite.

The dog at his feet lifted its square head to give me the once-over, then it lowered back down.

"Why's that?"

Why indeed. I'd lived in Marin less than two months, but sometimes it seemed like people here never worked. They were, however, wired into their cell phones, chatting away as they walked, shopped, or pumped gas. Bike riders chatted. Joggers, too. No one could possibly have that much to say so I assumed that was how and when these people conducted business.

Orion had one of the familiar Bluetooth earbuds attached to his left ear.

"How long ago did you work for Marc Upton?"

"I was the accountant of record when he sold off his last few businesses. That was about five years ago."

"What kind of businesses?" I asked, pulling out my notebook and pen.

A waitress with long wavy blond hair stopped at our table. "Another espresso, Orion?" she asked.

"Think I will, Cynthia. Would you like anything?" he asked me.

I ordered a cappuccino and waited for the woman to leave before I continued.

"Orion, a pretty original name," I said.

"My father's a sidewalk astronomer. Name a star, any star, and I can tell you more than you want to know about it."

"The only star I'm interested in today is Marc Upton. I could barely find anything on the Internet."

He laughed slyly, leaning forward in a conspiratorial manner. "I've heard he hires hackers to keep his name off it." He grinned and nodded. "That's why I can talk to you. I know this will never show up in print."

"You think he has that kind of power?"

"You've heard of the one percenters. Well, Upton is the top one percent of the one percenters. He has enough money to do whatever he wants. If money is power, then yes, he has that kind of power."

"You said he closed his businesses, but I understood he was an investor in a company called Primordium."

"Primordium? Where do I know that name?"

The waitress returned with our drinks. We were both silent while she set them down. Orion thanked her.

"Primordium burned down a few nights ago," I said.

"Right. Up on one-oh-one. Heard it was a hell of a blaze." He picked up the tiny espresso cup and downed it in one gulp. "That's what Upton does with his money. He invests in new technologies, but he doesn't own any companies anymore. From what I've heard, he also refuses to be on the boards of any. He's become kind of a recluse. Another Howard Hughes."

"Howard Hughes. A lot of myths built around the man," I said and took a sip of my cappuccino.

"Upton, too. He likes it that way. Very private."

"From what I understand, he was the main investor in Primordium."

"Doesn't surprise me. Weren't they doing stem cell research?" he asked.

I nodded. "Their primary business was storing cord blood for families. Is Upton married?"

"Never. The consummate bachelor. He'd be more interested in the stem cell research because of his illness."

Ah, the race for a cure. "What's wrong with him?"

"Not sure what it's called, but he's had a lot of liver transplants. In the two years I worked for him, he'd get pasty looking, really sickly and then he'd disappear and come back looking a hundred times better. Happened a couple of times."

The dog at his feet stood, its nose in the air. It watched a guy pass on a bike, then it turned to look at Orion.

"Usually after a few transplants a person's name is removed from the registry. How many do you think he had?" I asked, thinking the interview was coming to a close.

"He's been removed from the national registry, from what I've heard, almost fifteen years ago. Did I mention he was loaded? The woman I worked with figured he was buying black market livers, but there was nothing in the accounts to prove it." Orion caressed the top of the dog's head. "The reason he sold off all his companies was because he was dying. That was five years ago. He's probably at death's door by now. Before you, I hadn't heard his name mentioned in

182

well over a year." He scratched behind the dog's ears. "Lady wants to go for her walk now. I need to take off. Anything else?"

"Do you have any contact info for Upton?"

He chuckled. "I can text it to you, but don't tell him where you got it. He won't see you though. When I worked for him, he'd barely see me when it was in his best interest to do so." He stood and slid a ten-dollar bill under his cup.

I stood also and thanked him for the coffee. "Can you think of any reason why he'd burn down Primordium?"

"Are you joking?"

"Maybe to remove any link to him?"

"He can remove all links with his hackers. Doesn't make sense. Besides, Primordium was probably his last hope at growing new livers." He held out a hand.

I watched him and Lady as they headed south down the sidewalk, his voice carrying as he spoke to the device attached to his ear.

Upton had been a long shot, but he did seem to be one of the few people left alive that knew what Primordium and specifically, Vince Kerner, was working on. If Kerner's death would affect Upton's survival, maybe he'd want to talk. Probably not to a journalist if he was that secretive, but maybe to the police.

* * *

When I got home I had a text message to call Gerri Runyan.

"I'm at the courthouse," she said when I reached her. "The D.A. is releasing Conor to house arrest. The judge just signed off on it. He'll have to wear a monitoring device."

"So he's still charged with the murder."

"There's still the argument and fingerprint—"

"Circumstantial," I interrupted.

"Even so, he's too much of a flight risk. This is the best I could do for now. Will you be there for an hour or two? A deputy will drive him over, then wait until the guy shows up to put on the ankle bracelet."

I really didn't want him living here until his trial. More reason to help Dusty close this case. "I have to walk the dog, but I'll be here."

I threw the phone down on the sofa. I was tired of being Conor's keeper. Our marriage was over long ago and more than anything I wanted to start a new chapter in the tale of my mismanaged life. The cross-country move to California was supposed to be just that—a clean page—but here I was steeped in the past. It was enough to make anyone want a drink, but I didn't, not yet. I did want a cigarette though.

The Bracelet

Fifi was digging at something in the joint between the sidewalk and the retaining wall. I was finishing my second cigarette when Dusty stepped out on the deck of his boat. He was dressed in sweats so I assumed he was going to crawl around on all fours, something he referred to as yoga. I'd always heard yoga was graceful, but watching him contort his large frame was like watching someone trying to stuff a race horse into a Tupperware container.

"Hey," he called and waved.

I stubbed out the cigarette and stuffed the butt in my back pocket.

Dusty crossed the plank and came over to where I was standing.

Fifi looked up as he passed but didn't bark. Whatever she was digging at was more interesting and she went back to clawing desperately.

"What's up?" I asked.

"I wanted to let you know that UM Limited is owned by Marc Upton, the guy Eri Ikeda mentioned as being an investor."

"I figured as much. You need to interview this Upton fellow. He's the only one who knows what Kerner was working on before he died. I can't believe that the burning down of Primordium, the threats to the scientists, and, now, Kerner's death were all about stem cells from dead bodies. Something else had to be going on."

Dusty shook his head. "How did I do my job before you arrived?"

I sneered at him. "I was just thinking out loud. Don't get in a huff."

"I interviewed Upton this morning and Kerner's research was all about finding a cure for him. That's what I wanted to tell you. I don't want you bothering the guy."

"Sure. I heard he's a real recluse."

He stepped closer. "I mean it. Don't bother him."

"Did he look sick? My source said he should be on death's door by now."

A strange expression crossed Dusty's face, one I couldn't read. "You have a…source?"

"I'm not just another pretty face. It's called investigative journalism."

"You call it whatever you want. He will press charges and I'll have to arrest you."

As if on cue, a sheriff's cruiser pulled into the parking lot. Dusty must have assumed it was coming for him. He started toward it. The driver got out and greeted him.

"What's going on here?" Dusty asked, stooping to peer into the rear.

"Prisoner transfer," the deputy said. The deputy open the back door and a bruised Conor slid out. He didn't greet Dusty, but stepped around him, crossed the parking lot, and headed up the stairs to the apartment. The deputy followed.

I pulled Fifi away from whatever she was clawing at and walked over to Dusty. "Conor's on house arrest."

"Lucky you."

"You need to close this case before one of us does kill someone," I said. "Having him around twenty-four-seven would make Buddha pull a gun."

* * *

Conor and the deputy played cards while we waited for the guy to come attach Conor's ankle bracelet. Orion had texted me Marc Upton's address, but I didn't see the point of bothering the man. It was interesting that he funded a lab doing research to save his life, but it hardly seemed likely that he'd kill the person working so hard to save him. Sort of like shooting your hostage when you're surrounded by police.

Dusty had mentioned that there were similarities in the way Chaffe and Kerner were killed. He'd never told me what. I'd seen Chaffe's body. I tried to remember the details. A hand rake to the back of the neck. I remembered thinking it looked like a domestic situation. Why? Ah, a hand rake in a garage with other gardening equipment. The killer hadn't come prepared to kill.

Okay, what did that mean? The killer hadn't meant to kill him. An argument gone wrong. According to the D.A., that pointed back to Conor and his argument with the dead scientist over money. An argument Conor said never took place.

"Hey, can we get something to drink?" Conor called to me.

"Do I look like your servant?"

He held up his hands, cuffed at the wrist. "He won't take these off until I get the ankle bracelet."

I stomped off to the kitchen, took out two glasses, and filled them with cold water. I switched on the coffee maker and carried water glasses to the sofa, where the card game had ended. I handed the deputy one and Conor the other.

"Water?" Conor said. "Can't we get something a little stronger?"

"Thanks," the deputy said.

I bared my gritted teeth at Conor and walked back to the laptop. He mumbled something I didn't want to hear, so I didn't listen.

Orion had also sent me two links to articles about Marc Upton, which were still out there on the great World Wide Web. As I read both articles, I could see why Upton hadn't deleted them. They portrayed him as a philanthropic saint. Saint Marc. Wait, that name was taken. Saint Upton. Not pretty.

"What are you laughing about?" Conor asked. He was leaning back on the sofa, cuffed hands in his lap. The deputy was playing solitaire.

"Nothing," I said and went back to the email from Orion.

Fifi jumped up and ran barking to the door. Someone knocked.

"Halleluiah," said the deputy, gathering the cards together.

I picked up Fifi and opened the door. The man on the other side appeared to be in his early fifties and by the appearance of his crooked nose, he'd seen a lot of fights. He held a black tackle box.

"You waiting for me?" he asked.

I stepped back to let him to enter. "Not me," I said, closing the door. I nodded to Conor. "Him."

"I'll be glad to get these cuffs off," Conor said.

"Not so fast," said the man with the tackle box.

I headed for the kitchen. I put Fifi down. She dipped her nose in the empty food bowl, and then took off to examine our new arrival. I poured a mug of hot coffee and walked to the back window.

Agent Clark had arrived. She and Dusty were standing on the pier in front of his boat. Her lips were flapping and her hands were moving through the air as if she were conducting a symphony. Dusty's arms were crossed and his chest was out. A defensive stance. Clark didn't look happy.

Oh, a lover's quarrel.

I probably shouldn't watch. I took a sip and leaned into the cold glass pane. Too many layers of paint and sixty percent humidity had made the window impossible to open recently, so audio was out of the question.

Agent Clark raised her forefinger, then her middle finger; oh, she was making a list. Two, three, four. All the way to five. Dusty had done five things to make her angry. She half turned toward my apartment and pointed up at the window.

I jumped back even though I knew she couldn't see me. I'd once tested the view with Conor while walking Fifi. During daylight hours no one could see in. Only at night when the kitchen was lit and I wasn't even positive about that. I'd never tested it, but it made sense.

I inched back over to the window. Dusty had dropped the clasped arms and was speaking. Clark was still agitated as she leaned one way and then the other. Her hand rose up again and drifted back down.

Clark said one more thing, turned, and walked away down the pier. Dusty remained still, watching her go. When she was out of sight, I glanced back at Dusty. He was looking up at my apartment.

I stepped away and downed the rest of the coffee.

I reran their movements in my head, filling in plausible dialog. In my rendition, Dusty came out ahead. He may have even told Clark to *go to hell.*

"Briana!" Conor called.

"Ahhh." I wanted to scream. Instead, I set the empty mug on the counter and went to the other room.

Conor was standing, his pants rolled to his knee. A black plastic device was around his ankle. "This guy has some questions," he said, bouncing from one foot to the other as if to test whether he could tap dance.

"Where's your home phone jack?" the technician asked.

I shrugged. "Stop that," I said to Conor, whose soft shuffle routine was getting on my nerves. "I have a cell," I said to the tech.

"A place this old has to have a phone jack," the tech said, pulling back the blinds on the front window to check the wall.

"I'm sure it does, but I don't have service. Is that a problem?"

The tech looked at the deputy. The deputy shoved Conor down on the sofa. His dancing was irritating everyone. I was wondering how much a landline would cost per month and how many months I'd have Conor around. The biggest expense was probably the installation. No, the biggest would be the apartment down the street I'd have to lease to keep my sanity.

"I'll need to go back to the office and get an upgraded model," the tech said.

The deputy moaned.

The tech continued. "I've one of the new ones with the cell phone built in. You'd be the first to use it. Will you be going to work?" he asked Conor.

I answered. "He's not going anywhere."

"Oh." The tech fiddled with the bracelet on Conor's ankle. "In that case, I haven't tested the new model so I'll give him an older GPS unit that works with a cell phone. The phone will transmit the signal answered by the bracelet."

"How much longer is this going to take?" the deputy asked. "I'm getting hungry."

The Argument

The tech returned forty minutes later. I'd had enough of Conor's whining so I picked up Fifi and her leash and headed outside. I didn't see Dusty at first, but as Fifi sniffed closer to the pier I spotted him sitting cross-legged on the side deck of his boat. His palms were facing upward, one balanced on each knee. His eyes were closed and it sounded as if he were chanting something.

"Hey," I called.

"Meditating, go away," he said without opening an eye.

"Oh. Okay." I backed up and sat on the retaining wall while Fifi sniffed around. I could wait. It was infinitely more comfortable here than upstairs with both Conor and the deputy complaining about every little thing.

A minute or so later, Dusty opened one eye. "I thought you were leaving."

"I'm waiting for you to finish. I mean, how long can you possibly sit there and do nothing when lives are at stake?"

He huffed, closed his eye, and bent forward, touching his forehead to the ground. When he sat back up both eyes were open. He groaned as he unfolded and stood.

Brushing his hands together he crossed the plank to land.

"What's up?" he asked.

"I've been thinking about your interview with Marc Upton—"

"Well, stop."

I stood. "But, he's—"

"Damn it, Briana. What do I have to do? Lock you up? I told you to leave the man alone."

Whoa. Where was this coming from?

He pointed his finger at me. "Let me remind you that you are *not* law enforcement. You have *no* right to interview anyone involved in this case. Now, you need to back off and let me do my job."

I took a step forward. "Let *me* remind *you* that you came to me to bounce off ideas—"

"And I've already caught heat for that."

I took another step forward. I was almost in his face. "All I wanted to say was that—"

He snarled. "Stop! Stop now."

"You stop interrupting me." My fist clenched. I wanted to punch him. Fifi barked out a warning. I gritted my teeth and turned away from him. "Oh, forget it. Go back to your deck. Stand on your head. Maybe the blood flow will help you see straight."

I snatched Fifi up and stomped across the parking lot to the stairs.

* * *

The following morning I woke up angry, still rerunning the argument with Dusty through my head, trying to make sense of it. I hadn't slept well.

I shuffled into the living room. Conor was lounging across the sofa in his underwear, playing with one of Fifi's toys. She was trying to take it away from him. My stomach constricted at the sight of him. For moments at a time, I'd forget he was here. Those moments were becoming fewer and fewer.

"You need to sign those divorce papers," I said, passing him and heading for the kitchen. "You promised, if I got you out of jail."

"And I will, but first I have to be sure I stay out of jail."

"Not the agreement," I called from the kitchen. I smacked on the coffeemaker. There was about a quarter of an inch of old coffee in the bottom of the pot. I tossed it into the sink, rinsed the pot, and put it back.

I opened the cabinet to take out more coffee, but the bag was gone. I was sure I'd had enough to get me through this morning. "Conor! Where's my coffee?"

"I left you some in the pot." He strutted into the kitchen, the light on his ankle bracelet pulsing. "I couldn't sleep so I made some coffee. I left you enough in the pot for a cup."

I held up the empty pot.

He threw his hands in the air. "I swear, I left you some."

I slapped the off switch on the coffee maker and jammed the pot into place. I shoved Conor out of the doorway and pushed past him. I wanted to kill someone and he was all too near.

"Briana, it's not like I can go buy you more," he said, following me.

"No, you can't," I said, turning toward him. I should have kept walking, every cell in my body told me to, but this anger was bigger than I was. "And why's that? Oh, because you're in trouble again. Surprise! When are you going to grow up? It's time. Become a man."

His mouth dropped open. Hurt deformed his features. I was ready with more, but what was the point? I'd done the damage.

"Sorry. You know how I am without coffee." I headed to my room and slammed the door.

The View

Marc Upton's house was hidden down a private road on the side of Mount Tamalpais in Mill Valley. My GPS got me as far as two roads over, then told me the lane I was looking for didn't exist. But I was determined. I found it by driving down every turnoff and dead-end.

There looked to be only one way into the property and that was through a garage-like structure build into the mountainside. I parked on the street below and walked up to a mailbox with Upton's house address stenciled on the front. The box was metallic, tan, and large enough to hold several small packages. Protruding off one side was an intercom with a black button above the speaker.

I stared at the button for the longest time, imagining all kinds of responses to the inevitable question of "who's there?" None of my replies seemed like the magic bullet that would get me invited up to the house.

A concrete drive led to the garage. Oleander bushes grew against the side facing away from the mountain. A *No Trespassing* sign was posted on the front of the garage. Hard not to see.

I walked over to check the side of the garage and whether there was room to squeeze between the side and the oleanders. With my back to the wall, I inched into the high bushes, slowly making my way to the back of the garage. I scraped my forearms a few times and poked a hole in my pants when I jerked my leg past a thick branch.

So happy I'd decided to dress up. I'd hoped for an interview, but at the last minute, seeing how closed off the house was, figured Upton would never talk to me under any circumstances. A drive came out of the rear of the garage, making the garage more of a gateway than a parking spot.

I stepped through a patch of low-growing ferns and into the rear drive, which climbed up the steep mountainside. I hiked up the hill in full view of the house, wondering what I hoped to accomplish. I'd been so eager to get away from Conor that I hadn't thought this through. The closer I got to the house, the more nervous I grew. Dusty had said Upton was likely to file charges if I tried to get near him and I'd just given him my blessing by not announcing myself and visibly trespassing on his property.

A black town car was parked in a wide parking area near the entrance to the house. I peeked into the darkened car windows. Behind me the front door opened. I wheeled around, coming face to face with a very tall man in a nice black suit. His eyes were cold gray and his chin reminded me of Jaws from *The Spy Who Loved Me*. His broad shoulders hinted at muscle hidden beneath the—was it Armani?—suit.

"You're on private property," he said without emotion.

"I'd like to ask Mr. Upton a few questions."

"You and about a hundred thousand other people. Do I need to call the police?"

"Let her in, Frank," someone called from the house.

The tall guy looked down on me as if I was a spider he was about to squash. "God has spoken." He gestured toward the open door.

The entranceway was a tribute to Upton. Framed certificates and awards lined the upper part of both walls. Shelves, starting at floor level and rising to my shoulder level, held trophies of all sizes, shapes, and materials. A smooth crystal one, a pyramid-shaped pewter one, a colorful blown glass one: all similar in that they bore Marc Upton's name.

"Go on," the tall guy said, pointing to the other end of the entrance.

The corridor looked to continue a ways with a set of stairs off to the left, but I turned right, stepping into a well-lit living room. A red oriental rug contrasted a long, dark-green leather sofa and a matching side chair. The red-and-green drapes matched the accent pillows. A man, bent over a laptop on a glass and steel coffee table, was seated in the leather side chair.

He straightened and nodded. "Ms. Kaleigh, I admire your audaciousness. Oddly, no one has ever trespassed to get an interview before. Of course few people know my actual address so I commend you on finding it."

He was dressed in a peach button-down shirt and tan slacks. His skin and eyes were tinged with jaundice. His legs looked thick despite his narrow shoulders and thin arms. I wasn't a doctor, but I guessed his current liver was starting to fail.

"You did see the No Trespassing sign. Now that you have ignored it I'm in my right to shoot you. Frank, get your rifle."

Oh, shit.

Frank went to the hallway and came back with a large assault rifle.

"Nice scope," I said with a dry mouth.

Upton laughed. "He's not going to shoot you. I'm not a murderer. That's for groundhogs."

Frank left the room and I took a deep breath.

"How do you know me?" I asked.

Upton's glance went to the laptop screen. "The exterior cameras picked up your image. Facial recognition software matched it and brought up your credentials. Photographer for the *Plymouth Review*, crime desk reporter for *The District Dispatch*, and lastly, staff photographer for same daily.

Currently working freelance, I presume, since your last few articles have appeared in both the *Chronicle* and the *I.J.*" He grinned. "We no longer live in the dark ages."

"No, but I didn't think we lived in the Twilight Zone either."

"Would you like to take a seat?"

I walked over to the sofa and sat. Frank came back in and stood behind me.

Marc Upton leaned back in the leather chair, his arms on the armrest. "Why don't we start by you telling me how you found my address?"

"The old-fashioned way. A friend of a friend of a friend." Okay, maybe one friend too many, but I had to leave him guessing. "Your hackers can keep you off the Internet, but they can't erase memories."

He leaned forward. "My what?"

"Nothing. Just a rumor."

He relaxed. "There are lots of rumors out there about me. Few are true."

"Have you heard the one about you buying black-market livers?"

Upton's grip tightened slightly on the armrest. "Why would I need to do that?"

I didn't want to insult the guy by telling him how bad he looked so I let my gaze travel to the big open windows at the front of the room. "Whoa! Look at that view. I can see all the way to San Francisco Bay." I started to stand, but felt a firm pair of hands on my shoulders, shoving me back down.

I turned to look at the tall guy as he stepped back away from me. "I wanted to see if I could see my apartment."

Upton didn't say anything.

"I heard you've had a few transplants," I said, breaking the uncomfortable silence. "Might need another one."

"A friend of a friend of a friend." He paused. Looked as if he were studying me. "And if such a fabrication were true, you find it immoral that I would pay someone, a person who needs the money, for a piece of their healthy liver? Do you know that the liver is the only internal organ in our bodies that regenerates? In about two months a liver can fully regrow to its original size. Now, I'm not confirming I have bought black-market livers, but if I had, where's the harm?"

"You mean other than the fact that it's illegal in every country except Iran?"

"Illegal, perhaps, but done every day."

"How much money one has shouldn't be criteria for whether one gets a lifesaving organ."

"Ms. Kaleigh, don't be naïve. We are not all created equal."

Suddenly his face turned cherry and he punched on fist into the palm of his other hand. "Frank! Do something about that damn dog before I have to!"

"Yes, sir."

Frank rushed out of the room. I was tense from the sound of Upton's anger. I'd barely heard a dog barking in the background. Not close enough to be his. It must belong to a neighbor.

Had Frank taken the rifle?

Upton continued a little more forcefully. "While I was still in medical school, I devised a diagnostic test for sickle-cell anemia that is still used around the world today. How many lives have been saved because of me?!"

He took a deep breath, but didn't appear to relax. "I watched the first heart transplant performed in the U.S. at Stanford University. I was one of the top transplanting surgeons until I saw the value of research. Later, I started one of the first labs in this country to study the benefits of stem cells. So who deserves that available liver? Me—someone who has given valuable resources to humanity—or the twenty-something who lives on the street and has destroyed his liver with drugs and alcohol? Yes, you could argue that he has a longer life ahead of him—maybe—but I will save others in my remaining years."

Who have you saved lately? I wanted to ask, thinking about all those black-market livers. Poor people who had sacrificed so they could feed their families. How many had died from infection or liver failure so Upton could live another day?

I squirmed in my seat, holding back my question because I knew it would do no good. Neither would arguing. Black-market body parts were making donors think twice about giving for nothing and reducing the reservoir of legal organs for transplant. How many livers had his body devoured? "You've had your turn," I finally said because my mouth appeared to disconnect from my brain.

Calmer now, he rubbed his hands together. "So how much do I need to pay you to keep this conversation out of your article? I see that you have a little less than three thousand in your savings account. How about I offer you the same?"

My glance went back to the picture window and the breathtaking view of Marin County. He could pay more than three thousand. "That's very generous and I'd love to take you up on your offer because like your victims, I, too, need the money."

"They're hardly victims."

"You're exploiting their poverty." I exhaled as if to expel how powerless I felt before this man. "I don't need your money because I haven't come here to write an article. I'm here because my ex-husband is accused of killing Dr. Chaffe and I'm looking for information that might clear him."

Frank returned to the room, looking as well-groomed as before. I listened and heard no barking. What had he done?

Upton tapped a key on the laptop's keyboard. "Ex, huh. I have it here that Conor Nolan is your current husband."

"Whatever." I flicked my hand. "I'm sure the police have told you that all the cord blood stored at Primordium was removed before the fire. Other than its black-market value, which we've established you know a little about, why would someone want so much cord blood?"

"Research would be my first guess."

"I thought about that, but why take it all? And why kill Dr. Chaffe?" My gaze caught the buds of a neon pink bougainvillea on the other side of the drive. "Chaffe was worried that bad cord blood was coming in from Mexico. He wanted to test it."

"Actually, as I understood it, he wanted to close down Primordium's operation with Mexico until stricter controls could be put in place."

Oh! That was new information. "Still not a reason to kill him. In your experienced opinion, and maybe thinking outside the box, why else would someone steal all that cord blood?"

"Thinking outside the box," he mimicked.

"Yes. For example, cord blood is used to heal blood-borne diseases. Can it be used to heal anything else?"

He shook his head. "Possibly in the future, but not at this time, which brings us back to the research angle."

"But why steal so much? It was possibly enough to fill…" Oh, I had an idea. "What about this? If someone had a blood-borne disease, could they filter out all their blood and refill his or her body with this fresh new cord blood?"

"Sounds way too science fiction. And, the answer to your question is the same. Possibly in the future, but with medical resources today, such a thing wouldn't work. You are forgetting about the body's natural rejection mechanism."

"Like the way you keep rejecting livers."

He lowered his head, but not before I saw his jaw clench. A slight tremor ran through his hand.

Science fiction? Maybe, but he had the resources. Hadn't he bragged about how important he was to the world? But despite a first-rate mind, his body was failing him. His breathing was sometimes labored, his arms weak, and his coloring looked corpselike. He wouldn't have killed Kerner, the one person who might have had a chance at saving him.

I fished a card out of my camera case. "That's my number and address. If you think of any other ideas, no matter how farfetched, I'd like you to give me a call. Of course, I will respect your privacy. As far as I'm concerned, this meeting never took place."

He closed the laptop. "I appreciate that. Frank will show you out."

The Signature

I stopped at the market before heading home and grabbed two bags of coffee; one I planned to hide in the freezer. I also picked up two six-packs of beer for Conor. He'd been whining about beer since he got home and if I wanted to protect my coffee stash I needed to give in. Besides, without alcohol to dull his craziness, I might strangle him.

I threw some lunch meat and sandwich bread into the cart and headed toward the dog food aisle. Seemed like I was feeding everyone but me. I don't know if it was the lack of Dusty's company or the abundance of Conor's, but I hadn't been very hungry lately.

Before driving home, I called Gerri Runyan to see where she was on Conor's case and if there was anything she needed me to research. I was at a dead-end. This case stumped me like no other. The only principal who appeared to gain from Primordium's activities was Primordium or its CEO, Vincent Kerner, who was dead. Sure, Marc Upton might eventually benefit from their research, but who knew how many years that would take and whether Upton would still be alive. Nothing about this case made sense unless Chaffe's death and Kerner's were completely unrelated. But Dusty had said there was a similarity in the M.O. of both.

"Did you ever get any information on Dr. Kerner's murder?" I asked Gerri.

"I did, hold on."

I heard the sound of shuffling papers.

"Here it is," she said. "T.O.D. was between seven and nine p.m. Saturday night. Body found Sunday morning at, oh, you know all this. Let's see…"

"Cause of death?"

"Duh, duh, oh, here, cause of death, blunt force trauma. It says he was struck with an object weighing roughly four pounds. The blow ruptured an artery, causing an intracranial bleed."

"How was that similar to Dr. Chaffe's murder? Detective Arkansas said there was a similarity."

"Until they find the murder weapon it's hard to know, but what it looks like to me is that the murders don't looked planned. They both look like an argument gone wrong. Heat of the moment kind of thing. Have you come across anyone who can't hold his temper?"

I thought of Conor and his tantrums. Good thing I knew he was innocent.

* * *

Conor had been drinking steadily all afternoon. By seven, he'd finished the first six-pack and was well into the second. Clearly time to appeal to his softer side.

He was sprawled on the sofa, beer bottle in hand and earbuds in place.

"Can I make you something to eat before you drink yourself to death?"

He yanked an earbud out and I repeated my question.

"I don't want to put you out," he said, giving me his sheepish little boy look.

Too late. "No problem, how about some spaghetti?"

"Do you have any Swiss cheese?"

I headed for the kitchen. "I do. I remember how you like it."

He liked it cheap and easy. I dumped a jar of basil tomato sauce into a saucepan and filled another pan with water. The hardest part of his favorite meal was grating the Swiss cheese because I couldn't find it already grated. That's what I did while everything heated on the stove.

Fifi squeezed in between my feet and I dropped a piece of cheese on the floor. I filled her bowl with kibble and a tablespoon of wet food. While she gobbled it up, I set the table.

Conor was almost asleep when I plucked the earbuds from his ears. "Dinner's ready. Do you need another beer?"

He yawned and stretched. Fifi jumped up on his belly and he shoved her off. "Don't mind if I do. Lovie, I'll get it."

"I've got it. Go to the table."

While trying to sit, he knocked the chair over and bumped the table, splashing water out of the pitcher. As he tried to pick up the chair, I rushed to his side and lifted the chair into place, not to help him, but to stop any further damage.

He sat and I brought him another cold one.

"You sure you don't want one?" he asked, holding up the bottle. "There's plenty."

"No, thanks."

"Suit yourself."

I watched him dig into the spaghetti. He ate with the abandon of a child. I couldn't help but smile. He reached across the table for my glass of water. He paused.

"You mind?"

"Go for it."

He took a gulp and put the glass down. "Aren't you eating?" he asked, looking at my untouched spaghetti.

I picked up my fork and twirled some pasta around it. He went back to chowing down. When he finished the first plate, he refilled it from the bowl on the table. This was more than I'd seen him eat since his arrival. The beer was working its magic.

I carried my half full plate into the kitchen and put it in the sink. "I bought cupcakes for dessert. Are you still hungry?"

"Bring 'em on."

"Need another beer?"

"Not yet."

I carried the box of cupcakes and a brown envelope to the table. I placed the box in front of him.

"What's that," he asked.

"Cupcakes."

He took a draw off the beer. "No. The envelope."

"I see you still like spaghetti, I just wondered if other things were still the same."

He cocked his head, sensing that something was off, but too drunk to know that I was about to ambush him. "Like what?"

"Your word."

He grinned and shook a finger at me. "Are you trying to get me drunk so I'll sign those papers?"

"I know you better than that. You never get drunk." This was a lie, but one he ferociously believed. "You gave me your word and that used to mean something. Does it still?"

"I'm out of jail, but…"—he held his ankle in the air—"I'm still a prisoner."

"Not my problem. You said you'd sign if I got you out of jail. I've done my part, now, it's your turn."

He reached for a red velvet cupcake.

I had one more move. "Or I could call your aunt."

His eyes grew wide. "You wouldn't. She doesn't want us to divorce anyway." He dropped the cupcake on the plate.

Mrs. Macklin didn't want us to divorce, but she knew we weren't good for each other. Even in her big Catholic heart, she knew some people weren't meant to be together. "If she knew you gave me your word, she'd want you to honor it."

He held out a hand. "Give me the damn papers. I'm tired of hearing about it, but you better not let me go back to jail."

I passed him the envelope and handed him a pen. "I'd never let that happen."

"You almost did this morning." He pulled the papers out and turned to the last page. He signed next to the yellow "X" and dropped the pen.

He picked up the cupcake and I scooped up the papers. I read his signature to make sure he hadn't signed them with someone else's name. Something I wouldn't put past him.

I slid the papers back in their envelope and took a deep breath. I couldn't believe our marriage was finally over, and I couldn't have been happier.

The Apartment

In my dream, I was crouched over the starting line of a footrace track, but realized that I hadn't been given any information on how to run the race. I'd watched the runners before me take off and knew the route, but I wasn't sure who was dropping the flag for me to start. I saw the woman I thought was supposed to drop the flag, but just behind her was another woman holding up a flag. Both women dropped their flags, but not at the same time. I remained unsure what to do. The first woman called to me and frantically waved the flag. I took off.

I was flying, running so fast that my lower body passed my upper body until it was pulling my shoulders along behind my hips. Suddenly, Fifi was on the track with me. She was barking at me and nipping at my feet as they hit the ground. I was amazed that she could run so fast.

Then, my lungs started to burn with the exhaustion. I started coughing and coughing until I had to stop running. I dropped to my knees on the track and Fifi leaped up and barked loudly in my ear.

A loud pulsing screech jolted me awake. I coughed. Where was I? Fifi stood, two paws on my chest, barking frantically. The room was cloudy and smelled like…

"Conor!" I screamed, rolling off the mattress to my feet.

Fifi leaped to the floor, barking, but I could barely hear her over the pulsing alarm.

"Conor! I screamed again, running into the hall that separated our rooms. The image of him on his tenth beer popped into my mind. I rushed to his room, shoved open the door. Fifi still barking. I grabbed his limp arm and dragged him off the air mattress. He was naked except for a pair of badly fitting briefs.

He mumbled, then coughed. I, too, coughed fiercely, the effort of pulling him up more than my lungs could bear.

The alarm was deafening. The red light on his ankle bracelet pulsed and gave us a little visibility in the thick gray cloud. Conor gripped my arm as he realized what was going on.

"Come on," he said, picking up Fifi and running from the room.

I followed and we came to the source of the smoke. My front door was ablaze; flames licked over the walls on both sides. The pulsing alarm was coming from somewhere in the middle of the flames. It was the border strip that alerted the police if Conor tried to leave the apartment. The fire must have tripped it.

Conor handed Fifi to me and started for the door, but there was no going through it. He turned and ran past me to the kitchen.

"Come this way," he called over the roar of the flames and the scream of the alarm.

Once I reached the kitchen, he slid the door shut behind me and went to the back window. "Get away from the doorway in case the fire leaps."

Leaps? What was he talking about? Conor wrapped a dishtowel around his hand and grabbed a rolling pin from one of the drawers. I remembered wondering when I'd ever use a rolling pin. Then, I knew what he was going to do. He was going to break the window and the draft would draw the flames deeper into the apartment.

I thought of my laptop on the table. I knew it was foolish to worry about it, but it had all my work on it. My backup was in my closet so that was out of the question.

Before I could stop him, he slammed the rolling pin into the pane. Glass shattered to the floor. A loud roar came from the living room and dissipated as quickly.

I put Fifi down and while Conor cleared the rest of the glass from the window, I brushed the fallen shards under the cabinets. I went back to the door and pressed my hands to the wood. It wasn't uncomfortably hot, so I slid it open to see what the damage was. My laptop was untouched on the table. The fire had spread across the carpet and was slowly making its way along the wall near the sofa.

"I'm going to climb down so I'll be there to catch you," Conor said, one bare leg already through the opening.

It was now or never. I made a dash for the laptop, grabbing it and yanking the power cable free. I ran back to the window. Conor was almost down the downspout where two men I didn't recognized waited to help him off. Several people were crowded around him, including Dusty.

Dusty looked up. He motioned to me. "Can you make it?"

It was two floors. If the downspout could hold Conor, it could hold me, but climbing across the siding to it was the tricky part. Conor had longer legs and arms. I leaned out the window with the laptop.

"Catch this!" I called to Dusty.

He ran to a spot below the window. "I can try. Drop it."

I did and he caught it between his hands, fumbled, and then triumphantly held it up. "Your turn."

I was dressed in only a long tee shirt. It would be quite a sight, shimmying down the spout, but what else could I do? I looked down at the growing crowd. The loud cry of sirens filled the night.

"Come on," Dusty called. He was motioning with one hand. "I'm here."

Suddenly Conor was beside him. "Come on, babe, I'll catch you."

Dusty shoved him away and Conor, in his baggy briefs, launched at him. They started to tousle when the two men who'd help Conor down pulled them apart.

Dusty yelled something and pointed away from the building. The two men dragged Conor away.

"What are you waiting for? Climb out," Dusty called to me.

Smoke billowed through the kitchen. I threw one leg out and was balancing on the sill when a nagging feeling took hold of me. I was forgetting something. Something important. I looked down at the crowd. Dusty was motioning frantically. Several San Rafael police officers had arrived.

"Come on down," Dusty said. He motioned one of the officers over to him. "Briana, we won't let you fall." A fireman joined them and they pointed up at me.

Fifi!

I swung around and called her name. Conor had had her. No. He'd handed her to me. I'd put her down to grab the laptop. "Fifi?" I called, climbing back inside.

"Briana!"

I ran across the kitchen and looked in the living room. She lay curled on the other side of doorway, overcome by the smoke. I snatched her up and covered her nose with my mouth. I blew air in. I had no idea how to give a dog mouth-to-mouth.

Carrying her to the kitchen, I slid the door shut to cut the smoke. I rushed to the window, shoving Fifi out into the fresh air.

"The dog," Dusty yelled.

I massaged Fifi's tiny chest and felt her draw in a deep breath. Her pink tongue hung out, but her eyes were open.

She tried to lift her little head, but I kept a tight grip on her. The smoke was getting denser. I leaned farther out to breathe.

Dusty misunderstood my actions. "Are you ready?" he called and ran back below the window. "Drop the dog."

Fifi looked at me with an expression of pure fear. I've never seen her look so afraid. Dusty had caught the laptop, but barely. If Fifi wiggled, just a tiny bit, he might miss her. With only my tee shirt, I had no place to tuck or tie her.

I glanced over at the downspout. Realistically, I probably couldn't reach it. I held Fifi close and caressed her throat. "I won't leave you."

Dusty must have read my mind. He ran to the other police officers and pointed up at the window. The one officer stayed below the window as Dusty directed.

"Briana, you have to come down," he called, now surrounded by officers.

Off to the side, Conor gestured for me to jump. Someone had thrown a blanket around his bony shoulders.

A loud explosion ripped through the apartment. Despite the closed door, a thick ball of dark smoke rolled through the kitchen.

I coughed and held Fifi as high as possible, but the smoke rolled over her, too.

A bulky mass with thick arms pushed through the dark cloud. It reached for Fifi and I handed her over, knowing she'd be safe. I coughed again, hard.

I tried to follow the fireman out of the kitchen, but the next time I coughed, everything went black.

The Mittens

Dusty was arguing with someone. I couldn't make out the words, but the deep tonality of his voice left me feeling as though I were floating in a womb of protection. I lounged there a few minutes longer, but knew I needed to open my eyes.

My lungs felt as if tiny embers were burning inside them. The sparks seemed to flare and then subside with each inhalation.

Dusty must have moved closer because I heard him better.

"I won't," he said. "But I need to speak with her the moment she wakes."

My cue. I flicked my lashes several times before my eyes would open. I sucked in a lungful of pain and started to cough. As I brought my hand up to cover my mouth, I caught sight of a big white mitten. I raised my other hand. Both were covered in layers of gauze.

"What happened?" My voice was a hoarse whisper.

"Get the doctor!" Dusty said.

I felt his touch as he caressed my cheek with the backside of his fingers. I closed my eyes for a moment, overwhelmed by his gentleness.

"You're going to be fine," he said softly. "You started to fall and your hands got scorched on the rug. Nothing too serious. A fireman caught you so there aren't any other burns. Should have known that ugly shag thing was highly flammable. Probably a leftover from the sixties."

He'd always hated the carpet. Forest green. I'd never been too fond of it, but it didn't show dirt, which was why I'd kept it. Why was I thinking about carpeting?

I opened my eyes. "Conor? Fifi?" I wheezed out.

"Conor's back in jail. Fifi's fine. I'll look after her until tomorrow. Doc says you'll be going home soon. Maybe even today."

The thought of him and Fifi together on his boat sent a chuckle though me. I started to laugh, but ended up coughing.

"You need to stop smoking," he said.

I tried to laugh again, but only coughed harder. I'd just breathed in an apartment worth of smoke and he was giving me a hard time over a few cigarettes. I focused on calming myself and breathing slowly. It finally worked and I could breathe without coughing.

"Why is Conor in jail?" I asked. "He didn't do anything."

"It's the rules when his alarm goes off. Besides, he no longer has a viable place to live."

"With you and Fifi."

"Yeah. That's going to happen."

"Dusty, please."

"I own a gun. Legally, the judge won't allow him to live with me, and trust me, that's a good thing. The yapper is bad enough. I hate to bother you now, but I need to ask some questions. Do you mind?"

"I'm a little confused still. Not sure I can remember anything."

"The other day you mentioned that you had a contact that could put you in touch with Upton. I need that person's name."

Dusty's hair was longer. Not much, but he always shaved it at the full moon. He said he was a Buddhist monk in training, but the nubs on his scalp were longer than I'd ever seen. He hadn't shaved at the full moon. "You're growing your hair out."

"Clark didn't like it shaved, thought it made me look hard-assed."

I nodded. Nothing really to say.

Dusty gently sat on the bed beside me. The look on his face made my stomach tighten. I wasn't sure I wanted to hear what he was about to say. He started to say something, then paused. He started again, "Clark and I are done. It was a mistake."

"I'm sorry." But I wasn't. I wanted to leap up and dance a jig, but I'd probably start coughing again.

"I have feelings for someone else and she picked up on that."

I remembered them arguing beneath my window, the finger pointing and the angry expressions. "Me?"

He snickered. "You're pretty thick yourself."

"Like molasses."

He leaned forward and pressed his lips into mine. This time they were soft, and warm, and tasted like coffee. For a moment, I forgot about the fire, my burned hands, my painful lungs. It was only the two of us and it was good.

He pulled away before I was ready to lose him. "I was confused. You were there for me every day in the hospital and then I come home to find your husband living with you. I didn't know what to make of it."

"It wasn't like that."

"I understand that now. When I thought I was going to lose you in that fire, I had a moment of clarity. I'm sorry for not listening. I was hurt and not ready to hear what you were saying. Can you forgive me?"

"This is a mess." I saw how he had been hurt, and how he had in turn hurt me, and how our pain had caused a misunderstanding of epic magnitude. A kiss wasn't going to clear the air, but it was a start.

He sat up. "We'll sort of this out later. Right now I need your contact's name." His hand ran down my bare arm.

I leaned over and kissed his hand. "Confidential," I said.

Dusty slid off the bed so fast I felt a gust of wind.

"Briana. You're lucky to be alive! Someone poured accelerant on and under your front door and then set it aflame. If the stoner downstairs hadn't just gotten home, you would have died. Conor's alarm went off and your neighbor thought someone was stealing his 'medicine' so he called the police. Luckily, since the alarm went off at the station, the police were already en route. They saw the flames and called it in. So…I need that contact. As far as I can tell from your laptop, he was the last person you interviewed about this case."

"No, that's not—" I said.

"No, what? Sorry, I can't hear you," he said, stepping closer.

Arson. Interview. Accelerant. Death. Alarm. Smoke. It was all sinking in, but my brain wasn't processing. I was focused on Dusty's lips and my desire. "Wait," I said, trying to breathe.

Someone had tried to kill me. Got that. But to what end? I didn't know anything.

"Briana?"

"Give me a minute. I can't think straight."

My contact for Upton was the accountant. He was too far removed from this case to be of any interest. That left Upton, the last person I interviewed. Why would Upton want to kill me? To keep our conversation private? Would he go to such lengths to shut me up? Murder seemed excessive. The man only needed to make a few phone calls to discredit me and probably ruin my career. But he was one of the few people connected to Primordium who was still alive.

"This is Upton," I said, barely above a whisper.

"No. Can't be. Wait. You spoke to Upton after I expressly told you not to!"

Why did he sound so surprised? Not too long ago, I thought he was the one person who got me.

"I'm sorry," he said softly. "I didn't mean to upset you. Please, don't cry." He leaned down near my face. "I was just so worried. One exit to your apartment. You weren't meant to get out and that person is still running around free. I need to stop him before he comes for you again."

I sniffed and reached out to touch his nubs, but caught sight of my wrapped hand. "Could the arsonist have been after Conor? Maybe someone from jail?"

He straightened. That's when I noticed a deputy by the door.

"What did Upton say to you that would be worth killing over?"

I heard the skepticism in his voice. That was okay because I had my doubts, too. "Nothing. It doesn't make sense, but you should talk to him."

Dusty looked over his shoulder as if he'd heard something. "How do I find him?"

"I thought you already interviewed him."

"He came to the station."

So even Dusty didn't have an address for him. "In the Primordium file on my laptop. There's a document called H.E. His address is in there."

"H.E?"

"He. It's a Harry Potter reference."

Dusty shook his head and huffed. "What about your contact to Upton? I still think that's a good lead."

"He hasn't seen or had anything to do with Upton in years. Can't see a motive. Talk with Upton first. I'll do a little more research on my contact to make sure he's clean."

The door opened and a tall dark-haired woman, wearing a lab coat, stepped in. She pushed Dusty aside and stepped up to the bed.

"How are you feeling?" she asked.

I looked at Dusty.

"This is the doctor," he said. "I'll leave you to her and go talk with you-know-who. That's my Harry Potter reference."

The Ashes

The hospital released me after lunch. I looked like one of the homeless that hung around the boaters, hoping to scavenge food or beers. A nurse had found me some clothes in the Lost and Found. A pair of large sweatpants that I'd belted and rolled several times at the waist, a child's green plaid flannel shirt that was a little too tight across the breasts, and a pair of strappy gold sandals that squeaked when I walked.

What Dusty had failed to mention was that my long hair had gotten singed at some point, probably when I started to fall and now, it was in different lengths across my back. The nurse had tried to level it off with a pair of bandage scissors, which left it looking as if I'd tried to cut my own hair. I swept it all up in an elastic until I could get to a salon.

My car was at the apartment and I wasn't ready to talk with Dusty again so I called a taxi. I felt I should stop by the jail and explain things to Conor. I was sure no one had, but I really wanted to get home and see if any of my belongings could be salvaged.

The bandages on my hands would need to be changed every day and the burning in my lungs would get better, or so I was told. When I'd asked for pain meds, I was flatly refused. I blamed Dusty for that. It wouldn't be the first time he'd told medical staff that I was an ex-alcoholic. A label I firmly deny. Yes, I'd once drunk too much, but I'd had good reason to want the oblivion that whiskey afforded me. When I'd had enough, I'd stopped drinking. No intervention necessary. I didn't drink now because sometimes, when the world was dark and quiet, I still felt the draw of the abyss. Painkillers were never a part of that struggle.

A fire engine blocked the parking entrance to the apartments. Farther down the road, near where my car was parked, was another fire truck. The taxi let me out on the street and I walked over to the stairs where two firemen were milling around.

The fire engine in the lot held 500 gallons of water. The place couldn't still be burning after twelve hours. Nothing would be left standing. But from the looks of it, there was only smoke damage around my front window, which had been broken out probably by the firemen that rescued me.

The two firemen by the stairs weren't in full gear and I didn't see any water hoses going up to the apartment.

"Hi," I said. "Can I go up?"

"Who are you?" the good-looking one asked. His blue eyes looked like a place I'd like to float in if I weren't already floating because of another man. When I called him the good-looking one it was only because he had blond hair and I preferred blond-haired men and fireman number two was dark-haired. Fireman number two had sad lips that turned downward. His tee shirt hinted that he had abs I could bounce off of. Life was suddenly blooming with possibilities.

I pointed to the charred façade of my apartment. "I live there." I held out my arms as if to display my ensemble. "Want to see if any clothes survived."

After looking me over head to toe, the two men looked at one another, their eyes exchanging a silent message. That worried me.

"We'll have to ask. Wait here," the dark-haired guy said. Both men stomped up the stairs in heavy-duty boots.

I said a silent prayer that the fire hadn't reached the bedroom. It would be nice to have something that fit. I'd need a new leash for Fifi because hers had been by the door. Conor's cash was still being held as evidence so that wasn't lost. Maybe I could borrow some to replace the items that were destroyed.

I heard a familiar voice behind me.

"There you are," Dusty said, jogging over to me. "I went by the hospital, but they said you'd been released. Why didn't you call me?"

"Figured you were busy with Upton."

Dusty put a hand in the small of my back and stepped closer. He looked up at the apartment. Didn't look like he was going to be forthcoming about Upton.

"So," I prodded, "what did Upton have to say for himself?"

Still looking upward, he did something funny with his mouth. "Want me to see if I can get them to let you in?"

"Please. I'm hoping some clothes survived."

He looked me over. "Like the rolled sweatpants."

"It's a look.

He started for the stairs.

"Where's Fifi?" I asked.

"At the office. Being spoiled. You won't be able to stand her when you get her back."

"I can barely stand her now."

He chuckled and went up the stairs.

I watched him go and when I lost sight of him, I decided not to wait around. I followed him up.

The corridor between the two upper apartments was charred black, but the right side, my side, was burned out. The door and frame had burned to ashes and most of the wall was gone. Dusty stood just inside, his cell phone pressed to his ear.

"Good. Get the route," he said, then put the phone in his pocket. "Don't come in," he said to me, throwing out his arm to block my passage.

The highly flammable rug was gone, as was the floor for about the first four feet into the apartment. Dusty had said the arsonist had poured accelerant under the door before lighting it. The missing floorboards looked like a map of where the accelerant had reached. It was the heaviest damage. The rest of the floor was blackened, probably from the burning rug, but the firemen had gotten to it in time.

The two good-looking firemen were at the other end of the room and had just tossed something out the broken front window. It looked to be what was left over of the rug. A cloud of black ash swirled around them.

The sofa was a lump of charred cloth and thin wire. Yesterday it had looked like a rolled-up futon. It was curious to see its skeleton. The painting on the wall behind the sofa was gone and the wall had taken some flames, but hadn't burned through. That gave me hope for the bedroom.

Dusty was looking down at my feet. "You can't come in wearing those. It's too dangerous."

"Can you slip into my bedroom? There should be some boots by the outside wall."

He was very careful where he stepped. A third fireman came out of the kitchen, joining the other two, and the three stood silently, looking from wall to wall.

"Hey," Dusty called to them as he stepped back in the room, my boots held up as if they stank like a corpse. "Mind if I let her in the bedroom to get her stuff?"

"Let me lay some boards," said the man who'd come from the kitchen.

When Dusty reached me, I snatched my boots from his two-fingered grasp. "Why are you holding them like that?"

"How do you want me to hold them?"

I sat in the blackened hallway and pulled the leather boots over my bare feet. Not too comfortable, but I didn't plan on wearing them like this for long. "You never told me if you arrested Upton or not."

"Clark's looking into his holding company." Dusty stepped over me and headed for the stairwell. "I've got some boxes in the car. Let me get them so you can pack your stuff. You won't be allowed back inside once they condemn the place."

He was still in contact with Clark. "Who cares about Upton's company?" I called after him. *Condemn*. The word hit me like a strong wave knocking me off my feet. I was homeless. Where would I go?

The two good-looking firemen grabbed wooden slabs from a stack by the window. I'd seen them and thought they were the ripped-up floorboards. Now, I saw they were used but not scorched. They laid them end to end, creating a path from the front door to the hallway.

"So is the apartment below okay?" I asked the blond-haired guy. From what I could see the fire hadn't burned through.

He shook his head and shot me an expression that read, *are you kidding?* "We filled the place with a couple of tons of water last night. Where do you think that water is now?"

I stepped inside and looked down between the slats of wood that made up the ceiling of the apartment below. Whoever tried to kill me had ruined someone else's life. "Poor stoner guy."

"If you say so," blondie said.

"Hey, he saved my life." Wasn't that what Dusty had said? My thoughts were still somewhat jumbled.

Blondie, who was now a little less good-looking in my opinion, pointed to the path. "Stay on the boards. The supporting beams are sound, but we don't know about what's below."

The third fireman, who looked to be in charge, said he was finishing up and would stay with me. He ordered the other two to check out the lower apartment and assess the damage.

They headed out and Dusty arrived with about six flattened boxes and a roll of tape. "Let's see what's still good."

I started to follow him into my bedroom, but needed to see one last thing.

"Hey," I called to the remaining fireman. He was standing in the center of the main room. "Could you lift up the corner of the sofa?"

"If I do it'll fall to pieces."

"I don't care. I shoved an envelope with some papers under there last night and I need to be sure it's gone."

He laughed and stepped carefully towards the sofa. "Oh, it's gone. Hope it wasn't important."

He bent and lifted the corner. As he'd said, parts of the sofa broke off and crumbled to the boards. The carpet below was nothing but ash as was everything else. "Sorry," he said. "Paper burns the fastest."

"Thanks."

In the bedroom, the smoke smell was stronger since there were no windows to let air in. I threw open the closet door and was hit with another wave of burnt odors. Water damage on the back wall was visible. I dug through a stack of folded pants for my hard disk and found it dry.

"Hallelujah," I cried, holding it in the air.

"Drop it in here," Dusty said handing me a prepared box.

"Would you put the camera case in there, too?" I asked, pointing. The leather looked wet, but I'd wait until I had time to take everything apart to check the damage.

I pulled out the stack of pants, sniffed, and dropped them on top of the hard disk. I grabbed my sweaters next. Only one was dry. I loaded the box. Underwear, good. Socks, good. My tee shirts were on the top shelf and they'd gotten dowsed with water. I pulled out the only two I couldn't leave behind and put them over the side of the box since they were wet. I wondered how many washings it would take to get the smell out of everything.

"Here's your phone," Dusty said, holding it in the air.

"Is it dry?"

"Soaked. Want me to put it in this box with these books?"

I started to reach for it, but remembered the sweats I was wearing didn't have a pocket. "Sure."

We finished the third box with sheets and towels from the bathroom. I'd arrived only a few months earlier with three large suitcases. One of the suitcases was now ash because I'd used it as a coffee table. The other two had been in a closet next to the front door along with a vacuum cleaner that had come with the apartment. The closet was gone, as were its contents.

"I have three more boxes," Dusty said. "What's left?"

"Conor's room and the mattresses. Everything in the kitchen came with the apartment."

Dusty looked down at my brand-new mattress and box springs sitting on the floor. He shook his head. "You'll never get the stink out. Do you have renter's insurance?"

"Yeah, that's something I can afford."

He closed up the boxes and started to build a fourth. I went into Conor's room and let the air out of the air mattress. It was plastic and could be scrubbed. And I figured I'd be sleeping on it once I found a new place. Everything else fit into one box.

Four boxes. My life reduced to four boxes. I had a sense of déjà vu. When I'd moved here from D.C. my life had been reduced to three suitcases. Not much had changed.

Except the way I felt.

I'd always considered myself something of a modern nomad, able to up and move and start over without much fuss, but once I'd moved to California, I'd felt comfortable. This apartment had grown on me and felt like home. I knew my neighbors and their habits. I knew the boaters and their habits. They all knew me. For the first time since losing Siobhan, I was part of a community.

This uprooting hadn't been my choice. It was forced on me and I don't like to be forced.

"Dusty! What's going on with Upton?"

He started to hand me a box. "Can you carry this? It's light."

I looked at my gauze-covered hands. "Sure, they don't hurt."

"Ok. Careful," he said and handed it to me. He picked up the heavier one with the air mattress. "Let's go." He nodded to the doorway. "I'll get the rest."

"I want to talk to him," I snapped.

"I'm sure you do, but let's move you someplace first and then we'll have a long chat."

"You're not going to talk me out of it."

He huffed then exhaled. "You are what is observed, not what you observe."

"What does that mean?"

"Namaste."

The Hotel

Dusty and I argued over where I should stay, but in the end, I was determined not to inflict my inconvenience on anyone else. He'd offered me his boat and as much as I wanted to take him up on it, a nagging inner voice said, *It's too soon.*

The voice belonged to Mrs. Macklin so I had to respect it. Anyone else and I might have ignored it. Plus, I wasn't so keen on sharing the bed Agent Clark had just vacated. Especially since she was somehow still in the mix.

When Dusty had had enough of my rebuttals, he gave in and helped settle Fifi and me in the Marin Suites, the hotel where I'd first stayed when I was looking into the murder of my best friend, Haylee. Each suite had a kitchen and sitting room besides a bedroom and bathroom. There was also a large laundry room, which I planned to use immediately. I'd left all the boxes in my car. I wasn't about to bring that smell into my suite. If I wanted to ever drive again, I'd need to get the smoky stuff in the boxes cleaned.

The one issue with staying here was that they didn't allow dogs. Dusty had gone to negotiate with the manager, using the fact that I wouldn't be here long. That was true because I couldn't afford to stay long. The newspaper I'd been working with had paid for my last stay.

But how long would it take to rebuild my place? With both top and bottom apartments damaged on that side of the building, the owner might just tear them down.

Another wave of anger rolled through me, but I was determined not to let it take hold. I was alive and I had Dusty by my side. Now, I needed to focus and figure out how this had happened. I dropped down in the armchair that faced the door. I shoved the butcher knife I'd taken from the kitchen between the cushions. Dusty was hedging on telling me anything about Upton, which made me sure he was guilty and still free. Nice to be rich enough to hire powerful lawyers.

Maybe I could sue him for damages and mental stress. I glanced at Fifi, curled on the sofa, snoring. She looked terrified.

Why had he done this to me? With everything that had passed, I hadn't had time to figure out why Upton saw me as a threat, but he was the only possibility. Other than him, only two scientists from Primordium remained alive. Eri and Justin. Eri's fear was real; she was no killer. And I'd had absolutely no contact with Justin. I think he was gone, left like the email instructed.

That left Upton as the only person still connected to Primordium. And if the arson was linked to him, so was the fire at Primordium. The next leap would be that he was also involved in the deaths of Dr. Chaffe and Vince Kerner since the fire at Primordium was surely started to cover up something going on there.

The D.A.'s tinny voice in my head: *All circumstantial. No evidence.*

Now that the police finally had a direction, they'd find evidence, but I needed to help. I had to figure out what I'd missed at Upton's house.

Suddenly, Fifi was in my lap. She curled up and sighed. This was new.

Without disturbing her, I wrapped myself around a chunky pillow and let my mind wind back to that spectacular view on the mountainside. Three things had struck me as odd. The shrine to Upton's achievements as I walked through the door. A slap to the face, even to a dullard, that he was someone important. But with his top secret address, I assumed not many people saw the trophies, so who were they for? Was it to remind people that they were in the presence of greatness? Even his assistant had called Upton, God. I'd thought it was a joke because we were so high up on the mountain, but maybe he was serious. Maybe Upton thought of himself as God.

That brought me around to another idea. Maybe the trophies and certificates were to remind Upton every time he walked into the house that he was a great man. That he was needed. Maybe it was this adulation that kept him going. All those liver transplants couldn't be easy. I had no idea what the recovery time was or the side effects, but they had to be hard on a person.

The second thing I found odd was the way the assistant pushed me back down when I tried to stand. Had he taken it as an aggressive movement? Had he seriously thought I was going to leap across the table and grab Upton by the throat? Or did Upton have an aura that no one was to pass into? Possible contamination? It was strange to say the least.

And lastly, Upton's anger at the barking dog caught me off guard. He'd been so poised and controlled that the loss of said control was jarring. A cocktail of antirejection meds might make him irritable. Not to mention, he didn't look in the best of health. But anger? Not irritation.

My phone was trashed and Dusty still had my laptop. I needed to call my contact and see if Upton was known to have a temper. Both Chaffe and Kerner could have been killed in the heat of the moment. Dr. Chaffe was killed with a hand rake from his own garage. That screamed: argument gone wrong.

From what Dusty had said they were still looking for the weapon used on Vincent Kerner, but his death was due to blunt force trauma. Another argument?

* * *

Weaving through my tangled thoughts, I must have drifted off to sleep because when Dusty came through the door, I leaped up in a panic. Fifi jumped from the chair and lunged for his legs in a frenzy of fearless protection.

"I will shoot you!" he said to the dog.

Fifi tucked her pompom and turned to look at me. Satisfied I wasn't in danger, she trotted off to the bedroom.

I wobbled around the chair and headed for Dusty, way too much in my head to express at once. "I need a phone. I need my laptop. Do you have my laptop? I know what happened. I mean I think I know…"

Dusty caught me as I started to fall. "Whoa. Slow up."

I was fully conscious now and wrapped in his strong embrace. I took a breath to orient myself. "Oh, man. I must have fallen asleep."

I looked up into Dusty's warm eyes. He held my gaze for an uncomfortable few seconds then dropped his embrace. "We can't do this now." He took a step back and rubbed his palms together.

"Is something wrong?"

"No. Actually, I have good news for you." He looked at me and paused. "The charges have been dropped against Conor. He's being released."

Good news? Dusty was watching me; I was pretty sure he wanted to judge my reaction. He still didn't believe me when I told him it was over with Conor.

I nodded. "I want some water."

He followed me into the kitchen. "Against my better judgment, I gave his lawyer this address. He'll need someplace to stay."

"The charges are dropped? Completely?"

"That's what I said."

I lifted a glass. "Want some water?"

He shook his head.

I filled the glass from the faucet. "Conor won't be coming here. If he's being released, he won't want to wait around to see if the police change their minds."

"No one's changing their minds. He's no longer a suspect."

"Thing is…he won't believe it. He'll run for it. Dusty, let's forget about Conor."

"Gladly. Hard to believe you ever married him."

This wasn't the moment to mention Conor's Irish charm or what I had once seen in him. Not if I wanted Dusty's arms around me again. But one day I'd tell him. It was a part of who I was and where I'd come from. And yes, I had regrets, but regrets made the woman.

"Tell me about Upton. I know you didn't arrest him."

His shoulders tightened, his jaw squared off the way it did when he gritted his teeth. "Let's go sit."

Oh, boy.

I stumbled after him into the main room where he took my seat in the side chair, leaving the sofa for me. The distance as wide as the Grand Canyon. I tucked a pillow and sat, feeling the same way that I had the evening I'd broken a neighbor's car window playing stickball and my father had called me into the living room to scold me. He hadn't scolded me so much as made me feel ashamed by telling me how unladylike it was for me to be romping around with the boys. He said I should be cultivating more feminine virtues without telling me which virtues he meant. It wasn't long afterward that I was sent to Vermont to live with my spinster Aunt Eileen.

What had I gotten wrong this time? I crossed my hands in my lap and waited for the bomb to drop.

"You need to tell me about your conversation with Upton."

I quickly ran through the three things that had marked the conversation, finishing with my view on Upton's anger. "Other than that, the conversation was mundane. His views on body parts versus my view on the illegal black-market. He offered to pay me not to print anything, but I told him I wasn't going to. I saw no need to antagonize him."

Dusty looked down at the rug, pinched his lips together, and finally spoke. "I'd like to speak with your contact, too. He can perhaps validate the anger issues."

"Where is Upton now? Did you speak with him?"

He glanced up at me, then back to the rug.

Something was off. Why wasn't he over here on the sofa beside me? A slow heavy fear filled my solar plexus. "What's going on, Dusty? Why are you locking me out? My life is on the line here. You said so, this man wants me dead."

I wanted my safety knife, but it was in the chair with Dusty. I was moving now, pacing before the door as if ready to flee. "It's Clark, right. She doesn't want you talking to me. What a bitch! This is my life!"

"Sit down!"

His anger startled me. Was it the mention of Clark? I locked the deadbolt on the door and slowly made my way back to the sofa. I gave him my coldest smile and I sat.

"Agent Clark has ordered you a protective detail."

"I don't want—"

His phone chimed and he held a hand up. He reached for his phone.

Protective detail. I didn't want a bodyguard. I wouldn't
need a bodyguard is they'd arrest Upton. He truly thought he
was above us all and above the law. I had no doubt he argued
with Chaffe, probably over the Mexican operations, and
when Chaffe wouldn't give in, he nailed him with the hand
rake.

Dusty clicked off the call and put the phone in his pocket.
He looked down as he began to speak. "Both Agent Clark
and I believe Upton is our man."

"Then why haven't you arrested him?"

"Will you let me continue?"

He was looking at me now. It wasn't a happy look or an
angry look. More like a concerned look. Why concerned?

I pulled my leg up under me as if to make myself a
smaller target. "I'm sorry. Please."

"Upton's gone. That call was from the Feds. A flight plan
for the Maldives was entered at eleven last night. Including
the pilot, three adults were on the plane."

"I'm assuming the Maldives have non-extradition?"

"That's right. As you know, your fire was set after eleven,
but I never thought Upton set the fires himself. Someone, I
assume the same professional who torched Primordium and
your apartment, set fire to Upton's house, too. Probably to
destroy evidence. His fire was set while many fire stations
were responding to the one at your apartment. What Upton
forgot, or forgot to tell the arsonist, was that his house was
equipped with a fire prevention system."

"What do you mean? What's a fire prevention system?"

"Back in 1991 a huge fire ravaged the Oakland Hills.
Thousands of homes were destroyed. It was a nightmare. At
one point the fire consumed one house every eleven seconds.
Anyway, the point being that afterwards an investigation was
conducted to find better ways to deal with wildland-slash-

urban fires. One of the biggest problems in the Oakland Hills was the narrow mountain roads. The fire trucks couldn't get to the fires."

He leaned forward, resting his forearms on his thighs and interlacing his fingers. "When we have dry years, all those mountainside grasses are like matches waiting to be lit. The rebuilt homes over in Oakland and consequently many homes here in Marin that are built up into the mountains have added their own cisterns or water systems in case of fire. These cisterns are housed in the roof and contain a biodegradable gel that literally smothers the flames. Alarms are set around the property. If an alarm is activated, a jet of this gel is released from nodules all around the house, creating a safe zone. If an alarm is pushed inside the home, gel is released inside. That's what happened to Upton's. The arsonist set up several high-burning loads around the house, doused everything with accelerant, and left. His mistake was starting the fire upstairs, expecting the embers to continue the burn downward. The first high-burn load was a mattress and books in one of the upstairs bedrooms. This set off the alarm and the fire was extinguished."

"Doesn't sound like a mistake Upton would make."

"Maybe he was in a rush. Maybe he forgot about the system. I don't know how long he'd owned the house. We're looking into it. Either way, a neighbor smelled the smoke and called it in. Since the Oakland fire, people on the mountain are very paranoid about fires, especially because of the past dry winter. I got there as the fire inspector called it safe. My people have been going through the house all day. The good thing about the gel is it washes off easily."

"Have you found anything that can be used against him?"

"Possibly. Vince Kerner was killed by blunt force trauma. The S.I.S. guys think they may have found the murder weapon. A pyramid thing."

"I saw it! It was one of Upton's trophies in the entranceway."

"The shape is right, now it'll be tested for residue. Also, there were plenty of those canisters from Primordium, too. Can't figure out what he was doing, though."

"I think he was trying to replace his circulatory system. If he could get enough cord blood he could replace his blood with fresh healthy blood."

"Why?"

"So his blood would stop killing livers. Think about it. Chaffe wanted to stop the Mexican connection until they could look into the quality of the cord blood. Upton wasn't happy about it, he told me. I think they argued, it got out of hand, and Chaffe got bludgeoned. Next, your people started looking into Primordium, and Upton probably removed all the cord blood and burnt the placed down. For some reason that we may never know, Upton and Kerner then argued and Kerner ended up dead. My death would have wrapped up all the loose ends and Upton rides off into the sunset."

Dusty's phone chimed again. He stood to take the call. He drifted into the kitchen as if he didn't want me to listen. I wasn't listening. I was wondering how much trouble I was in. Upton's arsonist was still out there. Would Upton send him or someone else to finish the job? Dusty thought so or he wouldn't have asked Clark for a protection detail. I bet she jump at that. Wanted to see if Dusty and I…well, I wasn't going to give her the satisfaction. I thought back to the last phony smile she'd offered me. She probably wanted me dead as much as Upton.

Dusty rushed into the room. "The protection detail has been called off. That was Clark. Upton's plane left Madagascar and went down somewhere in the Arabian Sea. Rescue operations have found the plane and a body."

My chest tightened. "Is the body Upton? Maybe he'd died before the plane ever left California. He didn't look too good yesterday."

That would explain why the arsonist didn't have the information about the fire prevention system. Maybe Upton's assistant, Frank, cleaned up loose ends.

Dusty's phone rang again. My mind couldn't get around all that had happened. First, I was afraid; now, I was safe. Or was I?

Dusty put the phone in his pocket. "Come on," he said, reaching for my arm.

"Where are we going?"

"To the apartment. The officer there said Conor just arrived. I'll take you to him."

The Leash

When we reached the apartment we were greeted by a San Rafael police officer. His black-and-white was parked in front of my downstairs neighbor's apartment. The first thing I noticed was Conor's truck was gone. There were only two other cars in the lot.

"Took his truck and left," the officer said to Dusty.

Dusty looked at me, bewildered.

I shrugged. "Told you. He doesn't trust cops."

"He didn't even stick around to say good-bye to you."

Conor and I were so past civilities. We were linked through love and loss, and maybe our mutual distrust of others, but I'd grown. Conor, not so much.

"Now maybe you'll believe me when I tell you nothing was going on between us."

He shrugged.

"Yeah. While you were getting laid, I was putting up with dirty clothes tossed everywhere, being eaten out of house and home, and drunken arguments. It was a blast. Now, could you take me up the street to get a new phone? I want to see if I can recover my contacts. I have articles to write, income to earn."

Dusty looked at my bandaged hands. "That's going to be tough."

"I can take them off in a couple of days." I planned to take the bandages off as soon as I got back to the hotel, but I didn't tell him. I didn't like having my hands bound.

"I had another call from Clark," Dusty said as we drove to the strip mall.

"Should I be thrilled?"

"She spoke to some big stem cell researcher and gave him your suspicion about Upton trying to change out his blood. He said it was theoretically possible but not probable."

"That was once said about heart transplants."

He shot me a side glance. "He said too much cord blood would be needed."

"They've been collecting cord blood for four years," I insisted.

"That's just it. After four years some of that blood wouldn't be good."

"That's why the Mexican connection was so important. It probably doubled Primordium's intake. And Chaffe wanted to shut it down. Upton didn't. Even if half the blood they were getting from Mexico was bad, the other half was usable. Upton needed that blood. My guess is that Chaffe didn't know why Upton needed it so badly. So Chaffe held his ground and ended up dead. Kerner, on the other hand, had to know. His research revolved around Upton's illness."

Dusty shook his head. I figured he was far from closing this investigation.

"Hopefully, you'll find something at Kerner's home that will explain his research. Upton was using that blood. He knew that the families storing blood would never have a need for it. And if one day someone did ask for it back, Upton was smart enough to doctor something or come up with a scientific excuse not to give it back. Worse case, Primordium would be sued and die a legal death. Excuse the pun, but no blood, no foul."

He grunted and then went silent. He didn't say more for a couple of miles, then at the light, he started to say something and stopped.

"What?" I asked.

"Did you ever get your divorce papers signed?"

Oh, that was a turn. "I did. Last night at dinner."

He nodded, not really noting the significance.

"Last night," I said again for emphasis.

Dusty turned to me, looking surprised. "Oh, last night."

"I shoved them under the sofa in case Conor went looking for them while I was asleep. I was afraid he might take them back so he could blackmail me some more."

Dusty turned into the parking lot and parked in front of the phone store. "Under the sofa."

"Under…the sofa," I repeated.

Dusty grunted. "If he signed them once, he'll sign them again."

We got out of the car.

"I'm sure he will. The next time he needs something from me."

* * *

Dusty was on his phone much of the time that I worked with a cheerful salesgirl to buy a new one. The always-smiling clerk wore the same uniform as the other sales clerks and looked to be about fourteen. I told her about the fire and she said explained how I could get my contacts back. She also said I didn't need the SIM card to get my number back, that I could get my old number put into the new phone once the destruction was confirmed.

I pointed to Dusty. "He's a lieutenant in the Marin County Sheriff's Department. Can he confirm it for you?"

I didn't wait for an answer. "Dusty, can you confirm to this nice girl that my phone was destroyed."

With his phone held to his ear, he nodded to the clerk.

"Will he sign something?" she asked me.

"Whatever you need."

After about twenty minutes, I had a phone in my mittens. I handed the box with all the documentation to Dusty and took Fifi's handmade leash from him. Dusty had looped a belt around her collar to lead her around. It was tough on her neck.

"While you put the box in the car, I'm going to run into the pet store and get Fifi a new harness and leash," I said, cutting across the parking lot.

"I'll move the car to the front," he called back.

Fifi's last leash had been laced with rhinestones. I was looking for something a little more butch. She'd saved my life. She was a tough cookie and deserved to look like one.

Two rows of harnesses to choose from. Burberry to plain brown. I chose a matching turquoise print for both the harness and leash. I led Fifi to the checkout line. Four people ahead of me and several filing in behind.

My new phone pinged in my pocket. The sales clerk had told me to expect my old voice and text messages to arrive on my new cell. I was curious as to what I'd missed. Hopefully, something from an editor wanting an article. I'd be able to milk this case for enough money to pay rent for two more months. Wait…what rent?

I set the harness and leash on the unmoving conveyor belt and took out my phone. I set it on the conveyor belt, too, and looked for a way to access the new text message. Dusty was right. I couldn't press any of the apps with my bandaged hands.

I pulled a bag of doggy rawhide treats from a display. I ripped into it with my teeth and dumped out one pencil-sized treat. Using my bandaged hands, I put one end of the treat between my teeth and used the other end to tap the app on the faceplate.

Nothing happened.

I double tapped.

Nothing happened.

I was about to gag on the smoky taste of the rawhide soaking my tongue when I remembered the clerk saying something about the screen using the electricity of the fingers. She's made a snide remark about my bandages.

"May I help you?"

With the treat still between my teeth, I twisted to look up into a woman's face. She was in line behind me. I dropped the treat and straightened. "That would be great."

The woman wore a wool sweater despite the warm day. She had a kind smile and didn't hesitate. She reached for the phone and pulled a pair of reading glasses off her head and down onto her nose.

"If you could press the message app," I said. At my feet, Fifi growled. A teen had just entered the store with an unleashed black lab. I reached for the belt in case she had ideas of running off after the dog.

The woman held the phone screen up to my eyes. The number was unrecognized by my contacts. I didn't recognize it either. The message was simple:

Don't believe rumors

"Are you okay," the woman asked.

I reached to steady myself against the counter. "Yes. Thank you." I checked the time stamp. It had registered over an hour ago.

"Would you like me to put the phone back in your pocket?" the woman asked.

I took the phone between my bandages. "I can do it. Thanks for helping."

The line moved forward and I paid for Fifi's leash and the dog treats.

Dusty's car was idling at the curb. Fifi hopped in and I followed.

"Are you all right?" he asked, helping with the seatbelt. "Did something happen? You look funny."

"Did you get confirmation on Upton's body?"

He started to pull away from the curb.

"Stop! This is important," I said.

He looked at me and cut the engine. He huffed and slouched sideways in the seat. "Not yet, but the flight had three men on it when it left Madagascar. It's looking pretty sure all are dead, including the pilot. You can relax."

"What time did the plane go down?"

"Why does that matter?"

I leaned forward, offering as much of my back pocket as sitting would allow. "Pull my phone out."

"Now look at the top message," I said, sitting back.

"What does it mean, don't believe rumors?"

"It's from Upton. It's something he said to me when I met with him."

Dusty's glance went from the phone out the front windshield. He didn't say anything for a long time. Finally he handed me the phone and took out his own cell and punched in a number.

"Hey, can you tell me approximately what time Upton's plane went down?" he said into the cell. He turned to me and slid the mouth piece away from his lips. "I know what you're thinking. If Upton is trying to fake his death, though, why would he text you?"

"Haven't I mentioned that the guy is an egomaniac? His whole entranceway was a shrine to his greatness. Photos, commendations, trophies. Even if the whole world believes he's dead, he needs one person to know he's not. Maybe he's hoping I'll tell the world he isn't dead and the controversy will make him immortal, sort of like the Elvis sightings." I shook my head. It sounded crazy, but my gut told me it was true. "Honestly, I don't know what he wants, but that message was from him."

Dusty was back on the phone, listening. He disconnected and put his cell back in his top pocket. He ran his hand down my arm. "Three bodies have been recovered and part of the plane. Clark says Upton's manservant stayed behind in Madagascar and has confirmed that one of the three bodies is Upton's. Another body has been confirmed as belonging to the pilot.

"Good," I said, but felt a storm of fear gathering in the pit of my stomach. Why would Upton leave his servant behind? To give a false identification. Was Upton really dead and had the servant texted me to create the illusion Upton lived? Who was the third body?

"What was the cause of the crash?" I asked.

"Undetermined. Probably mechanical failure. A witness said it looked as if it just dropped from the sky."

Dusty turned back to the steering wheel and restarted the engine. He pulled away from the curb and headed for the exit.

Had Upton paid for someone's suicide? He told me himself he wasn't above it.

Upton's alive. I kept the thought to myself.

Dusty and I were about to start a new chapter and I was going into that with the fear of Upton shadowing me. If I published my suspicion about Upton, he'd have no further need for me. As far as he knew, I was the only person who knew he was alive. I had to keep it that way.

"Upton's dead," I said. "He may have died before the plane took off. He looked as if he were on death's door yesterday. That's why his manservant wasn't on the plane with him."

"How can you be sure?"

"Time will tell, but I'm pretty sure." I hated lying to Dusty, but why worry him. I thought about my apartment fire. What if Dusty had been with me? How much danger was I putting him in if I went forward with this relationship?

I needed time to think.

THE END
©2016

About the Author

Nicola Trwst has a gypsy heart. She currently resides in California, but has lived in Virginia, Georgia, France, and Canada. She loves languages and speaks several, including Pig Latin. Due to an overactive imagination, her stories thread many genres such as mystery, thriller, paranormal, and contemporary. Her short stories have appeared in several anthologies.

Discover more of Nicola's work at www.nicolatrwst.com

Also by Nicola Trwst
Bayou Nights (2013)

Briana Kaleigh Mysteries
The Belvedere Club (2012)
Bolinas Bongo (2013)
San Rafael Sizzle (2016)

Continue reading for the opening of Nicola's Fantasy adventure *Flames* due out in 2016

Visitor

"...and when one of them meets with his other half, the actual half of himself...the pair are lost in amazement of love and friendship and intimacy and would not be out of the other's sight..." Plato, *The Symposium*

I have yearned for Dominic every day during the past one hundred and thirty-four years.

For the first two of those years, he was as much a part of my life as the oxygen pumping my lungs. Some might call me obsessive, but I'm not. That's the tyranny of love. It grabs onto your heart, your soul, your essence, locking it in a stranglehold, only to release when the object of your affection is near.

I think of him now as I weave around my yoga students, obedient in their *Adho Mukha Svanasana*, or Downward-Facing Dog position. I press my hands on Susan's broad back, but imagine Dominic's powerful shoulder muscles and how he lifted me as if I weighed no more than a sparrow.

Sunlight has broken through the San Francisco fog, filling the studio's rear windows. My skin absorbs its warmth, knowing it will soon be gone. Such is summer in this city I've called home since 1932.

I glide past a vase of pink peonies, their scent sweetening the room with memories of afternoon strolls in Paris. Straddling Marla's mat, I adjust her hips, stretching those thick muscles where she carries the tension of running from place to place always ten minutes late. She thanks me and relaxes into the pose.

Posters of serene waterfalls, floral meadows, and meditating Buddhas decorate my modest studio, not because I worship Buddha, but because his presence, in some form, is expected in a yoga studio in this day and age. Today, my students are all women, a harried and over-pleasing bunch that find the class an oasis in their overburdened lives.

Some days, I am glad I have this to offer them. Other days, I too, wish to escape the weight of my unending life.

"Don't forget to breathe," I say. Air is sucked in like a chorus by those who have forgotten. "We'll hold for another forty-five seconds."

The studio door creaks. An odd odor catches my nose. I look up from Arlene to find the lumbering figure of a man shuffling in on lifeless feet, his arms and legs stiff from rigor mortis. His grayish skin is stretched into a death veil.

I should be afraid, but his anomaly, the pure impossibility of what I'm seeing, reminds me of other impossibilities such as that fateful day, long ago, when the Archangel Michael, the Lord's mighty warrior, carried my Dominic away.

Is this more of Michael's tricks? Has he not tormented me enough?

My students have probably heard the dragging feet propelled by some unimaginable force, making their awkward gait across the wooden planks. From curiosity or boredom, Arlene looks up. Her scream pierces my eardrums. With a collective thud, the other students drop knees first to their mats.

Another scream, then another.

At that moment, the corpse's chalky eyelids flutter. For an instant—one so short that I'll later question whether it happened at all—I'm looking into the eyes of my most beloved: Dominic.

As if that slight effort was all that was driving it, the body, clothed only in a simple blue hospital gown, tumbles forward, thumping to the floor. The gown falls away, exposing one buttock, but there's nothing sexual about the reveal. Indeed, it's comical, but I can't laugh. I drop to my knees beside the rigid form, the fetid smell of death rising around me.

"Dominic," I say, not expecting a reply. It's nothing more than a human shell—a heavy shell, I learn when I try to turn it over. Although I know there will be nothing to see, I want to look into the eyes one last time.

Several students dash past me for the door. Others huddle at the back of the studio. Some weep.

I stand to gather more strength. "Can someone help me?"

Blank stares. A whimper.

I grab the motionless arm, the skin clammy beneath my touch. It takes several tries, but I yank the body over. Something cracks. Maybe a bone; maybe a joint. Its face lies at an odd angle.

Behind me, someone yelps. Voices, rushed and anxious, leak in from the corridor beyond the studio.

I kneel and peel back the gray lids, but the pupils are frosted. The irises are dull and fading.

"Please step away from the body."

I look up. Two uniformed police officers are standing over me. A white man and a black woman. One of the students must have called from the phones they keep attached to their ears. Connected, they joke. But more like disconnected. Any excuse not to feel.

"Please, step away from the body," the female officer repeats in a voice laced with caution.

It's all too much. My head slumps forward, I close my eyes, and press my face against the cool floorboards. How I wish I could die.

* * *

Rosita's voice purrs with concern. Standing by my chair, she grips my hands tight enough to break a finger.

"Dana, speak to me. What's going on? I'm here now, *chica*. Talk to me."

"You're hurting my hands."

"She speaks!" Rosita, my dearest friend and only confidante, releases the pressure, but doesn't drop her hold, letting me know I can't escape her care. "Did that dead guy bite you or something? You're as white as a *cocodrilo albino*. What's going on around here? These police wouldn't let me in."

So many friends, like fireflies, have lit my life with their passion, only to be extinguished long before I was ready to lose their light. Rosita is one such friend. Born of a Mexican mother and an Australian father, she's petite, olive skinned, and so striking that men of all ages are drawn to her like broken hearts to ice cream. She passed my eternal age of twenty-eight years, a decade and a half ago. She's not happy that wrinkles begin to caress her face, but not mine.

Her glance sweeps my studio and absorbs the details that will help her form her own conclusions. Hopefully, hers are saner than mine.

"Dana, this is too bizarre for words. That guy there, the one in the suit, he's calling it a crime scene, yeah, a crime scene when the man was already dead. He was already dead, *sí?*"

Strangers, some in uniform, others in dress clothes, roam my sanctuary, touching my things like they have a right. They don't. I want them gone, but to guard my most precious secret, I must allow them unlimited access over my domain.

Two men, wearing identical jackets labeled San Francisco Coroner, lift the covered body onto a gurney. The scene is all too familiar. Yesterday, one of my students found a homeless man slumped across my front stoop, dead from the drink.

The significance hits me like a high-speed train on dark tracks. "Oh, Lord!" I yank my hands free and clutch my chest, my heart racing. "The homeless man. He must have been Dominic, too."

"Dominic?" Rosita glances over her shoulder as an investigator draws near. She lowers her voice. "You know the dead guy?"

"Dominic, my soul flame." I tilt my head to the gurney. "I'm absolutely sure. He must be trying to cross the spiritual plane. He's trying to reach me. Is such a thing possible?"

Of course, it is. If archangels exist, if soul flames exist, if I can live for over a hundred and sixty years without gaining a single one, other marvels must also be possible.

Rosita shoves her handbag off the teak chair next to me and sits. She has seen more than most in her short lifespan, but here, now, her doubt blankets me, thick and suffocating.

I understand her skepticism. Many years ago, it took a battle with a winged archangel to convince me that another reality exists beyond the veil of human perception. Had I trusted Dominic, had I believed him sooner, my life might have turned out very differently.

"It was him." Dizzy with emotion, I force myself to breathe. "Dominic was there, in that body. He's… It's… Rosita, believe me, he's trying to reach me."

Two of my students remain. They're speaking with a woman in the entrance corridor, their hands flying with words. Another woman is photographing tape markers on the floor, the spot that once held the body now being rolled away on a stretcher. I cannot think of what that poor man has lost; I'm too giddy at the prospect of seeing my beloved again.

"I don't know, *chica*." Rosita runs her palms down her thighs, smoothing her skirt. "It's just so…unnatural. Walking dead people?"

"Am I natural?"

She turns and the sienna ringlets that cover her head dance. "I've seen a being like you before and I'm told there are others."

"So you've said."

"You know, in some parts of the world your kind are called angels."

The door burps open. A brisk breeze excites my skin. "My friend, you've known me for eighteen years, would you actually call me an angel?"

The crease holding her eyebrows together relaxes. She probably remembers some of the bad, bad things we've done with my immortality. Amusement tickles her lips.

"I'm closer to a demon, no?"

She squeezes my arm. "One thing you aren't is a demon. For now, we'll stick with your Italian definition, *anima perduta*, lost soul."

She offers me a reassuring smile, but tension is tucked within the effort.

"And Dominic is my *anima germella*, my twin soul. He's trying to reach me."

www.ingramcontent.com/pod-product-compliance
Lightning Source LLC
Chambersburg PA
CBHW050022180626
46810CB00002B/527